HOUSE OF THE RISING SON

A Gabriel Ross Mystery

JOE HAMILTON

House of the Rising Son

A novel by Joe Hamilton

A Gabriel Ross Mystery

#5 in the Eye on You Detective series

978-0-99399994-9

Copyright ©2018 by Joe Hamilton

Published 2018 by Joe Hamilton

PRAISE FOR JOE HAMILTON

*"If you ain't a reader, you'll love
Joe Hamilton's* Gimme 3 Steps.*"*

*"This is the best book about a serial killer
trying to start a race war that takes place
in Biloxi in 1984...the best."*

*"If you're an outdoor-sie kind of guy, try
reading Joe Hamilton's* Gimme 3 Steps.
Just read it outside."

INTRODUCTION

This is the 5th book in the Eye on You Detective series.

- Book 1 *Murder in Biloxi,* takes place in 1979
- Book 2 *Rock You Like a Hurricane,* takes place in 1982
- Book 3 *The Mississippi Queen,* takes place in 1979
- Book 4 *Gimme 3 Steps,* takes place in 1984
- Book 5 *House of the Rising Sun,* takes place 3 months later in 1984
- *Eye on You - House of the Rising Son* has nothing to do with the megahit by the Animals.

While the novel may feature the song in some places, the title of the novel, with Son spelled differently, involves the theme of hope for a young man who was so traumatized by the violent death of his parents that he developed a debilitating condition called Mutism.

CAST OF CHARACTERS

Gabriel Ross - Main character, diminutive detective, and part-owner of the Eye on You Detective Agency

Jacqueline Ross - His beautiful, hot-tempered, half-Chinese wife

Benjamin Ross - Their 18-month-old son, also known as Jellybean

Rachel Henderson - Receptionist/Associate at the Agency

Ben O'Shea - Former Biloxi Police Detective who is part-owner of the Agency

Arnie Sims - A part-time associate at the Agency

Bourbon - A tabby cat who has been with Gabriel since the beginning; now lives with Arnie

Sheriff McDiarmid - Sheriff of Pearl River County

Tommy Huffman - A potential witness

Chevon - Ben O'Shea's girlfriend

Ralph Huffman - Tommy's dad

Mary Huffman - Tommy's mum

Dr. Marcotte - Tommy Huffman's doctor

William Friesen - An Alfred Hitchcock look-alike

Bonnie Friesen - William's wife

Hollis Huntley - Assistant Manager at Heritage Savings and Loan

Maisie Wilson - Glenn Wilson's mother

Fergus Wilson - Glenn Wilson's father

Agnes Flowers - Tommy's aunt

Bert Flowers - Tommy's uncle

Dixie Furlong - Slut

Madge Baxter - Mayor Baxter's sleazy wife

Frank Reznikov - Big trouble

PREFACE

During the mid-seventies, Russian immigration in the United States climbed to new levels. While most were hard-working people, it also gave rise to a particularly brutal organization called the Bratva or the Brotherhood. Former FBI Director Louis Freeh would say later that the Russian Mafia posed the greatest threat of any organization to U.S. national security. Over the seventies and eighties, this invasion was compared to an infestation of house flies infiltrating many American businesses.

It was like some fool left the door open.

PROLOGUE

September 17th, 1982

S eptember 17th, 1982
The house was just like all the other ghetto houses in Greenville, Mississippi. The bungalow was set back from the road in front of a patchy grass yard that had been over-taken by dandelions. A rusted-out Ford F150 was parked at an angle in the dirt lane. The house was made of dirty cream-colored clapboard with a roof that sagged in the middle like a well-worn saddle.

The full moon looked pale and wan, as if it shouldn't be up on a night like this. A solitary light bulb with a cluster of buzzing flies stood guard on the wooden porch. *This is where they ran to*, thought Kory, chewing on a toothpick. *I hate fuckin' runners.*

Kory Nantois, whose name, because he was from New Orleans, was pronounced NAN-TOY-ZZ, was sitting in his prized 1972 powder blue Plymouth Barracuda. Sitting in the passenger seat was his stupider-than-shit half-brother Kane. *The boy didn't have the brains God gave a pissant*, thought Kory, although he wasn't quite sure what a pissant was. *The guy's a psycho. A ticking, fucking time bomb. Just look at the guy – those ridiculous lamb chop sideburns, greasy black hair, and a three-day beard.*

While the brothers shared the same mother, they had different fathers. Their mother had remarried a half-dozen times, each time popping out another kid. She named all her boys with names starting with a K. In addition to Kory and Kane, there was Kiefer, Kerry, and two Kevins. The latter was because she couldn't think of anymore K names. She'd seen on the tube one night that George Foreman had named all his sons George. From that point on, she decided that all her future sons would be named Kevin.

Kane started playing the bongos on the dash to the Scorpions hit, *Rock You Like a Hurricane*. Kory just shook his head. *They wouldn't be in this mess if it weren't for the idiot sitting beside me. Now the mess needs to be cleaned up.* Frankie Fingers, their boss in New Orleans, didn't like people asking questions about his business. The word was that Frank got his nickname because one of his employees let him down, and as punishment, he had used tin snips to remove a couple of their fingers. Frankie was part of Bratva or the Russian Mafia. In the last ten years, they'd developed a reputation for brutality, and were involved in a huge web of criminal enterprises.

Kory looked up at the house, lighting up a Marlborough with his Zippo. He'd recently seen an ad in *Penthouse* featuring the *Marlborough Man*. Ever since then, he'd started wearing a black Stetson, a black fringe jacket, and kick-ass cowboy boots.

"Can I bum a smoke?" asked Kane.

"No. Sit still and fuck off the bongos. Make yourself useful and watch the street. We don't want any fucking witnesses." Kory pulled out his Smith and Wesson Enforcer from his shoulder holster and checked the ammo.

"Aren't we wasting time? Giving people more of a chance to notice us?" asked Kane.

"We're waiting until the street is clear," the *Marlborough Man* said, his tone reflecting his growing impatience. "You see that teenage girl walking towards us on the sidewalk?" She was leading a black miniature dachshund on a leash.

"Yeah, I'd like to show her my big black wiener! Ha-ha," sneered Kane.

"Your wiener's not black, numbnuts," Kory blew smoke out the side of his mouth.

"How do you know, you been peeking at my junk?"

"Shut the fuck up." *It's been five years since the killing in the woods. I thought we were in the clear until I got the call that there might have been a witness. That's why we're sitting here in Wankertown waiting for all these fucks to get off the street.*

Kane looked at his watch, "It's almost 9 p.m., time for everyone to go inside and watch *The Cosby Show*."

"Let's wait until she leaves. Do you remember what you're supposed to do?"

"Yeah."

"Tell me again what you're supposed to do."

"I'm going to go to the door and ask for Tommy Huffman."

Kory extended his index and pinkie of his right hand, turning to Kane, "You know what this is?"

"Yeah, that's like, *Rock on Man*," answered Kane, sticking out his tongue like the devil and copying the sign with both hands.

"No, that's what your hand is going look like if you fuck up again."

3

ONCE THE GIRL LEFT, the street was deserted. Taking the safety off the Enforcer, Kory opened the car door, "Let's saddle up."

Kane led the way up the cement path to the porch. He slipped on brass knuckles from his pocket. Kory followed, walking like John Wayne because the new boots were pinching his toes. When they got to the door, Kory took his post, out of sight to the left of the door. Kane, hand combing his greasy black hair off his face, rang the doorbell. They waited a few moments before Kane whispered, "I hear something." Putting his ear to the door, "Yeah, someone's coming." The adrenaline was kicking in. Kane's eyes were as big as saucers under the porch light.

The front door opened and Kory heard a woman's voice, "Can I help you?"

There was a pause as Kane just stared at the woman.

He forgot what he was supposed to say, thought Kory.

A moment later Kane said, "Tommy Huffman."

"What about Tommy? Who are you?"

Kane must have realized that he had fucked it up. He suddenly leaped forward and punched the old woman in the forehead. The force of the blow knocked the African American lady backward through the doorway.

Kory peeked around the corner. The woman was lying on the floor with Kane straddling her and banging her head against the linoleum tile. Kory, Enforcer in hand, rushed the door and surveyed the area. *Living room on the left, dining room and kitchen to the right. Bedrooms must be in the back.* He put his hand on Kane's shoulder. When his brother looked up, Kory shook his head. There was blood on the floor, and the woman was now unconscious. "Shut the door," Kory whispered in a stern voice.

Kane tried to close the front door, but the woman's legs were blocking the way. He then took hold of her legs and with some difficulty dragged her to the living room, leaving a river of blood on the floor.

They heard a man's voice from the back of the house, "What's going on Mary? Was that the paperboy? I hope you talked to him about not leaving the paper in the lane..."

A middle-aged black man abruptly stopped speaking as he took in the scene in the living room. There were two men, one with a wild-eyed look holding his wife's legs up in the air, and another dressed as a cowboy, pointing a huge gun at him.

"What's going on here? What are you doing to my wife?" The man's tone suggested to Kory that he was used to giving orders.

Kory walked right up to him and hit him savagely on the side of the head with the butt of the gun. The man fell to one knee, and Kory hit him a second time.

"He-he, fuck that's cool," said Kane.

"You need to take charge, show him right away who the alpha dog is." Kory boasted. He looked over at his brother, still holding up the women's legs and peering up her dress. Kory was sure that Kane was batshit crazy. "You can put the lady's legs down. I'm going to look for the kid. Keep your eye on them."

Both Huffmans were out cold. Kane looked at the woman. She was wearing a simple flower skirt and a pink cashmere sweater that accentuated her ample breasts. *"Mary the Milf,"* Kane said to himself.

Kory came back after a few minutes and said, "Fuck! The

kid ain't here." A *National Geographic* sat beside an easy chair. Kory picked it up and read the address label. "Ralph Huffman, 1933 Lebanon Lane, Wankertown, Mississippi."

"I thought this place was called Greenville?" asked Kane, sitting in a chair and pushing back, causing the footrest to rise.

"It is, fucktard. Go into the kitchen and find something we can use to tie them up." Kory lit a Marlborough and went to the front window to draw the drapes closed.

"Aw FUCK, what do we do now?" Kane whined. They had just finished using phone cords to tie the Huffmans to kitchen chairs. They used a pair of black socks and some black electrical tape to gag them. In a moment of exuberance, Kane encircled Mrs. Huffman's head with the tape at least a dozen times. "She looks like a mummy...a nigger mummy." He laughed, stepping back and proudly admiring his work.

"Get some water from the kitchen," commanded Kory.

Kane came back a few minutes later drinking a glass of water.

"Not for you, fucktard," Kory took the water glass and dumped its contents over Mr. Huffman. "Ralphie, wake up."

"Wakie, wakie, eggs and bakie," added Kane.

When the man didn't wake up, Kory told his partner to give him the brass knuckles. Kory put the knuckles on his right hand and went to punch the bound man in the head. At the last minute, as the man winced, he pulled back. Kory then walked over to the wife and hit her hard in the face. The blow was strong, causing her chair to fall backward. She lay on the floor making a strange gurgling noise.

"Whee, hee!" said Kane.

Mr. Huffman suddenly opened his eyes and struggled to untie himself.

"Oh, great...thanks for joining us old Ralphie, my boy," Kory said, using the Art Carney voice he'd heard on television. Kory gestured for his partner to lift the wife's chair back up. "Put it right here so Ralphie can see what I'm going to do to her."

Ralph's eyes went wide with fear for his wife. She was slumped in her chair, blood seeping through the electrical tape. "Take the tape off his mouth," Kory directed his brother. "Sounds like he has something he wants to say." Kane removed the electrical tape and pulled out the sock.

"Please leave my wife alone. She has a bad heart. Whatever you want, you can have. I have cash in my wallet, take the television, it's a Zenith."

"A Zenith?" repeated Kory, his tone showing he was impressed.

Kory went over to Mrs. Huffman and lifted her skirt revealing her white panties. He used his knees to spread her legs and then started to make a humping motion.

The husband renewed his struggle against his binds, "Please, please what do you want?"

"You know, I think she's wearing Fruit of the Loom," Kory said. "The man wants to know what we want," Kory said to his partner.

"Easy Peasy, Lemon Squeezy."

"Where's the kid? You know, Tommy. Where's he at?" Kory leaned into Huffman's face.

The man suddenly had a flash of realization. "Tommy...er

doesn't live here anymore. He ran away from home. He didn't like the schools here."

"Not convincing," Kory shook his head. He nodded to his brother, "Get me a sharp knife from the kitchen."

A few minutes later Kane returned with a Ginsu knife.

"Oh Ginsu! You guys have some cool stuff, a Zenith TV, Fruit of the Loom panties, Ginsu knives...I heard on late night TV that these babies are as sharp as Samurai swords. We're going to have to test that," said Kory.

"Ahs-hole," said Kane, bowing and then slashing the air as if he was wielding a sword.

"Get some more water and dump it on her, she needs to be awake for this," said Kory.

Kane came back from the kitchen and dumped half a glass of water on the woman, who immediately gave a start. Kory pulled some of the tape off so she could watch through the one eye that wasn't swollen shut. Taking the knife, he held it up, pointing it at Mrs. Huffman, "Last chance Ralphie boy...where's Tommy at?"

"Please leave her alone. Kill me if you want but leave her."

"Wrong answer." Kory pulled the bottom of her cashmere sweater and started to cut the fabric. Her mouth covered in duct tape, Kory had to be satisfied with the look of absolute terror in her one eye.

Ralph Huffman closed his eyes, no longer able to watch.

CHAPTER ONE

Monday, April 8th, 1984
"Alfred Hitchcock." That's what Gabriel thought the first moment he laid eyes on the man who said his name was William Friesen. The guy had a bulky physique; his balding head had a few thin wisps of hair dragged across the top.

It was a dank April day. Or as his wife, Jacqueline liked to say to their 18-month-old son Benjamin, it was an "umbie day." Gabriel had beaten his associate Rachel Henderson to the office and put the coffee on. He had just sat down behind his desk when the Agency door opened and in walked a man doing a pretty good imitation of Alfred Hitchcock, imitating a dog shaking off the rain. It was early Monday morning, too early for customers. Gabriel waited until the man had stopped his ministrations and then came out of his office, extending a tissue.

"Thanks," said the man as he used the tissue to wipe away the wet from his eyes. "It's like a monsoon out there."

The heavy-set man appeared to be in his fifties. He had a deadpan expression as he looked around the office.

"You know what they say about April showers," Gabriel extended his hand. "I'm Gabriel Ross."

"My name is Friesen, William Friesen."

"May I help you, Mr. Friesen?" said Gabriel, shaking the man's soggy dishtowel hand.

The man's eyes took in the empty offices. "All alone this morning?"

"The army will be in shortly."

"You're the guy that blew that killer away a few months ago." *A statement, not a question. The killing of Tyson Ulrich, better known as the Magnum Killer, had been national news. It had been self-defense, but that hadn't stopped the local paper from calling him Biloxi's Dirty Angel. Okay, so he might have overdone it by emptying all six bullets into the man.*

"Well, are you?" The man repeated, looking at Gabriel anxiously. Gabriel was momentarily taken aback by the question.

"Did you want to sit down in my office, Mr. Friesen?" After all the publicity he and the Agency had received, he'd been flooded with interview requests. "I was just going to have a coffee. You look like you could use one."

"Sure, black five sugars."

So, a cup of sugar with a splash of coffee, thought Gabriel as he went to get the coffee.

When Gabriel returned with the coffee, he found Friesen looking at the posters that Gabriel's wife, Jacqueline, had used to decorate his office. *Fix, or Repair Daily* was a picture of a Ford Pinto found dead along the side of the road. A subtle reminder of how dead Gabriel's career was at Ford before he'd come to Biloxi and met the person who would later become his wife.

"Had a Pinto back in 1975," said Friesen. "It was a piece of crap." The man had a gasping quality to his voice, like someone laboring for his last breath.

"I used to work for them as an accountant. That seems like such a long time ago now. Anyway, had the Pinto not been crap, my first wife wouldn't have ended up having an affair with the mechanic, and I would have never have left Detroit and moved down here."

The man fixed Gabriel with a look of understanding. "The Deadly Accountant...hmm, would make a good movie plot. Life can take interesting turns."

Friesen had a wistful look of regret as a flash of lightning illuminated the office. It was followed by a crack of thunder loud enough to suggest the heavens had split apart. Moments later, the lights in the office went off, plunging them into a blanket of darkness.

"That was nasty," Gabriel said nervously. "We haven't had a major storm for a while." He looked out at the parking lot. "We don't have any emergency lighting, so we'll have to struggle through it."

There was a glimmer of light from the window which allowed Gabriel to see Friesen in the shadows. "Have a seat and tell me how we can help."

Before he could answer, the Agency's door opened, and a shape walked into the dark reception area. "Geez, did you see that lightning?" asked a voice Gabriel recognized as Rachel Henderson's, his receptionist slash part-time investigator.

"Pretty nasty," called out Gabriel from his office. "Can you find some candles?"

"Sure, every time I hear thunder it reminds me of a boyfriend who once said I had thunder thighs," Rachel responded, shaking out her umbrella. She suddenly realized there was a man sitting in the office with Gabriel. "Oh, good morning! In the dark, I didn't realize …"

"Rachel, this is Mr. Friesen, another refugee from the monsoon happening outside," Gabriel said, using the man's word. Rachel shook the man's hand.

"I can't imagine a man being so rude as to say that to you," said Friesen.

"Thank you. That's why he's not my boyfriend anymore," Rachel replied. She went to her desk and quickly came back with a candle that Friesen lit and put on Gabriel's desk.

Both Gabriel and Friesen watched as she took off her raincoat, admiring the tall, attractive, dark-haired woman. Under the glow of the candle, she looked more sensual than normal. Rachel sensed the looks and smiled. Turning to Gabriel, "Did you get a chance to put the coffee on before the power went out?"

"Yes, we have a cup, it should still be warm."

Gabriel saw how Friesen was watching Rachel as she left the office and thought, *A womanizer. I'm guessing this is a divorce case. His wife, a high school sweetheart - lost her figure after having a dozen kids- he's bored, looking for something younger - she catches him cheating on her and sues for divorce.*

"Mr. Ross? Kind of lost you for a moment," Friesen got up and closed the office door behind Rachel. "Hope you don't mind, but my situation is kind of …delicate," he said, sitting back down across from Gabriel.

"Everything you say in this office is totally confidential."

Friesen nodded. The candle illuminated his face and Gabriel could see the man had the red bulbous nose of a heavy drinker.

"How's business?" Friesen asked.

"Good," Gabriel replied with a smile. The truth was that business was more than good. The Agency also had a part-time associate by the name of Arnie Sims working cases, and his business partner Ben O'Shea had recently left his job as a Biloxi detective.

"How many people have you killed?"

Odd question. Keeping his expression inscrutable, Gabriel answered. 'I don't know Mr. Friesen, why don't we talk about you?"

"I want to know who I'm dealing with." When Gabriel didn't answer, "You can't remember how many people you've killed?"

The man was wearing a sodden, off the rack gray suit with a red tie. *What kind of man goes around without an umbrella or a raincoat?* "I remember, but this is personal. I can say that I have never killed someone who wasn't threatening to kill someone else."

"How does it feel?"

This is getting creepy. "At the time you just do what you have to do, what you've been trained to do. After, when you think about taking someone's life, you wish it hadn't been necessary."

"Regret?"

"No, not regret. The people who died had to be put down. I guess you just feel sorry for whatever led them to the crimes they'd committed. Now, Mr. Friesen, what may we do for you?" *I don't know if it was the eerie candle-lit office, the rumbling thunder overhead, or maybe it was just that he looked like Hitchcock, but his response, as Gabriel would tell Rachel later, sent goosebumps down his spine.*

"I want you to kill me."

CHAPTER TWO

Arnie Sims parked his van in the busy parking lot of the Harrison County Detention Center and watched the rain pelt down on his windshield. *Someone should write a country song about rain falling like the tears of all of the mothers whose sons were locked up in this place.* He took a sip of his coffee, waiting for the rain to let up.

He had been surprised when Gabriel welcomed him back to the Agency with open arms. Three months earlier, Arnie had taken on a case involving some longshoremen who were scammed out of their New Jersey State lottery winnings by the son of a mafia kingpin. Despite finding the bad guy, the clients were still unable to recover their money and had not paid the bill, leaving the Agency with some significant out of pocket expenses. Making things worse, a couple of mafia thugs almost beat Arnie death. Then to top things off, Ben O'Shea, one of the two owners of the Agency, took a bullet in his shoulder trying to save Arnie. All in all, it had been a bad decision to have taken on the case.

Arnie had been deliberating returning to work when he'd

gotten a call from an old friend of his, offering an assignment that seemed safe and straightforward. Rodney Smith was a lawyer who Arnie knew from the old neighborhood. Smith was looking for an investigator to help him by visiting his client in jail. His client Geoffrey Motten was charged with conspiracy to commit murder, and the lawyer simply wanted Arnie's take on the case and didn't want to prejudice things by sharing too many details.

Before heading out that morning, Arnie had found the story in the *Herald*. The details were sparse, but apparently, Motten had tried to hire a hitman to kill his wife. It was Motten's bad fortune that the hitman was actually an undercover cop.

Realizing the rain wasn't going to let up, Arnie decided to use his newspaper as an umbrella and sprinted to the doors of the building. The Harrison County Detention Center was a medium security facility that served as a temporary jail for men and women who were awaiting trial. The cells were located on two floors with a common area where prisoners could gather, play cards, read or watch TV. As Arnie entered the security section, he was reminded that the jail had the highest ratio of guards to inmates of any in the state. The agency and its investigators had already completed the application for visitation and undergone the criminal record check. He followed the gray corridors to the interview room.

ARNIE once again showed his identification and was escorted to a prisoner meeting room where Geoffrey Motten was sitting at a metal table. "Mr. Motten, I presume?" Arnie asked, taking in the man across from him wearing the standard orange jumpsuit.

"You the investigator?"

"Name's Arnie Sims."

"I wasn't told you's was a nigger."

And I wasn't told you were a racist. Arnie let the comment slide and shrugged his shoulders as if to say he didn't have any choice in the matter. "Your lawyer asked me, as a favor, to come talk to you. I gather you're in a bit of a tight spot."

"Tighter than my ass in the showers in here." Motten was fifty-something, give or take a decade. As they say in the South, he was as thin as a poor man's wallet. The word wiry sprang to mind. His hair was long and stringy, and he had a chin strip of a beard that he'd allowed to grow too long. Motten's dark beady eyes darted around the room before once again focusing on Arnie, who had taken the chair across from him.

Arnie ignored Motten's comment, "Do you understand the charges against you?"

"Bullshit! They say I tried to hire someone to kill my wife." Motten looked away.

Arnie waited for a moment to see if he would continue. When the man turned back to him and glared, Arnie asked, "So did you?"

"Fuck, no."

"Okay, why do they say you did?" Arnie made a note on his pad.

"Anybody listening?" Motten looked around the room at the brick walls.

"I think we're good. They're not allowed to eavesdrop. Our conversation is privileged."

Motten seemed to chew on what Arnie had said for a

minute, probably not sure what privileged meant. "I was in a bar down by the waterfront. A place called McShay's. I was minding my own when this guy from work sat down beside me. We had a few, and I told him about my bitch wife. It was kind of like talking to a bartender. You know?"

Arnie nodded that he understood, knowing there had to be more, a lot more. When nothing else was forthcoming, "I've been in that bar. So, who was the guy?"

"Name's Drake, something; I don't remember his last name. I knew a guy who looked just like this guy. He was riding with the Sons back in the seventies. Anyway, not this guy, he's new at the paint shop."

Motten was referring to the Sons of Silence, a particularly violent gang operating on the Gulf Coast. "Paint shop?"

"Yeah, I work for a car painting place called who done it painting."

"There's a paint shop called who done it?"

"Yeah, but it's spelled Huedunit."

Arnie was surprised that this guy could spell. "Clever name. Was there anyone else around who might have heard the conversation?"

"Just maybe the bartender. Big Chinese guy."

"Wing?" Wing was the owner and used the name McShay's because he thought no one would go to an Irish pub named Wing's.

"I don't know. All zipper heads look alike."

Once again Arnie ignored the comment. "Did you say anything specific about wanting to hurt your wife?"

Motten looked up at the ceiling and bit his bottom lip like a kid about to tell a whopper. "I think I might have said that I wish she would go away."

"What did you mean by that?"

"Go away, like be gone. Go to wherever bitches like her go."

"Did you by any chance ask your drinking buddy to make that happen?"

"No, and if he said I did, then he's fucking lying."

CHAPTER THREE

"Kill you?" repeated Gabriel, looking quizzically at Friesen.

"I believe the going rate for rubbing someone out is $5 grand. I'm prepared to write you a check for twice that amount," Friesen said, taking a sip of his coffee.

"You're serious? You expect me to murder you?"

Friesen nodded.

"This is nuts," Gabriel got up from his chair. "I think you should leave."

"Don't you want to hear why? I think you might change your mind." Gabriel made a show of looking at his Casio before shaking his head and sitting down. He reluctantly nodded for Friesen to continue.

Friesen took a deep breath, "It all started six years ago. I'm in the jewelry racket. I specialize in importing precious stones. When I started the business, I put everything I had into it. I mortgaged the house, invested all of our savings. Once things got going, business was going pretty well. I was making money and had just started to pay off the bank loan."

Friesen lit a cigarillo he had taken from a silver case in his breast pocket. Taking a long drag, he sat back, "I suppose it was greed. I thought about how much more successful the business would be if I had more capital to invest. Thoughts of taking the business nationally, franchising and opening retail shops was all I could think about. To get the capital, the kind of money I would need, I decided to take on a partner. In return for two hundred thousand, I agreed to give him 50% of the net profit. This partner, let's call him Sam, convinced me to hire his bookkeeper. For the first 12 months, the expansion went well. Almost too well. Money was coming in faster than I had expected. One caution about success Mr. Ross, it's easy to delude yourself. I started to think I had a golden touch. Then I let a few things slide. Maybe more than a few. If you know what I mean."

"No, what do you mean?"

Friesen looked away, "I was partying with some of the suppliers and with some of the people Sam introduced me to. Before I knew it, I was living with a girl, sleeping with another, all the while still married to my wife. I know it's not an excuse but the drugs, the booze, things just got away from me. Finally, my wife left me and filed for divorce."

Friesen took a sip of his sugar coffee and continued, "I found an invoice at home from the Eye on You Detective Agency. So she had proof of my lifestyle. The proof, you, Mr. Ross, gave her. Also, she had information on my income the accountant was showing. The alimony she was asking for ...well it was ridiculous,"

He stopped for a moment before gasping, "Now this partner, Sam, he didn't think I was a very good partner anymore. I wasn't showing up for meetings with clients and well, blah, blah, blah, you probably can guess what happened."

"No, what happened?"

"Sam came to see me and said that he'd had enough. He said he wanted to exercise his right to buy me out. It turns out that the bastard had put this clause right into our partnership agreement. I thought if I could get my hands on 50% of what the company was worth then I could split the business with the ex and start fresh somewhere. At least that was what I thought in my perpetually half-drunk state."

"Can you get to the point where you decided you would be better off dead?"

"Sam said that I owed him a couple of hundred grand. It was my company, and he said I owed him!" Friesen yelled.

Gabriel nodded, still not understanding the punchline.

"Yada, yada, yada...I did what anyone would do in this situation."

"So, you went to the police..." Gabriel guessed.

"Not a chance," Friesen chuckled sarcastically. "Sam said he had a friend on the force and that he would know. He said he had all the records the accountant kept, showed that I had been embezzling."

"Were you embezzling?"

"Maybe just a tich."

"What did you do?"

"Like I said, exactly like anyone would do, including you. I went crying back to my wife and told her that my partner had stolen the company and that I had been planning to sell and split with her. I told her that I needed her to lend me the money to hire a lawyer."

"I wouldn't have done that."

Friesen just shrugged his shoulders, "She flipped out and called me a bunch of nasty names, but in the end, she said that she knew some people, said she'd take care everything. That was about a month ago."

Friesen stopped the story at that point and took a gulp of his coffee. Then, he dropped his half-consumed cigarillo into the mug. Gabriel waited patiently through the fizz, fizz. Finally, the man continued, "I know Sam did something to her. He more or less joked about it when I went to see him."

"Do you remember what he said exactly?"

"He said something about doing me a favor. That I had asked him to ...you know."

"No," Gabriel said in frustration. "Did you ask him to hurt your wife?"

"No, of course not. A few months back when she was talking about divorce and alimony, I might have said something. I don't know."

"You haven't gone to the police, even though your company has been stolen from you, and you suspect your ex-wife has been murdered?"

Friesen looked down at his shoes as if the answer might be written in the carpeting.

Gabriel looked at him in disgust for a few moments. "Interesting story, Mr. Friesen...So get to the idea of killing you."

"I don't have the money to pay the guy back. It's only a matter of time before he decides to punch my clock. I said to myself that if everyone thought I was dead, then I could start my life all over again."

"Why not just run away?"

"I've been looking into this Sam character, and he's involved in all kinds of things. He's not the kind of guy to just let me go. I would constantly be looking over my shoulder." Friesen shook his head in despair. "Look, I've thought this through. I have the use of a boat. Lots of people disappear out in the Gulf, and people say they've probably fallen overboard and were eaten by sharks. I have money to pay you and some cash for me to start over. All you'd need to do is tell people that I fell over in a drunken stupor."

"Why me?"

"I think it only fits since you started this mess with the surveillance."

"That's just bullshit."

"Because death seems to follow you, Mr. Ross."

"More bullshit."

"You're a celebrity around these parts. If you say I fell overboard, then people will believe I'm dead. I'll have a raft and can get myself ashore. You then sail back to Biloxi and break the news."

"Then what?"

"I'm going to start a new life. I have a new set of identification papers. Believe me; you won't hear from me again."

"But I don't know you. People would question why I would go out on the Gulf with someone I don't know."

"That's a good point. You can say that I'm a client and that I had engaged your Agency to look into my ex-wife's disappearance. The check I give you could be payment for work done."

"I'm sorry, Mr. Friesen. What you're asking me to do is to help you commit fraud."

"That's where you're wrong. It's not against the law in Mississippi for people to fake their death and disappear. It's done all the time."

"It's not done all the time."

"It's against the law for me to represent myself as someone that I'm not. But that's not your problem."

Gabriel remembered a case involving a man who'd faked his death during a hurricane. In that case, the motive had been to defraud the insurance company. "Do you have life insurance by any chance?"

"Yes, but I'm going to sell the policy beforehand."

"I understand your motivation. I can't be involved in this. I strongly encourage you to approach the Biloxi PD or the County sheriff. Maybe they can offer you protection."

Friesen got up and shook his head in disappointment. Just as he did, the lights in the office came back on. Without saying another word, the man walked out of the office into the monsoon.

CHAPTER FOUR

"Alright Mr. Motten, why would this person claim you offered to pay him to kill your wife?"

"I don't know! I wish I could figure that out," Motten got up from the table and wrung his hands in frustration, "It makes me so fucking angry. This is all horse-pucky. That Drake guy is an egg-sucking dawg."

"Mr. Motten, your lawyer asked me to come down to talk to you. This is a pretty serious charge. And my guess is that with maybe a few prior convictions, the judge might put you away for a long time. Now, come back to the table please." The prisoner reluctantly slumped back to the table, muttering about never having been in jail before. It wasn't just the lack of eye contact that set off Arnie's bullshit detector.

Once Motten was seated he looked down at the floor, "You got to believe me. I'm not the kind of man that would ever do that. Like I hate the bitch." Motten's eyes glazed over and he continued, "I had a dream once that I carved a hole in the back of her neck with a knife. Then I reached in and pulled out her spine."

Arnie took a moment to digest that before changing the subject. "Mr. Motten, what else can you tell me about the man from the bar?"

"Nothing. He started working as an apprentice at Huedunit. We've worked on a few jobs together, but I don't remember him ever saying anything important."

"He just happens to work for the same company, be at the same bar, at the same time, sitting on the next barstool, but you don't know anything about the man?"

Motten took a moment before his eyes lit up, "Fuck...he set me up."

"Why would he want to do that?"

Motten just shook his head. The guard interrupted them, saying the thirty-minute visiting time was over.

He's lying, like a no-legged dog, Arnie thought as the guard led Motten away. *But why would an undercover cop go so far as to get a job as a painter so that he could charge this guy with conspiracy? Doesn't make a whole lotta sense.*

ARNIE STOPPED at a payphone outside of a Peoples Drug Store and called Rodney Smith, Motten's lawyer.

"What do you think, Arnie?" asked the lawyer once they were connected.

"He's definitely lying. He wouldn't make eye contact, and well, you would have a lot of work to do with him if you want a jury to believe anything he says."

"Shit, this case just gets better and better. I just got a message from the prosecutor. They say they have a recording of Motten offering a grand to the cop to kill his wife."

"That's going to make his innocence a little harder to prove." After a moment Arnie asked, "You don't believe him do you, Rod?"

"Who would? But it doesn't matter what I believe, the man is entitled to a defense," the lawyer's tone was resigned.

"You should play the recording for Motten. It might make him a little easier to take."

"Don't have it yet, the DA has to release it to me as part of the discovery process. That might not be for a while. The DA doesn't seem to be in a hurry."

"Why not? Sounds like a pretty open-and-shut case."

"I don't know. He said he had a stack of other cases."

"There's one thing that doesn't fit." Arnie shared his doubt about why an undercover cop would go to that length just to nail someone like Motten.

"So what do you think that means?"

"I don't know. It's a real mystery. I'm not sure how it will help your client, but I'd like to check into why that cop would be moonlighting at a paint shop."

CHAPTER FIVE

B en was sitting in his usual booth at the Friendship Cafe when Gabriel walked in.

"Hey Ben, quite the downpour out there. Does the rain make your shoulder ache?" Gabriel shook his umbrella out and waved to the waitress as he slid into the booth across from Ben.

Ben rolled his shoulder, wincing slightly. "It's fine, like new."

Ben was old school. Didn't easily admit he was hurting. All those years with the police force had given his partner a crusty edge. Gabriel looked at his fifty-something partner. As long as he'd known Ben, he'd always worn his hair in a brush cut. Since going on disability though, he had let his hair grow into what looked like tufts of grass.

When their waitress Tweedy came by to take their orders, they both ordered their usual. Greasy burger, greasy fries, and coke without ice.

"Have you put on some weight, Ben?" Gabriel noticed his partner's rugged face was looking fuller.

"Have you gotten any shorter?" Ben replied with a grin.

"Ouch!" said Gabriel. Barely five feet in height, Gabriel had stopped growing when he was in high school. Since then he'd developed an immunity to wisecracks about his height. "Hardy-har-har, that's a good one. Something eating you, partner?"

Ben took a deep breath, "I'm bored. Bad enough I have no job, and a sore fucking shoulder, but Chevon gave me an ultimatum."

Gabriel struggled with what to say. Tweedy brought their cokes. Once she was gone, "Let's take things one at a time. What's the situation at work?"

"Chaos, with Chief Willis walking out because of Mayor Baxter; and me going on disability, there's all kinds of shit going on. They have a couple of new guys, former state cops. Murdock is still there, thank God, but the new people won't give me the time of day."

"What do you want to do?" Gabriel's tone was positive.

"I'm on disability. Once that's over, I could probably go through the union and get my job back, but that wouldn't go over well with the mayor. In all honesty, I couldn't go back while he's still mayor."

Gabriel felt bad for his friend. Especially since the bullet that had hit Ben's left shoulder had been meant for him. At the last moment, Ben had shoved his partner out of the way. "Why don't you come work at the Agency? We have lots of business."

Ben ignored the question. "How's Arnie?"

"He came back to work last week. Poor guy. Physically the plastic surgeon did a great job, but the whole lottery case rocked him pretty hard. I think he's going to stick to employee reference checks and insurance cases. Although, he's out meeting with someone this morning at the detention center as a favor to a lawyer he knows."

"He just needs time. I wouldn't have taken that case, but in all fairness, he didn't know he'd be dealing with the mob."

"So how about it, Ben? Will you come work at the Agency?"

Tweedy brought their meals, and Ben again ignored the question. They ate their meals in silence. Gabriel could almost hear the wheels turning in his partner's mind. He watched as Ben devoured his hamburger. Finally, when finished, Ben mopped the grease from his chin with a napkin. "Maybe a couple of days a week. I have to do physio every second day. After those sessions, my shoulder hurts like hell. I would shoot the therapist if I could lift my fucking arm."

"Alright, a couple of days a week works - when can you start?"

Once again Ben ignored the question. "How's Bourbon?"

Ben was referring to the feline associate that had adopted the Agency from the very beginning. "Arnie has him. The plan is that Arnie will bring him on the days that he works for us."

"Whose idea was that?"

"Rachel suggested it. She said that Bourbon was getting older and needed to settle down. She was worried about what he was getting into at night."

"Just like all women, trying to manage everyone's life." Ben chewed on one of the few remaining fries.

"Chevon?"

Ben had been seeing the young black woman off and on for the past couple of years. "Yeah, she's been my nursemaid. She took leave from her uncle's restaurant and visited every day. She bought me a TV, and she agreed to let me watch baseball as long as I watch *The Love Boat* with her." Ben took a gulp of his coke. "She finally went back to work last week. What's the secret, Gabriel - does Jackie make you watch that shit?"

"I watch whatever she wants to watch, but I'll let you in on something. Get a good book and read while she's watching her program. When she laughs, I laugh. Being in the same room and acting like I'm watching seems to be enough for her."

"Chevon's been busting my chops about moving to New Orleans and getting a real job. Whatever the hell that means."

"She doesn't want you to be a private investigator?"

"I think she and Jackie have been talking, and they think what you've been doing is crazy. You know, taunting serial killers on National TV?"

Gabriel's wife Jacqueline and Chevon had been friends since college. "Jacqueline would be fine if all we did were reference checks and insurance cases." After finishing a bite of his burger, Gabriel continued, "What are you going to do, then?"

Ben looked thoughtfully at the empty plate in front of him, "Part-time, a diet, new clothes, and Biloxi."

"Care to expand?" Gabriel smiled.

"I'm going to work at the Agency whatever days that Arnie doesn't come in. Since I've put on a few pounds, I need to eat better maybe get some exercise. Chevon wants to take me clothes shopping and force me to buy clothes that match. Lastly, I'm going to propose to Chevon as long as she is willing to accept me for who I am."

"Wow...that's a huge step. I didn't see that coming."

"Having someone to share my life with has somehow become more important than anything else. She makes me want to be a better person."

"You're going to move to New Orleans then?"

"I was thinking of taking a drive out to Picayune with her this weekend. Maybe grab some lunch; talk to people; take a look at some places. It's halfway between New Orleans and Biloxi."

"You've been thinking about this. I'm guessing you don't want me to tell Jacqueline?"

"Let's keep it to ourselves for now."

"Alright, what do you want to work on when you're at the Agency?"

"Where do you need help?"

"The publicity we've received has been great. Rachel has helped out and is doing surveillance pretty much every week. Arnie is back to work now. We could still use you on some of the bigger cases.

"Do you have any on the go?"

"No, I turned one down this morning," Gabriel told Ben about Mr. Friesen and his death wish.

"His check probably would have bounced. Did you tell him to go to the cops?"

"Yeah, he says he doesn't trust the cops. The guy who stole his business, and allegedly killed his wife, apparently has someone in the department."

"You know, the sad thing is that if he keeps waving that money around someone is going to do it."

"But not us. I think I've learned my lesson about big retainers. Okay, where does that leave us?"

"Well, I'm on disability, so I don't plan to mess that up

by taking a salary. I was thinking of working on a couple of my cold cases."

"Really? Are you allowed to do that?"

"No, and I'm also not allowed to copy a couple of murder books, which I did before leaving."

"What case?"

CHAPTER SIX

"Back in 1977 before you came down to Biloxi, there was a case; coincidentally it was in Picayune. A 14-year-old kid by the name of Glenn Wilson was found in the woods on the family farm. When the kid didn't come home for supper, his father went looking for him and found him at the base of an oak tree, a bullet hole straight through his temple. The case got lots of press, but they never found the shooter."

Ben continued after a sip of coke, "Since this was in Picayune, the Pearl River County sheriff caught the case. The old coot retired and died a couple of years back. Now an eager young guy named McDiarmid is the sheriff."

"Was the old sheriff the problem?"

"I don't know because it wasn't my case. My police chief at that time asked me to lend a hand. But the old fart sheriff didn't want my help. He ruled that Wilson's death had been an accident."

"An accident with a bullet in his head?"

"A bit of a stretch you say? The sheriff's working theory

was that Wilson was playing in the tree and that he fell, causing his the rifle to fire."

"A bullet right through the temple fired from a rifle while falling from a tree? Not sure if that would even be possible. You're going to look into it after all this time?'

"Thought I would give it a look-see."

"And the sheriff is on board this time?"

"Remember the Millard killing, where the car blew up last fall? McDiarmid worked with me on that. I mentioned that the Wilson case had left me with a bad feeling, and it hit a nerve. He knows the family and has agreed to work the case with me."

CHAPTER SEVEN

Later that evening, once a rambunctious Benjamin had fallen asleep, Gabriel and Jacqueline were sitting up in bed.

"Do you think Chevon and Ben make a good match?" asked Gabriel.

"She definitely cares for him, but I think she's getting resigned that he's not the marrying kind," Jacqueline was rubbing lotion on her arms. Gabriel fought back the temptation to tell her about Ben's plan for the weekend.

"What about you, now that he's left the police force do you think he might be ready to be domesticated?"

"Domesticated? You make him sound like a dog."

"Don't be silly; it's just an expression. Unless you think I treat you like a dog?" She was now rubbing lotion on her long legs.

"No, no," Gabriel said quickly, conscious of his wife's hair-trigger temper. "I had an interesting customer come to the Agency this morning. He looked and sounded just like

Alfred Hitchcock." He told her about Friesen and his desire to fake his own death.

"Gabriel, you're like a magnet for crazy people. I'm warning you not to get involved with any more psychopaths."

Gabriel skipped to a new subject like he was dancing across a minefield. "So how do your parents like living in Biloxi?"

"Pretty good, it's great to have them around for Benjamin," Then, after a moment, she put the lotion away and looked at him. "I've been thinking about going back to work. See if I can get my old job at the art gallery in Ocean Springs."

Gabriel nodded. "Have you stayed in touch with the guy that owns it?"

"His name is Peter. I've told you that a million times. He's a nice man. And yes, I spoke to him already."

"Already? You've already decided to go back to work, and then you bring it up now? Kind of asking my permission retroactively?"

"I wasn't asking your permission. I'm not your slave, Gabriel."

"It's our son."

"Are you saying that my parents can't be trusted to look after our son?" In response, Gabriel grabbed his nail clippers off the night table and started clipping his toenails.

"Oh...hey stop that! Is that what our marriage has dissolved to?"

"What does that mean?" He clipped a particularly long nail off his big toe.

"There was a time we used our bed for something more exciting than your personal toenail dump."

"Sorry," he said, putting the clipper away. He got up and went into the bathroom, leaving the door open. He sat on the toilet preparing to do his business.

"There's another thing. Leaving the bathroom door wide open while you gut out a massive dump, all the while staring at me. It's not only disgusting; it creeps me out."

Gabriel ignored her tirade and said, while using the bathroom tissue, "I think we should get a pet. You know, for Benjamin."

"He's only 18 months; he doesn't need a pet. Besides, you have Bourbon all day."

"Actually, I don't, Arnie adopted him."

"Oh, that's nice for Arnie. Whose idea was that?"

Gabriel thought about Ben's comment earlier that day about being managed. "Rachel's, she felt he was getting too old to be on his own, doing God knows what at night."

"Are you referring to Arnie or Bourbon?"

"Good point, maybe both."

"I'm allergic to cats." Jacqueline leafed through the latest *Cosmopolitan*. The cover promised a whole new way of dealing with men sexually. "What do you honestly think of me going back to work a couple of days a week?"

"If that's what you want, and your parents are okay with it, then I'm cool."

He came back and got into bed, turning out the lamp over the bed, plunging the room in darkness.

"That's the third thing that you do that bugs me; I was reading an article." She turned the light back on.

"I have an appointment first thing tomorrow morning," he whined, flicking the switch off once again. After a moment in the darkness, he added, "I was thinking of a dog, something small. It would be good company for Jellybean."

Jacqueline turned the light back on. "A dog's a lot of responsibility. You have to take it to the vet; you have to walk it; you have to feed it and then, of course, pick up its poop. Are you going to do all that?"

Gabriel shrugged and turned out the light again, not wanting whatever he said to come back to haunt him. After a moment, "I was thinking of a wiener dog."

"A dachshund?" After a moment she put her hand on his shoulder, "That's not the kind of wiener I've been hoping for."

"Bourbon isn't the kind of pussy I was hoping for."

CHAPTER EIGHT

Tuesday, April 9ᵗʰ, 1984

The rain finally stopped late in the evening, leaving in its wake a beautiful robin's egg blue sky. The weathermen were forecasting a week of clear skies and temperatures in the high seventies.

Ben drove west on Highway 10 to Picayune. One of the challenges of giving up his job with the Biloxi PD was losing the convenience of having a cruiser at his disposal. With the thought of moving to the country, he'd bought a used red and yellow 1980 F150 pickup. The truck had close to 100,000 miles on the odometer but was otherwise in pretty good shape.

For a city with a population of over 10,000, Picayune had a distinct country look. On the outskirts, there were plenty of red-brick farmhouses with old barns that had seen better days. As Ben got closer to town, he found country properties, all with large yards, set back from the road. Driving into downtown, he passed a strip plaza, a couple of greasy spoons, a Holiday Inn and an endless array of churches. *How is Chevon, a girl who grew up in New Orleans, going to react to living here?*

He had a 9 a.m. appointment with Sheriff McDiarmid in Poplarville, a small town of two thousand approximately half an hour north of Picayune. Ben remembered reading something about Poplarville that went back 25 years ago. An African-American man accused of rape had been abducted from the Pearl River County jail by a mob and shot to death. His body was found in the river 10 days later.

The FBI investigated and even obtained confessions from some of the eight suspects. Most important, however, the county prosecutor refused to present evidence to a state grand jury, and a federal grand jury refused to indict. The case had focused national attention on the persistence of this type of crime in the South and had helped accelerate the American Civil Rights Movement.

Ben parked his truck in the lot in front of the sheriff's office. A tall, wide-shouldered man in his mid-twenties, whom he recognized as Sheriff Cliff McDiarmid, was smoking a cigarette and drinking coffee on the steps of the building.

As Ben got out of the truck and approached, McDiarmid called out, "Ben, did you buy that truck cos you can see it at night?"

Ben smiled and shook Cliff's outstretched hand, "Only one they had left."

"If we have to go anywhere, we can take my car. Let's go in, and I'll fix you up with some bad coffee." Cliff took a last drag of his cigarette and then flicked it into the parking lot.

Once they were seated in the sheriff's small office, McDiarmid gazed at Ben and said, "You realize of course that the case you're interested in was before my time. At the time of Wilson's death, Sheriff Harrigan was in charge, and I was trying to figure out how to get Doris Pender to go to the dance with me."

Ben nodded then asked, "What have you heard about Harrigan?"

Cliff took his time answering, then got up and closed his office door. "There's still a few deputies around that worked for him." The sheriff grimaced as he took a big gulp of his coffee. "Fuck, that's bad coffee. Let's say we get out of here and go to a diner down the street."

"DID you go to the dance with Doris?" asked Ben as they grabbed a coffee and sat in a back booth of the diner.

"Nah! I've never been much of a lady's man. I asked her in my roundabout, bumbling jack-ass sort of way."

"Crashed and burned?"

"It was a Halloween dance. To Doris, October meant, *Only Me October.* Then, she followed up the rejection with *No Man November,* and then, *Don't Date December.* I'm a pretty persistent guy, but I finally got the message." McDiarmid had a southern drawl, pronouncing Halloween as Hallereen, and pretty as purdy.

"Sorry."

"Speaking of persistence. It's a small town, and I know the Wilson family pretty well. The case always had a bad smell about it. Most people hold the opinion that Harrigan was as crooked as a bag of copperheads. Nothing much ever got proven, but talk is, he protected drug dealers. I mean in a big way." Cliff lit up another cigarette. "Remember that corrupt sheriff in Biloxi a few years back? A guy named Cooper?"

"I helped bring him down."

"Hate to say it, but the two of them were buddies."

Ben took a long sip of his coffee. "If folks knew about him, why did they keep voting him in?"

Cliff stared at Ben for a moment. "Ben, you've got more experience in policing than me. But I was born here. I went to school here. You've got to remember that this is Mississippi. Folks around here like Harrigan and Cooper are the same people you see in church every Sunday. While they're busy organizing fundraisers, they're also thinking about how to make you disappear, all the while appearing to be your best friend."

"Understood."

"Tell me, how were you able to get Cooper?"

"Well first off, I had some help. There's a PI by the name of Gabriel Ross who did a lot of the groundwork. He also worked the Magnum case with me."

"I remember him, the short guy."

Ben took a sip of his coffee. "Cooper was into some pretty sick shit. Teenage girls were being abducted and sold to some creep on a cabin cruiser. Gabriel caught Cooper red-handed in a 'guns for drugs' scheme at Kessler Airbase. Gabriel was able to get under the guy's skin, and the sheriff went too far and tried to kill him. Cooper, faced with evidence not just of attempted murder, but also for conspiracy, made a deal to go into the witness protection program in return for his testimony about the Dixie Mafia."

"Wasn't there something about the sheriff's wife?"

"Gabriel developed a relationship with Cooper's wife. Kind of unprofessional, but she's quite the lady. When Cooper got relocated by the Marshalls to California, he snuck away and came back to town to take back what he thought was rightfully his. Gabriel shot and killed him."

"I remember reading about some of this. Listen, I usually have a donut around this time of day. They make great crullers, want one?"

"I'll pass. Trying to lose a few."

McDiarmid got up and quickly came back with a plate of honey glazed crullers. Ben took a look at the donuts and shook his head. "You do this every day? Why aren't you three hundred pounds?"

"Do you realize that stressed is desserts spelled backward? I just burn it off." Cliff answered with a smile.

"Alright, let's get to the Wilson case, what's your take?"

"I went over this file before you arrived." McDiarmid patted a binder he'd been carrying. "I called the Wilsons and told them that I was going to take another look at their son's case, and they'd be happy to meet with us."

"Anything jump out from looking at you?"

The sheriff lowered his voice, "To me, it sounds like a cover-up. Harrigan was up to his elbows in drug money. Christ, he might have been the one that pulled the trigger."

"The kid saw something?"

"That's what I thought."

"Too bad we can't interview Harrigan. He died a couple of years, back right?"

"Had a stroke. Wife is still around though."

The sheriff handed over the binder. When Ben opened it, he found the first few pages contained black and white photos of the scene. A spotlight was used to take pictures of a young boy sprawled on his back with death written on his face.

McDiarmid watched Ben's expression sadden as he looked at the photos. "In life, the kid was popular, full of teenage energy and life. He probably wanted to be an astronaut, a scientist, or an engineer."

There was a ghost-like picture of the boy lying on a steel gurney at the morgue. Ben quickly flipped through the pages and found a chronology report, a ballistics report, witness statements, as well as two medical examiner reports. Ben took a few minutes and read through Harrigan's timeline. "It doesn't say what the kid was doing in the woods that day."

"It was August, so no school. The family owned the feed store outside of Picayune, and when he wasn't at school, he was helping at the store. Lots of raccoons getting into stuff in August, so his folks say Glenn took the day to go coon hunting. The Wilson place is about 125 acres, and Glenn knew it like the back of his hand."

"It says his father found him later that evening?"

"The father started to get worried when Glenn didn't come home for supper, so he went looking for him. I believe that was around 7 p.m." Cliff stopped to swallow a whole cruller, making odd noises while chewing with his mouth open. Continuing to talk with his mouth full, "So the basic facts, *um,* are the Wilson kid, *um,* was fourteen and going to the local high school."

"That's disgusting. Finish your donut."

The sheriff swallowed and took a sip of his coffee, "Everybody around here knew the Wilson family from the feed store. The kid was bright, popular, outgoing,"

Ben looked in the file and read the Medical Examiner's reports. "Suicide?"

The sheriff nodded, "Most of what I know, I know, from growing up here. People talk, some of it might be people just speculating, but like I said there's something off about all this. The boy had a bullet hole in his temple. The bullet went clean through the left, exiting on the right. The gun would have to be held at his temple for it to pass straight through like that. The squirrel gun was lying there beside him."

McDiarmid ate the last cruller in one bite. When he finished, he continued. "Because the farm was outside of the city, Mr. Wilson called the sheriff's department. Harrigan and his deputies made it out there by 10 p.m. and roped off the area. It was dark, so not ideal for finding clues. From what I understand, within a few minutes, Harrigan declared Glenn's death to be an accident. A misadventure, he called it. His theory was that the kid fell out of that old oak tree and that his rifle fired as he fell."

"It looks like the first ME report supported that finding?"

"Keep in mind this is Mississippi, and the ME does not need to have any medical training to run for office. Most of them just do what they're told."

"What made the ME change his mind?"

"He said it was, 'after more thorough examination,'" Cliff used air quotes. "In reality, it was Glenn's mother. Mrs. Wilson was flying off the handle. She wasn't going to accept that this was an accident. She had a right old fashioned hissy fit, hollering at whoever would listen. She latched onto the *Herald,* and before you could blink your eye, there were vans of snoopy reporters driving around. I figure the ME just knew that the accident label wasn't going to fly, so he changed it to suicide."

The sheriff drained his coffee. "Forget the fact that Glenn Wilson was just about the happiest kid around. The ME said that because the bullet went in the left temple and out the right that it couldn't have been an accident. The new theory, of course, now supported by Harrigan, was that Glenn was standing and shot himself on purpose."

"Not impossible, but pretty hard to do with a rifle."

"The parents didn't believe it and smelled a cover-up. It says in the file that the mother claims she paid Glenn $40 cash for working in the store just before he set off hunting. When Mr. Wilson found his son's body, the wallet and money were missing."

Ben was going to say something, but Cliff raised his hand, "There's more. Mr. Wilson discovered that Glenn had a two-inch gash on the crown of his head and that there was blood on a branch nearby. Because of the location of the wound, it would be pretty hard to do that by accident."

"What did the ME say about that?"

"The ME said nothing, didn't include it in the report. Harrigan then said it was a combo. A combination accident and suicide. Don't laugh; it goes like this...Glenn was up in the tree looking for coons when he got excited and slipped, losing his grip on the branch. He then tumbled out of the tree and hit his head in the process. Once he regained consciousness, he wasn't in his right mind. He had lost his wallet in the fall, and in his depressed state decided to stand up and shoot himself in the temple."

Ben took a long sip of his coffee and looked again at the black and white photo taken of Glenn Wilson lying in the morgue. He had seen hundreds of similar photos in his career. The young ones were always the worst. They stayed with him and haunted his dreams.

"That's when they found the bullet."

"The bullet? There is nothing in the ballistics report about a bullet."

"It's not there. If you want to hear about that part of it best you hear it from the Wilsons."

CHAPTER NINE

In Gulfport, Rachel drove to the agency early, wanting to beat Gabriel into work. As was her habit when she was upset, she fell into a spirited conversation with herself. Beau Snyder, her professor and boyfriend, said he found no problem with the practice, just as long as she didn't start hallucinating that someone else was talking to her.

She spoke to her reflection in the rearview mirror. "It's okay to like Beau Snyder. There's nothing to feel bad about. He's twice my age, but he's fun in a kind of kooky sort of way." *Wait a minute girl ... what are you doing?* "Gabriel said the guy was old enough to have been in the Civil War. What kind of a future do I have with someone like that?" *Wake up, Rachel!! Tell him it's over.* "Beau, I really like you as a friend, but when I'm forty, I don't want to shop for a nursing home for you. Okay, okay...Beau stop crying, you can still find someone else...." On and on it continued until she pulled into the Agency's parking lot.

As she was opening the AMC Pacer's door, Rachel caught sight of her reflection and continued the conversation. "Working at the Agency is fun, but then there's Gabriel. I kind of missed the boat on him. Now he's back with Jacqueline; it's time to move on." *Yet I know there's something there. I need to get out of there before I make a fool of myself or mess things up for them... maybe I could get my old job back at the hospital."*

Rachel finally told herself to shut up and unlocked the Agency door, surprised to see that once again Gabriel had beaten her in. "My God, Gabriel," she said, walking into the office, "It's not even 8 a.m. yet. Did you sleep here?"

"Good morning to you too, Rachel. I didn't sleep well last night. Too much going on I guess." He noticed Rachel was wearing a cream-colored tight-fitting skirt along with a navy silk blouse. As usual, she looked incredible.

"Is there anything bothering you?" she asked with a smile.

"No, nothing specific. Arnie coming back to work feeling so bad about taking the lottery case; Ben deciding to come on board part-time; Jacqueline wanting to get a job; the office getting busier, Bourbon not being here when I need him.... lots of stuff."

"Oh, I see," said Rachel. "Anything I can do?"

"No, but thank God I have you. I don't know where I would be if I ...."

"Don't mention it, Gabriel," she interrupted. "I really like working for you." Rachel quietly shuffled papers on her desk.

"What's new with Beau?"

"I've pretty well decided that it isn't going to work out. He's just not right for me."

"I'm sorry. I hope it wasn't that crack I made about his age."

"No, nothing like that," she lied.

"What ABOUT when I made FUN of his Kermit the FROG voice?" The professor had an odd way of speaking. He emphasized certain words while simultaneously letting his eyes bulge as if he'd received a bolt of electricity.

"Ha-ha, no, that was funny, but that's not it either. I've been thinking about the future and, well I'm going to tell him that I just want to be friends. I'm not even sure about taking more history courses."

"I'm sorry it didn't work out."

"That's okay; I met a guy at a party last weekend who wants to get to know me. And you'll be happy to hear that he's more my age and doesn't talk like a frog."

"Sounds interesting. Who is Prince Charming?"

"His name is Dan, and he works for the Government of Mississippi as an analyst or an administrator doing some kind of bureaucratic mumbo-jumbo."

"Zzz." Gabriel faked that he had fallen asleep. "Sounds very interesting. Good luck with that. Hey, I meant to ask you. When you came in yesterday, I was talking to Alfred Hitchcock. Well, his name isn't Hitchcock, it's Friesen. He said we did surveillance on him for his wife. Does that ring a bell?"

"Friesen? I thought I'd seen him before. It was after Arnie got hurt. We got a call from a woman named Bonnie Friesen. Sweet lady. She suspected her husband was cheating on her and wanted to hire us to get proof. Arnie let me use his van, so I tailed him ...you're right he does look like Hitchcock. Anyway, he's a creep. I tailed him for three nights. The first night I got film of him making out with a blonde with big hooters at a local bar, then they went to a sleazy motel. The second night I followed him to this house in Biloxi where he had a sleepover party with a brunette with even bigger tits. I only followed him the third night to see if he had a redhead stashed away too. I was kind of disappointed it was just a business meeting with this creepy guy. I gave Mrs. Friesen the pictures and the bill for the work. It was a grand. I realize I should have told you, but you said you wanted me to get more involved and well there wasn't anyone else."

"She had huge tits?"

"Settle down boy, not your type."

"What's my type?"

Dangerous question girl. "I don't know, not skanky with big hooters. What did Friesen want?" Rachel changed the subject.

"He wanted to hire us to help him fake his own death." Gabriel related the previous day's conversation when he'd told the guy to take a hike.

"Wow, he sounds pretty desperate."

"Ben said that Friesen would eventually find someone who will do it for $10 grand." After a moment Gabriel asked, "So why was the guy creepy?"

"Creepy?"

"Yeah, you said Friesen had a business meeting with a creepy guy. So, let's hear your analysis."

Rachel closed her eyes and tried to visualize the man, "Friesen was excited, gesturing and standing up, but this guy just sat there drinking and smoking a cigar."

"What did he look like?"

"Short, but not as short as...well maybe five foot six, Round face, he had short hair in one of those widow things."

"A widow's peak?"

"Yes, that's it, kind of looked like Phil Collins, the singer. He was dressed in a black suit jacket, but I could tell he was muscular. Oh, and he spends too much time in a tanning booth because his skin had a kind of orange tint.

"I'll keep an eye out for muscular, short, orange looking man who looks like Phil Collins."

Gabriel then outlined Ben's return-to-work plan. "On the days that Arnie isn't in, Ben is going to use the spare office. For now, he wants to do his own thing and follow up on a cold case from ten years ago."

"I shouldn't book any appointments for him?"

"Not yet, just for Arnie and myself, and for you if you think you can handle it. Speaking of Arnie, this is Tuesday, is he coming in today?"

"I'm expecting him. He has an appointment at 10."

"I can't wait to see Bourbon."

ARNIE AND BOURBON arrived around 9 a.m. The tall African-American man had recently turned 63 but had the physique of someone twenty years younger.

"Bourbon," Gabriel picked up the tabby cat. "The agency hasn't been the same without you."

"Thanks, boss," Arnie's tone suggested he felt unappreciated.

"Oh, come here Arnie, it's great to have you back too." He put his arm around the older man, "The surgery didn't leave any scars," Gabriel said, looking at Arnie's face.

"There's a few, but makeup does wonders. I feel good though. I'm ready to roll."

"I understand you already have a case?"

Arnie quickly told him about the Motten case. "The guy's not what I would call trustworthy, but our client is the lawyer who already gave me a retainer. I made sure of that. The other thing is, this lawyer is looking for a new PI so there may be more business."

Since coming onboard, Arnie had proven successful at sourcing his own customers and bringing in extra revenue to the Agency. "Sounds great. Good work, Arnie. About this Motten case, how do you plan to proceed?

"The guy has pled not guilty. The DA must have pulled a favor because the judge refused bail."

"Sounds pretty severe for conspiracy when they just have a cop's word."

"Apparently this undercover cop has a recording of Motten offering him a grand to do the deed. The lawyer has hired us to look into this cop and the paint shop, and see if there's something the lawyer can use at trial."

CHAPTER TEN

The Wilsons lived on a farm ten miles north of Picayune. Sheriff McDiarmid pulled the cruiser onto a gravel road that snaked its way up to a red brick farmhouse. Rows of fruit trees bordered the lane. Behind the house, there was a barn which looked recently painted.

"Are they still farming?" asked Ben, as the sheriff brought the cruiser to a stop in front of a wraparound veranda.

"Nah, they're both in their sixties now. They quit farming and sold the store a few years back. Folks see them at church on Sundays, other than that; they keep to themselves. She used to call for updates on her son's death, but that ended last year."

"Is this going to rip open the wound?"

"Those kinds of wounds never heal. She sounded pretty pleased on the phone when I called and told them about you."

"You mentioned the mother, what about the dad?"

"He's not doing as well, health-wise. Not common

knowledge but in a town like this, people talk. Word is he's got cancer. Just to prepare you, she's a little feisty and pretty free with what she says. As for him, try not to get him riled up."

Ben nodded.

As they got out of the cruiser, the screen door on the porch opened, and a woman came out to greet them. "Morning, Sheriff."

"Good morning Maisie. Beautiful spring day," replied the sheriff.

"Surely is," Maisie Wilson turned her gaze to Ben. "You'd be this Private De-tec-tive from the big city."

The way she pronounced detective, and the tone of sarcasm when she said big city, made Ben wonder if she was happy to see him. The woman was five feet and a bit, with hair that shone like polished silver. "Yes Ma'am, thank you for letting us come by. I used to be a detective in Biloxi, but I'm now working privately."

"That's just special. Come on in, Fergus is waiting in the parlor." Once they stepped into the house, Mrs. Wilson went to get them some sweet tea. Sheriff McDiarmid led the way into the parlor where an older man was sitting on the couch. On one side of him was a colostomy bag, on the other an oxygen tank.

Fergus Wilson shook the sheriff's hand limply and nodded to Ben. "Sorry for not getting up. I could do it, but it's a big production."

"That's fine sir," Ben spoke loudly. "My name's Ben O'Shea. Can we sit and chat for a bit?"

"I'm going to have to turn down my hearing aid if you continue yelling, young man," Wilson said, as Ben sat on the couch. There was a picture of Fergus and Maisie standing under an apple tree with three kids in front of them, making stupid faces at the camera.

"How you been doing Fergus?" asked McDiarmid.

Fergus gave the sheriff a deadpan look before saying, "Pretty peachy, I think."

Mrs. Wilson came into the parlor carrying a tray of iced tea and a plate of what she called eeh-clares. "Help yourself; I got these miniature pastries from the Piggly Wiggly in town." Ben was just about to take one, but pulled his hand back as she added, "Got to eat them up as they expired a few weeks ago." She saw Ben's reaction. "Just messin with ya."

"Thanks for agreeing to meet with us. Now that I'm no longer on the police force I want to look at some of the cases that are unsolved."

"Bless your heart. Isn't that kind of you, Mr. 'I'm not a real cop anymore man," said Mrs. Wilson.

Her sarcastic comment was off-putting. "Please call me Ben. I remember your son's case from the newspapers, and well, something always struck me as funny about it."

"Ain't nothing funny about it, young man," wheezed Mr. Wilson, "but I get your meaning."

"The sheriff showed me the official file on the case and told me what he remembered about it. He also thinks there's something funny - I mean strange - about what happened."

"Hinky," said Sheriff McDiarmid.

"It was a goddamn cover-up," said Fergus, his voice going up a few octaves. He started hacking, which lasted about twenty seconds.

"Air, Fergus, air," yelled Mrs. Wilson, standing up in front of her husband.

The old man used the respirator, and after a few moments his coughing settled down.

"Sheriff McDiarmid was telling me that a bullet was found. There wasn't any reference to that in the official file." Ben commented.

Mrs. Wilson sat back down and flashed a look at her husband and said, "Shocker." Ben waited a moment for her to explain. "That Sheriff Harrigan," she rolled her eyes, "said the bullet we found, was, in his words, 'immaterial.' He just about accused Fergus here of planting the bullet because we didn't believe his malarkey."

"I found that bullet by doing the work that those good-for-nothing deputies were too useless to do. It was right there, buried in the dirt under where I found my son," said Fergus, his voice rising to a shout, fists clenched as he struggled to stand.

"Fergus sit, sit," yelled Mrs. Wilson. "This conversation might be a bit much for him."

"Are you saying that Harrigan was covering something up?" asked Ben.

"Ain't no flies on you. If he weren't crooked, then he was as dumb as a bunch of rocks."

"That must have been very upsetting for you, after all you've been through," commented Ben, feeling a little bruised by the woman's manner.

"You a Yankee?" asked Mr. Wilson, looking over at Ben. "Sounds like something a Yankee would say."

"I've lived here for over 10 years, but you're right, I'm originally from New England."

Mrs. Wilson gave him a fake smile and then tilted her head as if she no longer could understand him. "Ya'll from Bah-ston?"

"Providence actually. Rhode Island."

"Well, well, Fergus, this here crime's gonna be solved lickety-split on account of him being a Yankee."

Ben looked over at Sheriff McDiarmid, who was trying hard to stifle a laugh.

"So yes, Mr. De-tec-tive it was very upsetting. But not as upsetting as what that state ballistics man said." Ben again decided to wait the lady out. Mrs. Wilson took a sip of tea before continuing, "Fergus here drove up to Jackson and met with the state ballistics man. Some high fallutin muck-ety-muck. Fergus gave him the bullet and Glenn's squirrel gun and was told he'd get right back to us. We sat on our hands for near two weeks, waiting for that man to call. Finally, his secretary told us the test was inconclusive and to come pick up our property."'

"Inconclusive," repeated Ben.

"Yeah," she gave Ben an odd look. "It means the ballistics man didn't know shit and was in cahoots with the sheriff."

"When I went back to get our stuff they gave me back a different bullet," said Fergus.

"Are you sure?" Ben prepared himself for another sarcastic response.

Ben's question stimulated another bout of coughing, which of course led to more "Air, Fergus air." Once the coughing ended, Mrs. Wilson answered. "Of course, he's sure, I saw the bullet, and it weren't the same one he found. Then there was the man at Piggly Wiggly," the old lady pointed her finger at Ben, who nodded and gestured for her to continue. "It was about a month after we got the bullet back. I had done a piece with that lady from the *Herald*, bless her heart, she was killed this past fall, Debbie Sheehan was her name. The article went over all of the inconsistencies in the 'investigation.'" Maisie Wilson did air quotes to reinforce her scorn over what had been done to find her son's killer. "After that story come out, I was at the Piggly Wiggly one night loading up the pickup with groceries when a man I didn't recognize approached me. He said 'Maisie,' he used my given name, 'You have other children. You'd be smart to mind your own business and let the professionals do their job.' He scared me, and I called the Sheriff's Department, and they said there wasn't anything they could do. Harrigan blamed me for kicking up so much bad press."

"Then I found the radio," said Fergus.

"Go on," encouraged Ben. "Tell me about the radio."

"Fergus, I think you found the radio before that," interrupted Mrs. Wilson.

"No, I didn't," Fergus yelled.

Mrs. Wilson rolled her eyes again. "He found this radio before he found the bullet, I can fetch it for you." She got up and went to the dining room table that had boxes stockpiled on top of each other. It took her a minute, but she came back and handed it to Ben. It was a tin of *Spam*. Inside was what looked like a homemade transmitter. The device had an antenna along one side. Ben looked at it and then handed it to McDiarmid.

"Fergus found it in a clearing about a hundred yards from where he found our son," said Mrs. Wilson, sitting down again. "Once again, the sheriff said it was nothing. Based on some advice from a neighbor, we took it to a guy who used to work for the DEA, that's the Drug Enforcement Agency, you know. He told us it weren't a normal radio. He said it was a low range transmitter, the kind used by drug smugglers."

Ben nodded, "In the file, it says Harrigan said your son's death was a suicide."

"Yeah well, don't pee on my leg and tell me it's raining. We know our son, and he would never have killed himself."

"After all of this, what do you think happened to your son?"

Mr. Wilson spoke up. "I found his body. I figure Glenn was up in that tree and saw something he weren't supposed to see. Someone saw him and come upon him from behind. That person hit him on the head with a branch. And while my son lay unconscious and unable to defend himself, that same person put a bullet in his head." The old man cocked his fingers as if he was shooting a gun.

"Do you think that person was Harrigan?" Ben asked as he finished his sweet tea.

"Could be. I reckon Harrigan was involved. There's been talk about him being in bed with drug people from Orleans." answered Mrs. Wilson.

There was a break in the conversation and Ben noticed that Fergus' eyes were closed and his colostomy bag was filling up.

"Well Mr. Detective, what-cha-going to do about all this?" asked Mrs. Wilson.

"Thank you for meeting with me. I'm truly sorry for what happened and how long it has taken to get justice for your son. I can't make any promises, but I will give this my best. I'd like to start by looking at the site of your son's murder."

The use of the word murder seemed to impress the old lady. As Ben got up to leave, Mrs. Wilson cornered McDiarmid and whispered something to him.

CHAPTER ELEVEN

Arnie remembered he had an 11 o'clock appointment. He didn't know with who until he sat down at his desk and checked his day timer. Someone named Bernice. The only Bernice he knew was, *Oh my God!* He checked his watch and saw that it was a few minutes before eleven, much too late to reschedule. Bernice Cross, whom he knew from grade school, had shown up at the Agency unannounced one day last fall, coincidentally at the same time as her husband. They were both unaware of each other coming to the Agency, and had suspected the other of adultery. What ensued was pure chaos - with threats, accusations, and a swinging purse. Back then Arnie had been successful at sweet-talking Bernice into seeing a marriage counselor. With everything that happened since that fall, he had no idea whether Bernice and her husband Harold were still at each other's throats.

"Arnie, I'm sorry," Rachel came into his office. "When she called and left a message on the machine for an appointment, she just said it was Bernice. I should have clued in that Bernice was Bernice Cross. I would have given you a head's up. She's waiting for you out front."

"Not to worry, I need some practice at dealing with difficult people," Arnie said, giving her a smile and getting up from his chair. He followed Rachel out to the reception area. "Why, is that Bernice Cross I see here in our waiting room?"

A smile washed across Bernice's face like a beam of light. She was wearing a purple flower print dress and way too much purple eyeshadow. "Arnie Sims, my Lord I heard about your surgery, and I said to myself, 'Girl you'd better get in there and see if he's as handsome as ever... Gimme some sugar, honey." She gave Arnie a hug that went on a little too long. Bernice eventually released him and smiled, batting her eyelashes. "Arnie, you be finer than frog's hair split four ways."

Arnie smiled and caught a glimpse of Rachel standing behind Bernice and faking gagging. "Bernice, you're a sight for sore eyes, come into my office and tell me what you've been up to." Arnie ushered the heavy-set African American woman into his office.

When they were seated, he said "Bernice, I saw you back in the fall. You and Harold came to see me about..."

"Oh Arnie, Harold's cheating on me. He was cheating back then, and he's cheating on me now. He says he ain't, but that dog won't hunt."

"I'm sorry to hear that Bernice. What makes you think he's seeing someone else?"

"On account of him not wanting to be with me. He don't seem interested anymore. I go to bed, and he stays up watching the teevee. He always says he's too tired. Like look at this," she gestured at her body. "What man in his right mind wouldn't want to feed this kitty?"

Arnie smiled. "What happened with that marriage counselor, Bernice?"

Bernice stood up, hovering over the desk, "You mean that little slut y'all sent me to? She kept on taking Harold's side. 'Yo' reckon yo're bein' a li'l judgemental. Aren't yo' makin' an assumpshun? Assumpshun mah ass!" Bernice mimicked. She sat down again and said casually, "I told the little hussy I was gonna cream her corn."

"What would you like me to do, Bernice?"

"I've had it with Harold. I tried. Lord knows how hard I tried, Arnie." She pulled a Kleenex from her pocketbook and dried her eye. Finally, she said, "Enough is enough, I want a deevorce."

"Have you spoken to Harold about how you feel?"

"I can't talk to him anymore. I could really use someone like you to talk to." Then after a moment, she asked in a sultry voice, "You still a bachelor, ain't you?"

"Actually ...I live with ... someone."

Bernice's expression changed 180 degrees. "You mean, you getting kitty?"

"You could say that."

"My God, I should have jumped your bones years ago," Bernice said wistfully.

"Bernice, I want you to go home and make a special supper for Harold, open up a bottle of wine, and work your magic. You're too much woman for any man to resist."

That seemed to perk her up, and after a few more minutes of Arnie talking about her husband's fine qualities, Bernice reluctantly nodded. "I think I'd better leave now. Thank you for the advice, Arnie." Before leaving the office, she turned back and said, "What's your gal's name?"

"Bourbon."

CHAPTER TWELVE

"Quite the couple," Ben said as he got in the cruiser beside Sheriff McDiarmid.

"Like I said, feisty. After all, that's happened, she can come across a little crusty."

Ben smiled and rolled his eyes. "Do you know where to go?"

"Yep, been in those woods plenty of times myself. The easiest way to go is to drive up ahead to a small clearing and then take the trail into the woods."

"What did Mrs. Wilson whisper to you as we were leaving?"

"Just that I should keep an eye on you, on account of you being a Yankee."

"Seriously?'

"No," McDiarmid smiled. "She told me to tell you about Tommy Huffman."

"Who's Tommy Huffman?"

McDiarmid took his time answering. "What I'm going to tell you is not written down in any police record, and it's known only by a few people. They came to see me the day I was elected Sheriff. When I tell you, you'll understand why folks might want to keep this secret." He drove in silence for a couple minutes, seemingly weighing whether he should continue. "Glenn Wilson wasn't alone that day in the woods."

McDiarmid had Ben's full attention.

The sheriff lit a cigarette and cracked his window. "He was with this colored boy who lived on the next farm over." Ben waited as the Sheriff McDiarmid steered the cruiser into a small clearing. He turned off the engine and continued the story. "I think he was younger than Glenn, maybe a year. They were best friends, rarely seen apart, so I guess it stands to reason that he might have been in the woods that day."

"So, Tommy saw what happened and is hiding some-where?" asked Ben.

"Close, but not quite. The presumption is that he knows what happened to Glenn. We may never know though. You see after Glenn died, Tommy and his family moved away. Left in a big rush. That day when I first got elected sheriff, Mrs. Wilson came to see me, she was upset and told me about what had happened to the family."

CHAPTER THIRTEEN

Arnie had a contact in the Harrison County Police Dept. The man was some kind of cousin, maybe 5th or 6th, it didn't really matter on account of folks around the neighborhood were called your cousin even if they weren't. He dialed the number for Deputy Amos Croome. Arnie was in luck; the deputy was just returning from being out on patrol.

"Hiya Arnie, heard about that mess at the drydock, been meaning to come pay a visit."

"That's okay Amos. We're about due for a get-together anyway."

"How you making out, cousin?"

"Pretty much recovered. Only hurts when I smile."

"Ha-ha. Something I can do ya for, Arnie?"

"I'm working a case for Rod Smith. You remember him? His family lived on High Street?"

"Yeah, High Street where everyone got high."

"I went to see a fellow up at the detention center on

Rod's request. He's in there for conspiracy to commit murder. His name is Motten."

"Yeah, I heard something about that. I guess the guy's a bit of a cracker, throwing the nigger word around at the guards."

"Who did the arrest?"

There was a pause on the line before Amos said, "It doesn't say, just says to refer all inquiries to Sheriff Bragg."

"The sheriff?"

Amos lowered his voice just above a whisper. "Be careful here Arnie. This likely means it was an undercover arrest. When these happen, it's entered into the file as Sheriff Bragg. I reckon that has to do with confidentiality." He said the last word as if it was new to him, making it sound like 7 separate words.

"But won't the arresting officer's name come out if it goes to trial?"

"Yeah, but I think they probably kick everybody out for that. What they call a closed session."

"You taking law courses Amos?"

"Nah, just picking up a thing or two."

"That so? If I want to get more information about the arrest who would I have to speak to?"

"Sheriff Bragg, but he won't tell you shit."

IT TOOK Arnie ten minutes to get to Huedunit Painting. It was located in an out-of-the-way, industrial part of Biloxi, on McElroy Street. The place was a large metal hanger surrounded by a ten-foot-tall perimeter fence. About a dozen cars and trucks were parked in front. A painted sign showing an image of a man wearing a peaked hat and staring at a paint job with a magnifying glass hung above the double garage doors.

Arnie parked his van outside of the entrance. A sign on the front door said Yuri Chekhov - Proprietor. The reception area was small and opened up to the hangar where a man wearing a face mask was spray painting a Mustang. Arnie watched for a moment before another large man noticed him and walked over.

"Help you?" The man was tall and built like a Frigidaire.

"Do you paint vans?" From the man's name, Arnie figured he was Russian.

"Yeah, but we're busy."

Arnie looked into the hanger, which was big enough for at least a dozen cars. Other than the Mustang, there was a Lincoln with brown paper being taped to the windshield. There were maybe half-dozen guys working. "I don't mind a wait."

"Show me van."

The man was wearing navy blue coveralls with the name Yuri embroidered over his breast pocket. He had a rugged complexion and wore his long dark hair tied in a ponytail. "So you're Chekhov?" Arnie asked as the man ducked through the front door. The man ignored the question and walked quickly over to the only van parked on the property.

After a quick inspection, "You have nice van. Carousel, always like. Where you get tint?"

"Someplace up north."

Chekhov nodded as if he was okay with the vagueness. "You know, illegal this tint?"

"I didn't know that."

"Cops need to see into van. Too dark. Good for some things eh?" Chekhov smiled lecherously at Arnie.

"I'll keep that in mind. My name is Arnie Sims, by the way." He held out his hand, which Chekhov reluctantly shook. The man's grip was a bone crusher and went on a fraction too long.

"So what's deal, Mr. Sims? Your van is fine. No nick."

"I know, but I'm getting bored of the color. I was thinking black. How much would that cost me?"

"Not cheap, maybe $2,000. Not this month, too busy."

Arnie figured the price was double the going rate and likely meant to put him off, which just made him more suspicious. "How many people do you have working for you, Mr. Chekhov?"

"Enough."

Obviously not. "Okay, Mr. Chekhov. I'll get back to you."

CHAPTER FOURTEEN

B en waited for Sheriff McDiarmid to explain.

"They moved to Greenville, which is up north in Philadelphia County. Not exactly a great place to live. Lots of crime and unemployment, but Mrs. Huffman had family there.

One night, when Tommy was at his cousins for a sleep-over, there was a home invasion. From what I learned from the cops up there, the neighbors reported seeing a blue car parked in front of the house. The cops said that based on the crime scene there had to be at least two of them." Cliff McDiarmid paused for a moment and put out his cigarette.

"Mrs. Huffman was found in the living room with her throat slashed. There were signs of sexual assault. The husband was found bound and gagged, hanging in the closet. There were clear signs of torture. Their son Tommy was the one that found them the following day. Cops up there thought it was a case of mistaken identity. There was a known crack house in the same neighborhood."

"Shitfuck. What happened to Tommy?"

"Mrs. Huffman's family took him in. He was understandably upset. He tried to commit suicide a number of times before the family had him committed. Northshore Psychiatric Hospital in Slidell, Louisiana. That's where Tommy is. I drove over there and tried my best to get him to talk. Nothing, the people down there say it's hopeless. He spends the day looking out the window."

IT TOOK about twenty minutes for Ben and Sheriff McDiarmid to hike to the old oak tree. Ben couldn't imagine the horror, the shock, and the agony, of finding your son's lifeless body. *How much of what happened did Tommy Huffman witness? If he was able to talk, would he be able to identify the killers? Do the killers know where he is? If so, have they tried to get to him?*

"This here is the oak tree. At its base is where Mr. Wilson found Glenn's body." McDiarmid bent down and pointed. Ben nodded and looked up at the tree. It was an ideal climbing tree, with heavy branches interspersed almost like a ladder.

"Here, I'll give you a boost," said Ben.

"Me?"

"I have a sore shoulder. Not sure I could manage it."

After two or three tries at coordination, Ben was able to boost McDiarmid enough so the sheriff could reach a low branch. "I think you might want to cut back on the crullers," cracked Ben.

McDiarmid managed to pull himself up and then used another branch to climb to what was a split in the tree about forty feet above the ground. "I can see a clearing from here."

"How far would you say it is?"

"Eighty, maybe a hundred yards."

"This is April. Would you still have the same view in August?"

"I think so. The foliage is pretty thick." The sheriff was about to get down when he noticed two sets of initials carved into the trunk of the tree. "GW" and six inches off to the side, "TH." He ran his fingers over the carving. Somehow the initials made what had happened seemed all too real. "They were up here. They carved their initials in the tree. By the way, that clearing is where Wilson found the radio." McDiarmid started climbing down, jumping the last five feet and falling flat on his ass. "Fuck, I'm getting too old for this shit."

Ben helped him up. "I want you to run as fast as you can to the clearing."

"Man, I'm still trying to catch my breath. Why?"

"Because I want to see how long it would take someone looking back from the clearing to get here. Has anyone else told you to lay off the crullers?"

Sheriff McDiarmid gave him a sarcastic grin. After a moment he took off and ran full speed through the trees to the clearing. Ben had the time at twelve seconds.

"Okay, run back now," Ben called out.

Ben heard the sheriff yelling at him to fuck off. A short time later Mcdiarmid arrived back at the oak tree. "Why did I have to run back?"

"No reason, just messing with you. I bet there was a drop scheduled for that afternoon. The kids were here, Glenn up in this tree, Tommy waiting at the bottom. Not sure if they saw the drop, but I bet one of the men saw Glenn up in the tree. Glenn then tells Tommy to run for it. As he hustles down the tree, he falls on his ass just like you did. Now it takes approximately the same amount of time to climb down the tree, that it took you to get here from the clearing. The men get here, there's a struggle. One of the men hits Glenn with the branch, probably from behind."

"Tommy is hiding. Otherwise, they would have heard him. While Glenn is lying on the ground one of the men shoots him in the head. Tommy's watching, sees it happen. Does that play?"

"Or maybe they heard Tommy running and couldn't catch him."

"If that were the case, they would have killed him that night."

McDiarmid nodded. "You're pretty good at this."

"Did the M.E. estimate the time of death?"

"Sometime late afternoon to early evening, which would fit with the Father saying the body was still warm."

"Let's assume it went down that way and that Harrigan was in on it. Who were the major dealers back then?"

"That was before my time. But as I said, there are still a few old-timers at the station. They would know."

CHAPTER FIFTEEN

On the way back through town, Ben stopped at the real estate office called Let me Pick-A-You a Home. He was met by an attractive woman in her thirties wearing a gray business suit, with her blonde hair piled up in a beehive hairdo. She professed to know everything about the town. "My name is Anita. Anita Sayle, get it? When Ben didn't laugh, the smile fell from her face, and she said, "And you are?"

"Ben O'Shea. My girlfriend and I are thinking of settling here. What can you tell me about apartments?"

"There's not much inventory of decent apartments. Most folks tend to buy. Probably because of the incredible home prices I can get for my customers,"

"What's do bungalows go for?"

"The average house last month sold for just under $35,000. I have a nice 2 bedroom place on Chestnut that I think you could get for $50,000. I can get you all the financing you need," she smiled. When Ben didn't answer, she asked, "When's the wedding?"

Wedding, who said anything about a wedding? He was going to say in a couple of years but caught himself. Living in sin might be frowned upon here. "We don't actually have a date yet. I haven't even asked her. I thought I could take her around on Saturday, let her get a feel for the place and then maybe at a nice restaurant ..."

"Oh, how precious is that? You should take her to a place called Stonewall BBQ on Canal Street; it's just about the best restaurant east of New Orleans. I can call them and see if I can get you a table?" Anita Sayles' voice bubbled over like a glass of champagne.

"I don't know."

"There's the Chick N' Stick. Folks like that place too. It's just not what you'd call romantic."

"Tell me, what else should we see in Picayune?"

"Oh, at this time of year? The Arboretum is open all day. You must take her there. She'll go crazy. What's your gal's name?"

"Chevon."

"What an unusual name! You must bring her around on Saturday. I'll be working all day. Then you can take her to the Teddy Bear Museum. That's a lot of fun. Then, let me think, there's the shooting range, lots of people check that out. What kind of guns do you carry?" She spoke with a Mississippi drawl, pronouncing gun like it had a dozen "n's."

Ben avoided the question, "Is there a lot of crime in Picayune?"

"Every town has its share. Picayune has a population of almost 10,000 people. Sixty percent are white, the rest well," she let her voice trail off, a sneer of disgust on her face. "The Chestnut area is very safe. It's in a development called the Crossroads. Most of the darkies live on the other side of the highway. I wouldn't let any of my customers buy there."

What if I was shacking up with a black girl, half my age? How would you feel about that, Anita?

CHAPTER SIXTEEN

Arnie sat in the Pacer looking at Huedunit Painting. It was after 9 p.m., and there was a first quarter moon casting a glow on the activity outside the hangar.

"So, tell me again about this?" asked Rachel. When Arnie had approached her about swapping vehicles, she'd readily agreed on the condition that she go with him.

"This is where Geoffrey Motten worked before he was arrested for trying to hire a hitman. What happened, in a nutshell, is that one of those guys over there is an undercover cop and apparently, he recorded Motten trying to hire him to kill his wife."

"What are we doing here?"

Arnie didn't answer right away. From the spotlights illuminating the yard, he spotted at least five different workers in addition to the owner. They'd seen a dark BMW being driven into the hanger about five minutes earlier. "Trying to figure out why an undercover cop would be moonlighting at a paint shop, and why he would be interested in a two-bit punk like Motten."

"One of those guys at the paint shop is a cop?"

"Yep, and that's not a paint shop. They weren't interested in painting my van. If they were just a paint shop, they wouldn't be working this late. No, this is what they call a chop shop, you know, stolen cars."

"I always thought a chop shop sold pork chops," Rachel replied sarcastically.

"Ha-ha. I have a cousin who knows more about this than he should. There's usually a couple of guys with a shopping list of relatively new cars that the owner knows he can sell quickly. Inside a bunch of guys take the cars apart. Sometimes the cars are sold for parts, but many times they're reassembled with different parts that have a new serial number. Then if the buyer wants a red BMW, they have a painting crew. The whole operation might take three or four hours. At some point, someone is going to take delivery of a red BMW for a fraction of the price."

Arnie watched as a black Camaro passed them and was driven onto the lot.

"But I still don't get it. If the cop is in there, and we've seen two cars being driven in, why doesn't he just have the place raided? Why bother, like you said, with Motten?"

"I don't know."

They sat quietly trying to come up with a theory. Finally, Rachel broke the ice. "So, Arnie, are you going to go see Bernice Cross tonight?"

"Watch it, girl," he laughed.

"You must have said something. She was all over you when you came out of your office," Rachel said playfully.

"I told her to go home and seduce Harold. She's too much woman for any man to resist."

"Any man? You're the one who'd better watch it. She might think you're interested."

"I told her I was living with someone."

Rachel started to laugh when Arnie told her he'd been referring to Bourbon. "I can't believe you used your cat as an excuse. Better hope she doesn't find out."

"What about you? Are you still seeing the Professor?"

"No, I told him that I really liked him, but that it wasn't going to work out."

"How did he take it?" Arnie asked sympathetically.

"Not well. He asked me if I was in love with Gabriel. Apparently, he got that impression because I talk about him so much."

"Wow. I knew you guys used to hang out back when Jacqueline was away, but I didn't think it was anything serious."

"We ended it before it could get serious. I told Beau that Gabriel was just a great boss."

"Relationships can be hard sometimes."

"Said the bachelor who lives with a cat."

"I've had my share of broken relationships. Even if you know it's the right thing to do for everyone; it's still hard..." They were interrupted by a set of headlights that turned towards them. "Shit! Get down." Arnie pulled Rachel towards him and under the dash of the car. A few moments later they could see the interior of their little car illuminated by a set of headlights.

"Do you think they saw us?" asked Rachel.

"I suspect so since they're stopping. I should have been watching."

"Shit, Arnie!!!" Rachel cried out. They heard a car door open, and then footsteps approaching.

Arnie quickly sat up and saw a man he didn't recognize looking through his window at him.

He rolled the window down, "Help you with something?"

Rachel, who'd had her head down in Arnie's lap, sat up and said, "Can't people get a little privacy?"

CHAPTER SEVENTEEN

Wednesday, April 11ᵗʰ, 1984

Gvozdana Novak was a middle-aged lady that liked to mind everyone else's business. She had raised snooping to a fine art. She liked to peek out from behind the living room curtain and watch the comings and goings along Travina Avenue. Her recently retired husband Baldo would admonish his wife that she was acting like a busybody.

"Baldo, why don't you go talk to that man over at #14? Maybe suggest to him that the hedges are not going to prune themselves. Baldo? Baldo, are you hearing me?" As usual, Baldo was sitting in his favorite La-Z-Boy, his nose buried in the *Morning Herald*. He was using the paper as a force field to shield himself from his wife. "Baldo, are you listening to me?"

"Why you not come away from window? Make some coffee." Baldo replied in his heavy Croatian accent.

Dana, as she preferred to be called, decided to let it drop, her attention now distracted by the mail carrier walking down the opposite sidewalk delivering the mail. "Here comes that darkie letter carrier. I have a mind to complain. I spoke to him at least three times in the past month about delivering the mail earlier. I like to have the mail before noon."

"It is before noon," Baldo said, looking at his watch, "11.53. What you making me for lunch?"

"He's delivering to #12. I wonder if he knows that the woman moved away." *Friesen, was that her name?* "Maybe he should not be delivering her mail." A few weeks ago, Dana had watched from the upstairs bedroom as a small U-Haul was backed into the laneway of the house across the street. She'd seen the woman and a strange man move some big boxes and suitcases out. *Was this man her secret lover? Was she slipping away in the night when her husband was off doing God knows what? Was she leaving him because he did nothing around the house other than complain about her goulash not tasting as good as his mother's?*

She had suspected that the couple was having problems. When she had seen the U-Haul across the street, she'd called out, "Baldo, Baldo, wake up!" As expected, he'd rolled over and put his fat head under a pillow. "Maybe I should go out and tell the boy that she moved out."

"Who moved out?" asked the voice from behind the paper.

Not bothering to respond, Dana quickly ran out the front door, saying, "I'm going to talk to him." She hailed the mail carrier, who was now walking back down the laneway. "Yoo-hoo," she called to get his attention.

"Yes, ma'am?" the carrier replied from the end of the laneway.

"I don't know if you're aware, but the woman who lives in that house moved."

"Moved?" He repeated, starting to cross the street towards her.

"Yes, a few weeks ago. I think the couple broke up."

The man looked unsure and turned back to look at the house as if there might be a sign telling him what to do. "They haven't submitted a change of address notice, and someone's been picking up the mail."

Dana looked at the man and displayed her frustration, "Young man, I didn't say he didn't live there anymore. Just that she moved out." The words had no sooner left her lips when a giant whoosh-bang sounded, and the ground beneath her shook, knocking her to the ground. It was like the oxygen had been sucked out of the air. From her vantage point on the ground, she heard a deafening explosion followed by flames shooting up to the sky. Pieces of drywall, eavestrough, and shingles started raining down. Dana covered her head until Baldo, who had heard the commotion and felt the house shake, came running out and started pulling her back to safety.

When the fire department arrived, they found the letter carrier under a pile of rubble, still breathing but in serious condition. The house at #12 Travina was gone, along with parts of #10 and #8 on either side.

CHAPTER EIGHTEEN

Thursday, April 12th, 1984

One of the ways the *Eye on You Detective Agency* made money was by performing employee reference checks. Some of the largest Biloxi employers had begun contracting out parts of their hiring process. It was a sign of the times, someone had explained to Gabriel. With rates of unemployment nationally at high levels and particularly bad in Mississippi, there were hundreds of applicants for every job. This made the task of hiring the right person more challenging. With this competition, applicants sometimes exaggerated their skills and experience. Gabriel was winning this reference check business for the Agency by providing excellent service, guaranteed turnarounds and a reputation based on honesty. Rachel had proven indispensable, responding to the seemingly endless number of fax requests.

Gabriel arrived at the Agency later than normal that morning, having just returned from visiting an HR rep with one of the larger hotels. "Good morning, Rachel," he said as he walked into the Agency. "Any messages?"

"Ben called and wanted to know if we would both be here this afternoon for a meeting. And then Jacqueline called and would like you to call when you get a moment."

"Alright thanks," replied Gabriel. "Hey, is Bourbon here?"

"Sorry, it's Arnie's day off. By the way, we were on surveillance last night." Rachel told Gabriel about how they'd almost been caught.

"The guy thought..."

"Yep, he thought I was doing something naughty," Rachel said with a smile.

Gabriel laughed. "Thank you for going with him. What's Arnie's next move?"

"He was going to call his client today and update him on the surveillance. He's still stumped about what to do next."

"He'll come up with something," said Gabriel. "So Motten said that the guy that had him arrested was an undercover cop who was working at the paint shop?"

"Yeah. Arnie called his contact at the Sheriff's Department and got nowhere."

Gabriel went into his office and called Jacqueline. He could hear Benjamin yammering on in the background when she answered the phone. His son was talking a lot more these days. A week ago, Gabriel had taught him to say "blah, blah, blah' Now Benjamin was saying "blah, blah, blah" and then giggling hysterically.

"Hi Gabriel, I'm feeding our son, and he is not cooperating."

"Try the peaches. Rachel said you called?"

"We can't feed him peaches every day. Did you happen to read the *Herald* this morning?"

"No, the paperboy hadn't delivered it yet, and I left early for a meeting at the Edgewater."

"How did it go?"

"Pretty good, they agreed to give us a shot at their employee reference business. Is there something interesting in the paper?"

"Maybe. That guy you said reminded you of Alfred Hitchcock, was his name, William Friesen?"

"Yes, that's right, but I'm not taking the case."

"Maybe someone else did. His house blew up yesterday."

CHAPTER NINETEEN

Sheriff Cliff McDiarmid had told Ben that he didn't have a snowball's chance in hell of getting an interview with Widow Harrigan. He described her as another of the County's colorful personalities. Maybe because McDiarmid gave him zero chance of success, or because as a private investigator he was no longer limited to following police procedure, Ben decided on a cover story.

Parked in his truck in front of the widow's house, he practiced his approach. The old lady lived in a beautiful, two-story, stone home off of Highway 11, just on the outskirts of a town called Carrier. The property was immaculately maintained. The green grass would have made the groundskeeper at Augusta National Golf Club envious. Tall magnolia trees dotted the front and side lawns. In a couple of months when the trees bloomed, the house would be worthy of the cover of *Better Homes and Gardens*. *The old lady must spend all her time out here, or maybe she has a gardener?*

While his script might be straddling the truth, Ben had no intention of lying or misleading her. His goal was to get a sense of her late husband and whether he might have had anything to do with Glenn Wilson's killing.

"GOOD MORNING MISS, my name is Ben O'Shea of the *Jackson Clarion-Ledger*," he said to the blonde woman who answered his knock. She was wearing beige pedal pushers and a plaid shirt tied in a knot above her waist.

"And what can I do for you, Mr. Ben O'Shea from the *Clarion-Ledger*?" She smiled, leaning on the door jam. The woman was attractive if you liked well-built blondes wearing skimpy outfits.

"I was hoping to talk to Mrs. Harrigan."

"Yeah? Okay so talk."

"Mrs. Leona Harrigan?" This woman, Ben figured, was at most forty.

"God! How I hate that name!" She exclaimed dramatically. "I go by Lee Harrigan now."

"I called earlier and left a message about a story I was working on for the paper."

Lee looked at Ben appraisingly. After a moment she said, "I've been busy doing my nails." She flashed fingernails at him that were painted with black nail polish. "I'm having my period. I like to do my nails appropriately. Are you going to come in, Mr. Reporter?"

"Yes, thank you." The front door opened into a large foyer finished in pine. Stairs on the right led to a loft. To the left was a spacious living room dominated by a large circular couch.

Lee pointed at him. "You know your outfit, I mean the red pants and yellow plaid shirt, goes well with your truck.

Pretty funky if you ask me." She led him into the living room and sprawled on the couch, kicking off her sandals. He noticed that her toenails were also black.

"Are you really the widow Harrigan?"

"I think there's a joke that starts like that. Yeah, I'm sure. My husband, the late Sheriff Thaddeus Harrigan, liked younger women with big hooters." Lee suddenly bounced off the couch, "Now, where are my manners? Would you like some cranberry juice? I'd offer you something stronger, but that would be breaking the rules. No booze for Leona."

"Sure, if it's not too much trouble." He followed her into a large kitchen. There was a certain quirky sensuality in how she moved.

"You want to do a feature on old Thaddeus?"

"Yes, my editor wants to highlight some of the county sheriffs in the state and some of their accomplishments. A different sheriff each week...you know, their philosophy, how they did their job...."

"Blah, blah, blah." Lee poured a large glass of juice. "Sounds as boring as fuck, Mr. Reporter. Can I call you Benny? I've never been with a Benny before," she said, as if she had a scorecard. When Ben nodded, she continued. "Do your readers; I'm assuming you have some, actually read that crap?"

"Maybe I can write this article from your perspective. Like through your eyes?"

"I'm a lot more interesting. Do you think your editor would go along?"

"I don't know," Ben replied, "I'm kind of new at this."

"Kind of old to be starting out aren't ya?"

"It's sort of a second career." Ben took the glass of juice from her.

"You look more like a policeman. The way you carry yourself, the paunch. My late husband used to have a belly like that. Too much sitting in your car, eating donuts. I have to admit the truck, clothes ... the hair - all a little odd. Are you a homo?"

"No." *This lady's game is to try to shock me into a reaction. Not sure why. Maybe she just likes messing with people.*

"It's okay Benny. I'm not going to turn you into the homo police."

"I have a fiancée." Ben lied. The woman was rattling him. "A female," he added.

"Name?"

"Name?"

"Yes, name. She must have told you her name before you proposed," she admonished him.

"Chevon."

"Oh," she gave him an appraising from with the bluest eyes he had ever seen. "That fits."

"Why does that fit?"

"You're just a little off center aren't you Benny? Marrying a darkie, that's why you're wearing the outfit and driving the truck. You're making a statement. I like that." Lee took a large swallow of her juice before pointing him back to the living room.

Ben picked up his juice and tried to change the subject. "So, you like black nail polish."

"No, only when I'm having my period. When I'm playful, I use yellow...kind of mood polish. You should come visit when I use red," she winked.

Ben quickly jumped to another subject. "You have a beautiful home, Mrs. Harrigan." He stopped and picked up a photo of a man dressed in a sheriff's uniform. The man was bald with a big face, a handlebar mustache, and a serious expression on his face as if he was pissed at the photographer. "This him?"

"Yep. You can take it if it helps. Not the best picture, but he wasn't what people would call camera-friendly."

"Thanks." Ben could see out the patio doors that there was a huge swimming pool with a statue of a naked woman writhing in ecstasy off to the side.

Following his gaze, Lee nodded at the statue. "I modeled for that, can you tell?" She stood and positioned herself in the same pose. "I think he did a great job on the tits." She sprawled on the couch again like a cat. "Do you really like the house?" She didn't wait for a reply. "I was approached by a movie company to rent it out. You know that Tom Cruise movie that came out last year?"

"Risky Business?"

She nodded and drank some more juice, "They wanted to film it here, but they backed out when I insisted on being in the movie and playing the part of the whore."

Ben pulled out a pencil and a small spiral notepad from his back pocket. He sat down in an armchair.

"Isn't that cute, you even have the little cop notebook. Fire away, Bennie."

"What kind of a sheriff was your husband?"

"Old. Really fuckin' old, but he had lots of moolah. We had fun together until, you know, he keeled over."

"He keeled over? He had a stroke, right?"

"He did. One minute he was on top of me plowing the cornfields, and then his eyes kind of went cross-eyed, and he collapsed." Lee pantomimed the act, including crossing her eyes.

"That must have been awful." Ben tried to keep a straight face.

"It was. At first, I just thought he had the mother of all orgasms. Did you know Benny, that when you die your bowels let loose? My God, I started freaking out. Like just imagine it. It was really gross."

"Is that a true story?"

She smiled. "I would check with your editor about putting that in the article. People down here are such prudes."

"Do you live in this big house by yourself?"

"Yes, that is if you don't count the male sex slaves I have locked up in the bedroom."

Ben chuckled. "You mentioned he had a lot of money."

"Honey, every guy I've ever been with might have had an Andrew Jackson or two. Old Thaddeus would pull out this roll the size of a fucking honeydew."

"Was he born into money?"

"Just the opposite. My Thaddeus knew how to play his cards right. There you go, use that. He knew how to play his cards right. That says just about everything."

"He was a gambler?"

"Sometimes, but more than that, he liked putting himself in a position to make money. That's the American way. You're not from Mississippi, are you Benny?"

"I moved from Providence about 15 years ago."

"Is that where you met your Chevon?" Lee reached for a cigarette from a pack of Tareyton's on an end table.

Tareyton's, whose smokers would rather fight than switch. Ben watched as she lit up and took a puff, blowing smoke out of the side of her mouth. "No, she's from New Orleans."

"New Orleans, I love that town!" Lee said dramatically,

stretching her legs out again. She repeated the city name, this time pronouncing it with a southern twang. "Thaddeus had lots of friends in Noo Orleans. We had lots of great times there."

"There must have been quite the difference in ages between you and your husband."

She looked up at the ceiling as if trying to pull down the math to answer his question. "Twenty-three years, but that number is getting smaller as I'm getting older and he is, well, dead."

"How did you two ever meet up?"

"I was dancing at a club in Carrier. The Pussy Willow Inn, you believe it? I had noticed him a few times. You always notice the ones with rolls of cash the size of fucking honeydews. One night we got raided. The deputies arrested a whole bunch of us girls, but Sheriff Thaddeus Harrigan pulled me aside and put me in his cruiser. He took me home, didn't lay a hand on me. Next night the girls and I were back dancing. This time when Thaddeus came in, he just said I was going home with him."

"Was your husband a good man?"

"Oh, excellent question." She held up her juice glass in mock salute. "That would depend on what you mean by good. He was a pretty good lover, a good provider. He was very good at pulling the wool over people's eyes when it came to Election Day." Then after a pause, "Are you going to put all of this in your article?"

Ben nodded, "If you're okay with it." Then after making a couple of notes, "I meant good, in terms of character."

The woman seemed a little conflicted. "That's a difficult question. He did what he wanted. He wanted to be re-elected, so he was constantly helping little old ladies cross the street, volunteering at bake sales, or going to some lame-ass career day at school. Not because he gave a damn about anyone. You see, he also had another side to him that wanted other things."

"Other things?"

She gestured around her, "Material things, money, younger women who made him feel manly."

Ben thought her tone had become emotional. "What makes you say that?"

"I tried my best to not listen to his conversations with people on the phone, but it's hard when a person likes to eavesdrop," she smiled. "I stayed in my room when he had his pals over. I wouldn't ask him about it if he came home late smelling of another woman. I tried not to watch from the bedroom window when someone would drive up to the house late at night."

"Was he a fair man?"

"Fuck, you're good at this reporter thing Benny." Lee lit a new cigarette with the butt of her old one. "Yeah, he was fair, as long as you understand that being fair down south might mean treating people differently. Like if you stopped a darky in a speeding car, you might think, 'Hey that nigger is running away from something.'"

"I heard talk... I'm sure you have too, about your husband and some of the people he dealt with. What would you like to say about all those rumors?"

"People around here are pretty two-faced. I bet you most folks in town think I was a gold-digger. They're all sweet as cherry pie to your face, but when your back is turned, that's another story."

"What about rumors about your husband?"

"You mean that he was on the take, he was crooked, a

racist, a drug dealer? I even heard that he might have killed someone. Some folks probably think he did JFK."

"He didn't, did he?" Ben deadpanned.

Lee drained her juice and said, "You have many more questions, Benny? I need to get back to the sex slaves upstairs."

"Just a couple...Did he have it in him to kill someone?"

Lee gave Ben a serious look. "My husband was arrogant. 'The most fucking powerful lawman in the County,' he called himself. He thought he could get away with anything. If someone tried to stop Thaddeus from getting what he wanted, they'd be dead meat."

"If I wanted to do more research on your husband, who were some of the people he was closest with?"

"I would probably talk to the deputies, but most have moved on, I hear. Of course, there were those brothers; I believe their name was Nantois. Fucking losers if you ask me, but they were some of those nighttime visitors that I didn't see."

CHAPTER TWENTY

Arnie called Rod Smith to pass along what he'd learned from his surveillance of Huedunit.

While the lawyer listened intently until the end, he said, "I'm not sure how this fits together Arnie, but it smells worse than my gym socks."

Arnie sensed his friend's frustration. "I'd like to stick with it for a few more days."

"I should never have agreed to this," Smith said, with more than a touch of irritation.

"What's crawled up your nose, Rod?" asked Arnie.

"In no particular order, this case, the District Attorney, my client, my wife. Take your pick."

"Okay, let's take one at a time. What are your thoughts now on the case?"

"I don't know. You say Motten was working at a chop shop, so what? Why didn't the undercover arrest him for that? The guy's a convicted felon. Why does he all of a sudden show up at the bar and arrest Motten for conspiracy?"

"I don't know yet. How is your client doing?"

"According to Motten, he's the victim. He's just a peace-loving car painter trying to make a living. To hear him say it, he was just enjoying a beer at a local bar with someone from work, then all of a sudden, he gets handcuffed and put in a cruiser. After today, I realize now that I have a complete scumbucket for a client. Do you know what he asked me when I went to see him?"

"What's that?" Arnie was growing concerned about the lawyer's state of mind.

"He offered to pay me, an officer of the court, his own fucking lawyer, a $1,000 bonus if I could take care of this undercover cop."

"Oh my God! That guy is a piece of work. Are you going to ask the judge to appoint another lawyer?"

"Believe me I've thought about it. With this judge, I'm not sure he would grant it; plus, I think it would be prejudicial to the case. I'm sure he would say something like, 'You aren't the first lawyer to realize that you've got a guilty client, he's still entitled to a defense."

"You said you were upset with the DA, why's that?

"Yesterday, the judge denied bail again. That is unheard of for this kind of charge. I objected of course, but the judge ruled that given they had the defendant on tape offering money to a co-worker to kill his wife, bail was out of the question."

"This tape, have you heard it?"

"That's the next thing. The judge has heard it but doesn't seem to be concerned that this hasn't been turned over to the defense." The lawyer's frustration came over the phone. After a moment he continued, "Arnie, have you found out anything about why a cop would be working undercover and for that matter, wearing a wire to talk to Motten?"

"I'm getting closer. It could be that the cop is onto a stolen car ring and Motten might have just been an easy target. Motten said something about the guy looking familiar. Maybe the undercover cop wanted him out of the way."

"Familiar from where?"

"He wasn't sure it was the same guy, but Motten used to ride with the Sons of Silence."

"Hmm, I guess that makes sense."

"You said you were upset with your wife?"

"Yeah...you know she's best friends with Bernice Cross, don't you? Clarissa and Bernice talk every blasted day. Now Clarissa wants me to take on Bernice's divorce case against Harold. Poor Harold, the guy is a saint," said Smith. "Do you know Arnie, Bernice never shuts up about you? Arnie did this, and Arnie said that. Then a couple of days ago she started ranting and raving about you being shacked up with some new gal. Is her name really Bourbon?"

CHAPTER TWENTY-ONE

After Jacqueline's call, Gabriel ran down to the corner store and purchased the *Herald*. *This couldn't be a coincidence. Friesen had found someone who could help him disappear.* The front page of the paper was dedicated to the coverage of the explosion.

Emergency response teams were called to a quiet neighborhood after a home on Travina Avenue exploded into flames. The massive blast and subsequent fire were seen as far as Pascagoula. While there was some damage to the surrounding properties, the house owned by Mr. and Mrs. William Friesen was obliterated.

Authorities had no comment on whether anyone was in the house at the time of the explosion. Acting Police Chief Murdock indicated that they were trying to contact anyone who might know the whereabouts of William Friesen or his wife, Bonnie.

Mrs. Gvordana Novak, who lives across the street from the house on Travina, told this reporter that Mr. Friesen was a shady businessman, coming and going at odd hours of the night. According to Mrs. Novak, Mr. and Mrs. Friesen, who had no children, were recently separated. "Since the wife left in a rented U-Haul, there's been a steady stream of loose women going into that house. Like Sodom and Gomorrah, this is a sign from God."

Gabriel walked back to the Agency, relieved he'd told Friesen to take a hike. Since he didn't believe in coincidences, he needed to tell the police about what Friesen had asked him to do. When Gabriel got back to the office he went straight to his phone. He was about to call Ben's number when he realized that Ben didn't work for the Biloxi PD anymore. The article in the *Herald* quoted Murdock, an officer Gabriel had met once at a press conference early the previous year. He dialed the main number, asking to be connected to Acting Police Chief Murdock. After about three minutes on hold, he was put through.

"Acting Police Chief Murdock's desk, this is Officer Moyse."

"I was looking for Murdock; my name is Gabriel Ross, I'm a private detective and a friend of Ben O'Shea's."

"Whatcha got? We're kind of busy here."

"I have some information about the house that blew up last night."

TWO HOURS later Gabriel was sitting across from Murdock. The middle-aged man who, according to Ben thought he was God's gift to women, was leaning back in his chair with his shoes up on the desk. "Gabriel Ross? Yeah, of course, I know who you are. You're the guy the *Herald* calls Dirty Angel. The newspaper said you killed two bad guys in a week last fall. Pretty fucking righteous if you ask me."

"Didn't have much choice in the matter."

"You heard how some states are introducing anti-handgun laws? All rifles and shotguns need to be registered. What is this country coming to? The only fucking gun control you need is to use two hands." Murdock laughed.

When Gabriel didn't laugh, Murdock took his feet off the desk and leaned forward, his expression growing serious. "How's Ben?"

"Pretty good, kind of hard sitting on his ass all day though."

"What's the deal with you two? How come you're always working on stuff together?"

"No reason. He and I just like to bounce ideas off each other."

"Tell him we could use him here, everything is upside down. I might be the new Chief, but a couple of newbies were hired from the State police, and they don't do a thing I tell them to do. Real assholes."

Gabriel gave him a sympathetic look, "I wanted to talk to you about the explosion on Travina. Any theories yet?"

Murdock looked around as if to make sure they were alone, then lowered his voice and said, "I remember a case where a person's barn burned down. The wife called the insurance company the next day and asked the agent to send a check for $60,000, the amount of insurance on the barn."

"Is that what you think this is about, insurance?" Gabriel interrupted.

Murdock ignored his question and continued. "Anyway, the agent told the lady that insurance doesn't work that way. They hire people to rebuild the barn, and then they replace the equipment. The wife was very upset. When she heard that, she said if that's the way it works, then I want to cancel the insurance on my husband." Murdock laughed heartily once he finished the story.

"Very funny, Chief Murdock." Gabriel waited for him to stop laughing, "What else is there to this that wasn't in the paper?"

Murdock gave Gabriel a serious look. "Nothing. If you read the paper, then you know as much as I know. We might get something later if we can locate either of the owners of the house, or if the Fire Chief finds something."

"You likely won't find either of the Friesens."

"Sounds like you have something to tell me about all this."

Gabriel told him about meeting with Mr. Friesen this past Monday morning, and his plan to fall overboard.

Murdock took notes on a pad he had on his desk. "You think this guy got someone else to help him stage his death?"

"Maybe. I don't know. It just sounds a little too coincidental."

"Why would he bother asking you to get involved? He could have done this all himself."

"I believe he thought that I would make the story more credible if I said I saw him go overboard."

"I don't see that. Anyhow, I'm not sure what else we can do. We have an APB on the Friesens, and we're waiting to hear from the Fire Chief."

"What about checking into his story? Investigate his business, find his partner?"

Murdock's lip curled in distaste. "Sounds like a lot of work. A little out there, if you know what I mean. But listen, Mr. Ross, I'll keep all this in mind."

CHAPTER TWENTY-TWO

When Gabriel got back from his meeting with Murdock, he found Ben already sitting in his office, chatting with Rachel.

"Sorry I'm late," Gabriel said, grabbing a chair in front of the desk.

"Do you guys remember that news reporter who was in that bad accident? He was paralyzed and put up in Gulf Oaks?" Ben asked, once Gabriel was seated.

"Mr. Dermody?" replied Rachel. "He's still there."

"That's the guy. Do you still go to see him, Rachel?"

"Not as much as I should, maybe once a month now."

"Any change in his condition?"

"No, still non-responsive. Although, I have always thought that we had a special way of communicating."

"It was through Rachel's work that we were able to uncover an important clue," said Gabriel with more than a touch of pride.

"I might need you guys to help me." Ben brought them

up to date on what he'd learned about the death of Glenn Wilson, and the deaths of Tommy Huffman's parents.

"You want Rachel and I to get Tommy Huffman to tell you what happened that day in the woods?" asked Gabriel.

"I know it's a long shot. I'll go there first and speak to them about his condition, but to be honest, I don't have the right bedside manner."

"Does he have any physical trauma that is preventing him from communicating?" Rachel stood up and started to pace as she often did when thinking.

"No, I don't believe so. I think he's scared that people who killed his parents, and I'm assuming Glenn, are looking for him."

"But I worked with Mr. Dermody for years, built up trust, sat with him day after day. I can't imagine that I could go up there and bingo, Tommy Huffman spills his guts to me."

"I realize it might take time... a week?"

Rachel rolled her eyes. "Of course, I'll try, but I'm going to have to give this some thought. I'll want to speak to people who knew him before he got sick."

"Sure, I'll try to find his Uncle and Aunt. I believe they moved to Slidell to be near him."

After a few moments, Ben changed the subject. "So what's going on here?"

"I saw Murdock today, and he said to say 'Hi.'" Gabriel said.

"Did he tell you a joke?"

"Yes, as a matter of fact, he did."

"That's his thing. He kind of weaves it into a story, and if you don't know him, you think he's telling you something that really happened." Ben shook his head. "Why did you see Murdock?"

"Have you seen the *Herald* today, and the story about the house blowing up?"

"Yeah, I read it, sounds like a gas explosion. I guess everything was atomized."

"The guy that owned the house was William Friesen. He was the guy I told you about the other day, that wanted to hire me to kill him." Gabriel recapped the story.

"You didn't take that case, right?"

"No, but, I think someone did. It's too much of a coincidence."

"Did Murdock have anything more to say?"

"He's waiting to hear back from the Fire Chief. If I'm right, he won't find anything."

Ben thought for a moment. "If I remember correctly, Friesen wanted you to be on hand so you could help convince people that he was dead...right?"

"Yes, so if this is all staged, then someone will be coming forward," replied Gabriel, anticipating Ben's point.

"And that person is guilty of conspiracy," said Ben. "Have you considered that the explosion might have been the work of the partner? The guy he said killed his wife?"

"Friesen said the man's name was Sam, but I'm not sure that's his real name. The way he said it was like, 'let's just call him Sam.'"

"Is Murdock going to check that angle?"

"Yes and no, he said it sounded like too much work. He told me that he'd get back to me once the Fire Marshall finished his report."

"That sounds like Murdock. I used him on a witness canvas, and he spent all his time chatting up one woman."

"In cases of house explosions like this Ben, would they even be able to tell if someone had died in the explosion?" Rachel asked. She'd stopped pacing and was sitting on the edge of Gabriel's desk.

"Hard to say, they might find bone fragments."

"Ben, there's another case you might want to hear about," Gabriel said after a moment. "Rachel and Arnie are working it.

Rachel told Ben about the surveillance she'd done with Arnie on the chop shop, and about Motten being held on an attempted murder charge. "Arnie's trying to figure out what the undercover cop was trying to do."

"Is this a Harrison County operation?"

"I don't know, Arnie called a friend in the sheriff's department and was told to speak to Sheriff Bragg."

Ben picked up the phone and dialed the number for the Harrison County Sheriff's Department. It took a few minutes to be connected. While he was waiting, he put his hand on the receiver and explained, "I worked on a couple of cases with Sheriff Bragg. I'm sure he'd know what's going on." After a minute, Ben was connected and pressed the speaker button so all could hear. "Hi Peter, it's Ben O'Shea."

"Hey Ben, I heard you went on disability."

"Yeah, I'm not quite back to normal."

"You thinking about retirement? I could always use someone like you here...I'm up to my ass in crocodiles."

"Alligators. I think the expression is up to my ass in alligators."

"No, I can see them, and they're big fucking crocodiles."

"Thanks anyway, I'll keep it in mind." Ben figured that Bragg had to have heard about Mayor Baxter wanting to get rid of him. "Listen, Peter, I know you're busy, so I'll get right to the point. There's a guy at the detention center by the name of Motten; he's in on a conspiracy rap."

"Oh yeah? Why is this of concern?" Sheriff Bragg's voice grew cold.

"Friend of a friend thing."

"Tell your friend he should get a new friend. This guy's really bad news. Remember that thing a couple of years back with the motorcycle gang, Sons of Silence?"

"The lug nut killers?" The case the sheriff was referring to had involved a couple of paid killers who rode with a motorcycle gang. The newspaper had called them the 'lug nut killers,' as they liked to loosen all the lug nuts on someone's wheels, sit back and watch the accident.

"Yeah, that's them. Motten was mixed up with them."

"Do you have an operation going on at the paint shop where this guy was working?"

"Not us. But why would that be important to your friend?" Bragg asked, suspicion creeping into his voice.

"He's just trying to find out what he's up against."

"Ben, you're a good guy, so I'll tell you this, and only this. They have Motten on tape offering to pay a hitman $1000 to kill his wife."

"Why would there be an undercover wearing a wire in a bar?"

"Sorry Ben, I've already said more than I should. There's a lot of heat on this one."

CHAPTER TWENTY-THREE

F riday the 13th. Ben didn't like Friday the 13th. Not that
he was superstitious, but he remembered that as the
date his first wife had left him. That memory led to
thoughts of Chevon, which stayed with him from the
moment he got in his truck, to one hour later when he
pulled into the parking lot of Northshore Psychiatric
Hospital in Slidell.

*Chevon is a wonderful woman. At my age, I should be counting
myself lucky that she wants to be with me. It feels great to have someone. When I was in the hospital, she came to see me every day. Maybe
it's love. When I first got married, there was so much I didn't know
about living with a woman. If I was to do it again, I'd need to be
more aware of her needs. There's no question that Chevon and I are
compatible. We both like jazz, old movies, and Chinese food. Could
there be a better recipe for marriage?*

There was still a nasty little voice in the back of his
mind. *Get real, O'Shea. She's half your age. By the time you're
sixty, she'll want to start a family. Let me tell you something else.
Remember your first marriage? She left you because she didn't want*

to be married to someone who was already married to his job. And not just any job. When you were working at the Providence PD, she worried every night about whether you would be coming home in a box. And how is life going to be any different as a private detective? Look at your partner Gabriel; his wife was almost buried alive, twice. Is that what you want for Chevon?

Ben tried to shake those thoughts out of his head and concentrated on how he was going to handle the conversation with Tommy Huffman. But as he sat in the parking lot, the thoughts came back like a door that wouldn't stay closed. *Ben, have you noticed she's black? I know you don't care, but how about those neighbors in Picayune, Mississippi? Do you think they'll have a parade when they see a middle age white man with his twenty-something black girlfriend moving into their little racist community? The town where darkies live on the other side of the highway? And what kind of a world would you be bringing little Benny into? Think it through before you do anything foolish. You'd be doing her a favor if you just remained friends.*

Ben looked up to the heavens hoping for an answer. The high sunlit clouds drifted across a clear blue sky. He put the radio on. The temperature was expected to peak at 75 degrees in New Orleans, another day without rain. He pulled into the hospital's parking lot.

He'd had to turn in his shield and weapon when he went on leave, but he hadn't surrendered his identification. *I'm Detective Ben O'Shea of the Biloxi Police Department, and I'm working on a murder case. I believe you have a potential witness that I need to speak with. Oh yeah, are you the Ben O'Shea who is on disability, the one that's dating that nice New Orleans girl, Chevon? Oh, you are? Aren't you old enough to be that girl's daddy? Why would you want to destroy her life? Make her miserable like a water moccasin in the desert?*

Ben's daydreaming was interrupted by a rap on his side window. He looked over, and a heavy-set, middle-aged, black woman was staring at him. He rolled down the window. "Yes."

"Are you okay sir, did you want me to bring you into the hospital?"

"The hospital?"

"Yes, you really shouldn't be driving in your condition. You're at Northshore Psychiatric Hospital," she said, a look of concern on her face.

"No, no I'm okay. I was just thinking."

The woman gazed at him, seemingly considering whether to run for a straitjacket or leave him be. "I was starting to worry. I saw you just sitting here and lips moving, but there was no one else in the truck."

"Thanks, Ma'am, I'm fine," Ben said.

"Seriously, maybe you should come in and have a chat."

"I said, I'm fine." To punctuate the point, he rolled up the window and looked away. Ben looked at his surroundings as the woman stomped away to the hospital. The hospital was nestled in a park-like setting with tall pine trees. The building itself was a sprawling one-story. Ben knew one of his challenges would be the confidentiality of patient care. His plan was to use his Biloxi PD identification simply as proof of his name. Technically, he was still employed by the police department, but he knew that if he announced himself as a police officer and it somehow got back to the wrong person, he'd be risking his pension.

After a few more minutes he got out of the truck and went into the front doors of the hospital. Approaching a young woman in a nurse's uniform, he flashed his identification and told her he wanted to speak to someone about

Tommy Huffman. The nurse escorted him to a set of double doors leading to the long-term care unit. Using a swipe card, she directed him to follow the long hallway.

When Ben made it to the right area, he approached another woman working at a nursing station. She wore a name tag on her left breast announcing her name as Jo-Anne. "Excuse me, Jo-Anne, my name is Ben O'Shea." He flipped his wallet open and made sure she got a good look at the Biloxi PD identification.

"What can I do for you officer?'

"I'm from Biloxi and looking into a crime that was committed some years ago. I believe you have someone here named Tommy Huffman. I'd like to talk to him."

A look of confusion came over the woman, "I have to call the clinician, Dr. Adrienne Marcotte...she might be able to help you." The nurse picked up her phone and pressed an extension. Ben stayed close enough to the desk to hear her speak to someone on the phone. "I have a Biloxi policeman here who says he wants to talk to Tommy Huffman."

WHILE WAITING FOR THE DOCTOR, Ben checked out the bulletin board. He was reading about Easter festivities when he heard someone approach from behind. He turned around and was face-to-face with the African-American lady from the parking lot.

A flash of recognition washed over her face and was replaced with a suspicious look. She looked him up and down, no doubt wondering about his beige trousers and his yellow shirt with blue paisleys. "You're a policeman?"

Ben pulled out his ID again and showed it to her. She

took it in her hands and inspected it. "You don't look like a policeman."

"Kind of an uncover operation," he replied officiously, lowering his voice to a whisper.

She gave him a look like he was trying to sell her the Twin Span Bridge. Finally, she said, "If that's the case, maybe we should talk in my office."

"WHAT DOES this have to do with Tommy Huffman?" Dr. Marcotte asked, sitting down behind her desk. She had a file folder in front of her.

"Back in 1978, Tommy's parents were killed in a home invasion. Tommy was staying with relatives but found what was left of his parents the next day."

"I know all of this."

"I believe that Tommy has information about the killers."

"You just said he wasn't there. How could he help you?"

"It's a little more complicated than that. Tommy's parents were from a town called Picayune and were hiding out in Greensville because their son saw someone kill their neighbor, a kid named Glenn Wilson. The killers found out about Tommy witnessing the killing a couple of years ago, and somehow found out where the family was living."

The doctor gave him a blank look. "You haven't told me anything that I didn't already know. But even if I let you visit Tommy, it would be pointless. He hasn't spoken or communicated in any way since he was brought here."

"Maybe he's scared? Worried that if he speaks up, the killers will come."

"Really?" Dr. Marcotte said sarcastically. "Has he just

been biting his tongue for two years? Do you have a medical degree? You haven't got a clue, do you? Are you even a real policeman?" She stood up from her chair and hovered over him.

"Yes, yes, I am, and I'm sorry I upset you. I wasn't trying to..."

She cut him off. "We've been caring for Tommy for two years. When we first got him, he tried to kill himself. Did you know that? Then he tried to starve himself. It has taken all this time to get Tommy to trust us enough to let us feed him. And you think he's faking? You're an ass."

"Won't you please sit down, Dr. Marcotte? I can see from all of the diplomas on your walls that you are infinitely more qualified than me. Do you have children, Dr. Marcotte?" When the woman nodded, Ben continued, "Yesterday I visited the parents of Glenn Wilson, and their pain is real. They have never accepted the official explanation for their son's death. Their twelve-year-old son was murdered, taken from them. Just like Tommy's parents were taken from him. I know that type of pain never goes away. I won't stop until I catch the people responsible for this. Won't you help me?"

Dr. Marcotte finally sat down. "I can't let you see Tommy; you are not properly trained to handle these situations. You could end up ruining all the good work we've done."

"Can you at least tell me what he has?"

"Tommy is a very sick young man. He has mutism; it's an affliction where his anxieties are so severe they rob him of his ability to communicate. Many have tried to get him to speak, even his Uncle and Aunt. The trauma that Tommy endured when he found his parents was so horrible he must relive it every day."

"Can he communicate by writing or through sign language?"

Dr. Marcotte shook her head. "He's non-responsive. We feed him; we help him in and out of bed."

"If I was a trained nurse, closer to his age, with a background in working in a hospital like this, working with people like Tommy. Would you let me spend time with him?"

"But you aren't any of those things. I'm not an idiot."

"I have an associate, a young woman with impeccable credentials and experience."

Before she could answer, Jo-Anne, the nurse who was working reception, opened the door and said, "Dr. Marcotte, your 11 a.m. appointment is here."

"Okay, I'll come out and explain to them that I won't be much longer." The doctor got up and said to Ben, "Excuse me for a minute."

As she slipped out of the office, Ben looked at the file folder on the desk. It was labeled Huffman. He knew he only had seconds and had to act fast. Ben found what he was looking for and slid the file back to its original position just as Dr. Marcotte re-entered. She came around the desk and then stopped, looking at the folder questioningly. She seemed to shrug it off.

"Officer O'Shea, I'm very busy. We've had speech pathologists and all kinds of clinicians working with Tommy. All to no avail. Your associate would be wasting everyone's time."

"Would you at least meet with her? You'd be helping to solve multiple murders."

CHAPTER TWENTY-FOUR

The owner of Huedunit Painting had already seen Arnie's van. At the stakeout the other night, Rachel's Pacer might have also been noticed. In the end, it was Rachel's idea to borrow Gabriel's VW beetle and to go get a look at the undercover cop. Gabriel and Arnie were both reluctant, and together they insisted that she stay in Arnie's eyesight at all times.

As Rachel turned on to McElroy Street, she thought, *this isn't a car, it's an accident waiting to happen. The steering constantly pulls to the left as if it wants to throw me into oncoming traffic. The brakes are soft, the clutch slips and the engine sounds like a tank. Why doesn't he get a new car?*

In broad daylight, the place looked different. It was deserted, no cars being driven on or off the lot. Unlike the other night, the hangar door was closed. Rachel turned into the parking lot and pulled up to the front door. As she turned off the ignition, the little car did a death rattle that seemed to go on for an eternity. When she got out of the car a large man wearing navy blue overalls came out of the front door. He went to the back of the VW and lifted the hood. Rachel walked back and saw that the man had taken it upon himself to adjust something.

Without looking up, he said, "Try now." Rachel went back and turned on the ignition and revved the engine. "Okay, turn off." She turned off the ignition, and to her surprise, there was no death rattle. As she got out of the car, the large man closed the hood.

"Thank you, that was very nice of you." Rachel was wearing a sleeveless summer dress that hugged her body and showed off her legs.

The man's name tag said "Yuri". He was big and towered over her. His dark hair was unkempt, and judging by the dark stubble on his face, he had a casual relationship with his razor. He nodded as if to say it was nothing. "Help you?"

Rachel felt the man's eyes x-raying her body. "Is Drake around?"

"Drake? He works in back. Come into the office, and I get him."

The office had third-generation dust everywhere and smelled of paint, grease, and oil. A selection of dusty, dog-eared, *Collision Repair* magazines from the past decade sat on a table in the waiting area. *Who would want to read that?*

Yuri went to the doorway and waved to someone, "He come." He turned to leer at Rachel.

"Thanks again for fixing my car, Yuri." Rachel gave him her best smile.

"You...girlfriend?" he asked, nodding back to the shop.

"No, nothing like that." Arnie, who was parked in his van down the street, had told her to say that Drake had been recommended by a friend of a friend. She was to get him to come outside so that Arnie could see him through the binoculars. The plan was to inquire about painting the VW. She was looking out the window when she heard a voice behind her.

"Can I help you?"

She turned and then gasped. The man looking at her was Dan, the guy she'd met at the party last weekend. "Dan?"

Dan must have picked up on her confusion. Yuri was standing off to the side watching the interaction. "Hello, welcome to Huedunit, my name is Drake," he said, emphasizing his name and pointing to what was stitched on his coveralls.

"Yes, Drake. I'm sorry, you reminded me of someone else."

"What can I do for you?" Drake was tall with a muscular body. He had short dark hair and a funny dimple in his chin. He was even more handsome than she remembered.

"Miss?" he repeated.

"Rachel Henderson, you were recommended by a friend. I wanted to see about getting my car painted." Yuri caught Drake's eye and shook his head.

"Come outside and show me your car." Drake walked out the door and held it open for Rachel. As they walked out to the parking lot, Drake whispered, "He's watching us from the door. He wants me to get rid of you." Once they got to the car, Drake made a show of looking at the car from various angles before shaking his head.

"I'm sorry, this piece of shit ain't worth painting," he smiled.

"Is your name Dan or Drake?" Rachel asked crossly. "And you were supposed to call me."

"Drake. You must have misheard me. And I lost your

number. I searched everywhere for it," he said, now looking under the car.

"Funny, I'm in the book."

"Okay, I'll call you. We'll have a drink, maybe see a movie."

"I thought you said you worked for the Government of Mississippi. I'm pretty sure I didn't mishear that!"

Drake must have sensed the office door opening behind him. Speaking loudly, he said, "So, I'm sorry Miss Henderson. I'd like to help you, but the car is probably only worth a few hundred dollars."

Yuri walked up to Rachel, wiping his hands on an oily rag. "What color you want car painted?"

This wasn't supposed to happen. Arnie said they would just make some excuse and say no thanks. "I was thinking pink."

"Very nice, beautiful color for beautiful lady. You leave car with us, and I drive you home. I show you good time."

"Ah, how much? I can only afford a couple of hundred dollars."

"Not to worry pretty lady. I give you special price." Yuri took Rachel's keys and gestured to Drake to take her into the office.

Shit, Shit, Shit thought Rachel, as she watched Yuri get in the Bug, starting it up. He honked for the hanger door to be raised.

Once Yuri was inside, and the heavy door came back down, Drake turned to her and said with an urgent tone. "You don't want to let him drive you home. Start walking, in a few blocks you can catch a bus. I'll call you later."

WHEN RACHEL GOT to Arnie's van, she looked around and then climbed in beside him.

"Where's Gabriel's car?"

"Being painted pink."

"Oh. He's not going to like that. Was that dark-haired guy you were talking to Drake?"

"Yes, he's also Dan the dirtbag I met at a party, who was supposed to call me."

CHAPTER TWENTY-FIVE

While Rachel and Arnie were driving back to the Agency, Gabriel was manning the reception desk. If Rachel was going to get more involved in the business and help Ben with his witness in Slidell, he was going to have to come up with another plan. In the two hours since they'd left, he must have answered a dozen calls. At least half of them only wanted to speak to Arnie.

Bourbon jumped up on his desk, looking for some attention. "I know, big guy. You miss coming in every day. But Arnie needs you." Ben gave his feline partner a scratch on his back. Bourbon let his back rise and started up his purring machine as he pranced back and forth in front of Ben. The kitty massage was broken off when the agency door opened and Acting Chief Murdock walked in.

"Figured you'd be playing with pussy, but I thought maybe something...you know, human."

"Ha-ha Murdock. Meet Bourbon, my feline associate. Can I get you a coffee?"

"Sure, unless you have something stronger."

Gabriel went into the kitchen and came back with two cups of coffee. He found Murdock standing by Gabriel's desk admiring a picture of Jacqueline in a bathing suit on Biloxi beach.

"Quite the babe," Murdock commented.

"That's my wife Jacqueline; she's half French Canadian and half Chinese."

"Can I borrow this picture?'

Gabriel handed the man his coffee and put the photo in a drawer.

"You ever see Johnny Carson do his *Carnac the Magnificent* bit?" Murdock sat in a chair in front of Gabriel's desk.

"What do you mean, Murdock, is this another joke?"

"No, I have an envelope here with a question, a very important question."

"Yeah? What is that?"

"The answers to the question are a house, your mouth, and my ass."

"Murdock..."

"A house, your mouth, and my ass," Murdock repeated, holding up the white envelope to his forehead and closing his eyes. He then ripped open the envelope and blew into it. He extracted a piece of paper and looked at Gabriel as he said, "Name three types of gas explosions?" Murdock began to laugh as he read the question.

"I still don't get it. Are you saying that the explosion on Travina was caused by gas?"

"Yep, and you were right. It wasn't an accident. Someone deliberately started the gas leak and rigged an ignition device that was set to go off once the pressure from the gas got high enough. Then boom." Murdock made a gesture with his hands signifying a massive explosion.

"So, Friesen staged his own death as I told you."

"You see, there's your mouth spouting bullshit theory #1. The Medical Examiner found bone fragments in what was once the basement."

"Oh my God! The partner must have killed Friesen."

"Bullshit theory #2. We checked this guy Friesen out. No jewelry business, there is no record of any business. No record of him having a fucking partner. Want to know his occupation? He's a manager at the Heritage Savings and Loan in Biloxi."

"What? How could that be?"

"Seriously Ross, are you that dumb? Some guy walks in here and feeds you a line, and you bite just like a catfish in a fishing pond." Murdock stuck his index finger in his mouth and pantomimed being a fish caught on a hook.

"So, this guy made all this up? He couldn't have. I have an associate who did some work for his wife. The wife suspected him of cheating, so we tailed him and took some pictures."

"Bull shit theory #3. The ME says he's 99% certain that the bone fragments belong to a female."

"The wife?" Gabriel was dumbfounded.

"Maybe, and guess what? He also thinks she's been dead for a while."

"Are you thinking Friesen killed his wife and decided to fake his own death to throw off the investigation?"

"Not sure how it could be anything else. We have an APB still out on the guy. We'll get Friesen, and then he can answer to a murder charge."

"Hmm. Listen, Murdock, would you mind sitting on this for a couple of days? You know about the ME's findings."

"Why would I do that?"

"I think we're supposed to believe that William Friesen died in that explosion. He was willing to pay me $10,000 to vouch for him dying. If he's still following the same plan, I wonder if someone might come forward to corroborate the story."

Murdock gave Gabriel a stern look. "I don't know. You haven't been right about anything."

"As you said, you have the APB on Friesen. Just hold off telling the press about the ME report, let him think he got away with it."

CHAPTER TWENTY-SIX

"Pink what? You're getting my car painted pink? I don't want a pink car!" Gabriel whined.

"Actually, you really should be buying a new car. That ride is a deathtrap." Rachel told Gabriel about the visit to Huedunit Painting and the confusion surrounding Drake / Dan, and how Yuri the owner wanted to show her "Good time."

"This has been a crazy day. Apart from how I get my car back, what do we do now?"

Arnie had Bourbon nestled on his lap and spoke up. "We still need to find out where this Dan guy really works. Remember when Ben was talking to the Sheriff Bragg the other day? The sheriff said that the undercover operation wasn't theirs. Who does that leave?"

"Could be Biloxi PD. Murdock was just here. I think, for now, he has his head up his ass. I suppose we could ask the Feds, but Wil Graham retired, so I wouldn't know who to ask." Gabriel put Jacqueline's picture back on his desk. A questioning look washed across Rachel's face, which Gabriel dismissed with a shake of his head to suggest it was a long story.

"What happened with Murdock?" asked Arnie.

Gabriel told them about his conversation with the Acting Chief of Police.

"I can't get over what a liar that Friesen is! What's wrong with people?" Rachel stood up from her chair. "I can't believe he made all that stuff up!"

"Let's go with what we know to be true," said Gabriel. "We know his name is William Friesen, and his wife Bonnie hired us to check up on him. We know that he was having multiple affairs. We know that he asked us to help him pull off a staged death. We know that they lived on Travina in a house that just blew up. He may have lied about being a jeweler and having a partner, but the best lies are 90% truth."

Arnie picked it up from there. "So maybe he steals money from the bank somehow. The cops are about to close in, and he thinks it's time to disappear."

"Good thought Arnie," complimented Gabriel. "Might be someone other than the cops, maybe he has an accomplice."

"What about the woman they found in the house?" asked Rachel, now pacing the floor. "He finds out that his wife had him tailed and that she's threatening him with a costly divorce. So instead of sharing any money with her, he kills her. We can't let him get away with this!"

Gabriel looked at Arnie, who nodded his head. "There is just one slight problem."

"What's that Arnie?" Rachel asked.

"We don't have a client."

CHAPTER TWENTY-SEVEN

The Flowers' house was on Edgewood Drive in Slidell. As Tommy Huffman's next of kin, their name, and address had been on the admission sheet at the top of Tommy's file. Ben pulled his truck up to the curb facing a gray bungalow with a large white balcony. He figured that when Tommy had been admitted to the hospital, the Flowers' must have decided to leave the bad memories of Greenville and move closer to him.

Ben didn't get a chance to knock on the door, as an elderly African American woman came to the screen door and spoke to him. "Help you with something?" There was a touch of suspicion in her eyes.

Ben pulled out his Biloxi PD identification and showed it to her through the screen. "Mrs. Flowers? My name is Ben O'Shea, and I'm working with Sheriff McDiarmid on a murder that took place in Picayune some seven years ago."

The woman was thin as a rail and wore a purple pantsuit with cat's eyeglasses. She was about to say something when a tall, slim black man came up from behind Ben and said,

"That's got to be the ugliest truck I've seen in my day." Ben turned around and smiled at an old man who was as tall and lean as a skyscraper.

"Bert, this man says he's a policeman from Biloxi looking into the Wilson kid's murder."

"I thought the official cause of Glenn's death was suicide?"

"It was, but the official explanation always stuck with me like a bad meal," replied Ben.

"Well, then come on in. Agnes, do we have some lemonade in the fridge? Judging by this man's rainbow truck, you better make it pink." Ben gave the black man a quick look before realizing from his smile that he was joking, "Just joshing ya, my name's Bertram Flowers." The man extended a hand, his grip firm. "Any man after the truth is welcome in our home." Ben introduced himself and Bert led him into the front room. "Have a seat, Detective." Bert pointed to a couch with a loud floral pattern.

As Ben sat down, he noticed that they had picked out floral wallpaper, as well as white curtains with multicolored roses. Even the vase on the coffee table containing fresh-cut petunias had a floral pattern. "I've just come from the hospital, checking on Tommy's condition. Poor kid. This must have been awful for him, and for you."

"It was. Hardest on Agnes. She and her sister Mary were pretty close. Is there any new evidence that prompted you to look at the case?"

"I've recently left the force and am working as a private detective. Glenn Wilson's death was outside my jurisdiction at the time but was heavily covered in the local paper. I've developed a friendship with Sheriff McDiarmid, and we both felt that the killing needed to be re-looked at."

"Re-looked at? I don't think it was ever investigated," said Bert.

"I'm afraid that Tommy isn't going to be much help." Mrs. Flowers entered the living room with a pitcher of pink lemonade.

"I understand from his doctor, that he is making some progress," offered Ben.

"Dr. Adrienne Marcotte and the staff at Northshore have been wonderful. I was just telling Bert the other day how amazing Tommy was doing." Mrs. Flowers poured the lemonade into floral glasses. "But there's no sign of him being able to communicate."

"Do you see Tommy very often?" Ben took a sip of lemonade.

"We take turns. One day I go, the next day Bert makes the trip. We moved down here to be close to him."

"Was Tommy's mutism something that came on him gradually, or was it all of a sudden when he discovered what happened to his parents?"

"The police found him wandering the streets. From his library card, they took him home and found his parents. I don't believe he has said anything since," said Bert.

"Before the killing, was he a well-adjusted boy?"

"Pretty much,'" answered Agnes.

"Did he ever talk about what happened to Glenn?"

Bert interrupted. "That's what you want to know, ain't it? Ben nodded, and Bert continued. "We have twin boys, Aster and Basil are close to Tommy's age. They're away at Ole Miss now, but they formed a close bond with him when his family moved to Greenville. The night of the murders the boys were having a sleepover in our backyard."

"Did your boys ever say anything...."

"About the murder?" Mrs. Flowers inserted. "I'm afraid not."

Bert spoke up again. "I think Tommy saw the men that killed Glenn Wilson that day in the woods. I think he was hiding and watched as someone put a bullet in his friend."

"I think that too, Mr. and Mrs. Flowers. The sheriff is dead now, I spoke to his widow yesterday. It sounds like even she thought he could have been involved. But to find the others responsible, I need help. Do you think you could ask your sons if Tommy ever mentioned the name Nantois?"

CHAPTER TWENTY-EIGHT

Rather than drive back to Biloxi after the meeting with the Flowers', Ben thought he would pay a surprise visit to Chevon. *Maybe we could grab dinner. Since we're going to spend the day together tomorrow, I could spend the night, and we can head out to Picayune from her place.* Chevon played saxophone in a band that performed at a place called *Les Trois Muses* in the French Quarter. The cafe was owned by her uncle and was popular with tourists.

Ben thought about what he had learned that morning. First, the interaction with Dr. Marcotte meant that getting anything from Tommy was going to be a longshot. Second, while the conversation with the Flowers' had confirmed his own thoughts, it yielded little new information.

It was just after 4 p.m. Chevon had told him she performed at the Cafe from noon to 3 p.m., and then again from 8 p.m. to 11 p.m. She often crashed midday at her apartment on Treme Street. Ben was able to find a parking spot and made his way to Chevon's apartment. On the way, he passed a street vendor selling cut flowers, and he thought about Bert and Agnes. They'd seemed pretty content in their old age. He bought Chevon a bunch of Easter lilies.

Chevon's apartment was on the top floor of an old two-story, pink clapboard house. Ben huffed and puffed his way up a long flight of stairs to the second floor and knocked on the apartment door. He was leaning on the door jamb trying to catch his breath when the door suddenly opened. He went from anxious to confused in the blink of an eye. Before him stood a tall black man wearing dinosaur pajamas bottoms and nothing else. Ben turned around, thinking he'd knocked on the wrong apartment. The problem was that Chevon's apartment was the only one on the floor.

CHAPTER TWENTY-NINE

"Y ou'll be surprised to hear that we're getting a new car," said Gabriel as he helped Jacqueline with the dinner dishes.

"Seriously, after all this time...you're going to get rid of the Bug?"

"Sort of."

"What does that mean?"

Gabriel shrugged his shoulders, "You'll see soon enough."

"Gabriel Ross, you tell me right now what you did," she commanded.

Gabriel responded by pantomiming that he was using an imaginary key to lock his lips.

"Don't give me that guff, what are you talking about - a new car?"

"Newish."

"Newish....you tell me right now!"

Gabriel kept it up for a few more minutes before relenting and telling Jacqueline about what had happened at the chop shop, and that they would be getting a freshly painted pink VW Bug in return.

"You bum. Stringing me along like that," she splashed him with dishwater from the sink. "Now you'll have to get rid of it. There's no way 'Gabriel Ross' would be caught dead driving a pink car," she laughed.

"I thought I could start driving your car and you could…"

"Forget it, Mister!" she said firmly, cutting him off.

Gabriel took refuge with his son on the living room carpet. Benjamin was playing with some trucks that Jacqueline's parents had given him.

"What do you really think of Chevon and Ben as a couple?" he asked.

"Didn't you ask me that the other day?" Jacqueline was putting away the dinner dishes.

"Yeah, but I don't remember what you said…it was something about being domesticated." Gabriel's tone suggested he was searching for the answers.

"I think they must enjoy each other's company…. but …you know."

"No, I don't know," said Gabriel

"There's the race thing, which I don't think either of them cares about. But depending on where they live, there might be problems."

"I guess old attitudes live on in the next generation. Anyone ever give you any grief over being half Chinese?"

"No, I get lots of looks, but not that kind."

"What do you mean, lots of looks?"

"Do you remember when you first saw me in that elevator?"

"Oh, that kind of look. You were wearing that tight-

135

fitting red dress that reminded me of a Ferrari hugging the coastal highway. Say, where is that dress?"

"Sorry, the Ferrari ran off the road when I gave birth to your son."

During a lull in the conversation, Gabriel wondered to himself. *Will Benjamin have to suffer through discrimination once he starts school? Being mixed breed in Mississippi, plus having his Father's height?* "Hey, do you think Benjamin is short for his age?"

"Don't be silly; he's only a year and a half."

After a moment Jacqueline came back to the issue of Ben and Chevon. "There's the age thing,"

"I'm older than you."

"Two years, but you're young for your age. Ben is twice her age."

"Is that a way of saying I'm immature?"

"You know what they say, if the shoe fits..."

"How's this...how old would you be if you didn't know how old you were? Satchel Paige said that age doesn't matter."

"He was saying that right up until he keeled over and died of old age. The real reason I don't see it ever happening is that Ben is into catching bad guys and Chevon, well, she's a homebody who's interested in music...they have different interests."

"As you said, they like each other's company."

Jacqueline gave Gabriel a contemplative look. "Why are we talking about this again, Gabriel? Is Ben going to ask Chevon to marry him?"

"You can't tell her. Or let on that I told you anything."

"Are you for real...this is huge!" She ran into the living room and straddled him where he lay on the floor. "Tell me what you know, or I'll squash you like a bug on a windshield."

Jelly Bean started laughing, seeing his mother astride his father. The young boy crawled over and sat on Gabriel's head, saying, "Blah, blah, blah."

Gabriel wrestled with his son for a few minutes. Finally, he told Jacqueline about Ben's resolutions and his plans for the weekend in Picayune.

"Wow, I have to confess. I didn't see that coming."

"Will she say yes?"

"Maybe, I think she would be touched that he even asked. I know she really cares for him. She enjoys that the four of us are friends and can hang out, but here's the bottom line: I love Ben; he's a great friend. She'll have a lot of work to do with him."

"Really? First, you suggest that I'm a dog needing to be domesticated, now Ben is a horse that needs to be broken."

CHAPTER THIRTY

Since Ben hadn't seen his ribs for twenty years, the sight of the well-sculpted body in front of him rendered him speechless. The young man had muscles on top of his muscles. He looked back at Ben and broke the stare-off that was now growing weird. "Help you with something?"

Ben felt a twang of awkwardness. An old man, interrupting something. He felt like a fool standing in Chevon's doorway with his miserable bouquet of flowers.

The young man looked down at the flowers. "You delivering flowers, is that it?"

Ben managed to nod.

"That's okay fella. Great to see you've got a job. I can take them."

"They're for Chevon."

The young man held out his hand. "She's taking a shower. I'll make sure she gets them."

"A shower?"

The young man gave Ben a sympathetic look. "Yeah, a shower, you know, something you do to get the sweat off?"

Ben gave the young man the flowers and turned and walked away.

"Wait, buddy, let me give you a tip." A few moments later as Ben continued to walk to the staircase, he heard, "Hey buddy, there's no card. Who are they from?"

"Just from a friend," Ben answered. From behind him, he heard Chevon's voice ask, "Who was at the door Tray?"

"Just some old retarded guy delivering these flowers."

As Ben was about to lumber down the stairs, he heard Chevon call after him, "Ben? Is that you?"

He turned to look back at her, and after a moment responded, "I'm sorry, I didn't know you had company."

Chevon was wearing a mauve Oxford shirt and little else, but she ran out to the hall and gave Ben a hug. "What's wrong, Ben?" She pulled away. "That was like hugging a statue."

Ben tilted his head then nodded to the young man who had turned to go back into the apartment, showing Ben that his back muscles were no less impressive than the front.

"Oh Ben, did you think...? Oh my God," Chevon started to laugh. She called out to the young man. "Trayvon, come over here and meet my boyfriend." Turning to Ben, "Tray is my little brother. Tray, I want you to meet Ben, he's the guy I've been seeing."

A smile crossed Trayvon's face, and he extended a hand. "Sorry man, you didn't say anything, so I thought, you know, you were just delivering flowers."

Ben shook the man's hand. Relief came through his voice, "No apology necessary. I should have seen the family resemblance."

"Chevy told me a lot about you...you got shot in the

shoulder or something. Geez, that must have hurt." Tray winced in empathy.

"Your sister nursed me back to health. It's much better now." Ben flexed his muscles like he was Arnold Schwarzenegger. "Listen, you two are both half-naked. We should either go into the apartment, or I'll have to take my pants off."

Once they were in the apartment, Chevon said, "Tray is crashing at my place until he gets a place of his own."

"I knew you had a younger brother," Ben answered. He turned to Tray. "She said you were getting an arts degree at Ole Miss?"

"Just finished my undergrad a week ago. Mom and Dad said I could have my old room back, but I'd rather bunk with Chevy."

Trayvon eventually left them to take a shower. Ben turned to Chevon. "Sorry, I should have called. I guess when I saw him at the door, with no shirt on, and then you wearing this, I jumped to a conclusion."

"Ben O'Shea, you should know I would never dump you for a younger, slimmer, dynamic, well-built, handsome guy."

"Funny," he said sarcastically. Ben then noticed the shirt she was wearing, "Nice shirt. It looks familiar."

"It should; it's one of yours. You left it here. I think it looks better on me. Don't you think?"

"I've been looking for it in my giant pile of laundry. I like wearing it with my plaid slacks."

"Maybe I better keep it."

"Maybe I'll have to take it back by force," Ben smiled. Chevon raced into her bedroom and jumped on the bed, Ben following closely behind.

After snuggling in bed, Chevon gave him a kiss on the cheek. "Hey, have you lost weight? Your face looks thin."

"I've started exercising. And I'm no longer having the large fries with my Big Macs."

Chevon nodded and gave him an impressed look. "So, you came here because you were just missing me?"

"Yes, well, sort of." Chevon rarely wore her brown hair the same way twice. Today she had it tied up on top of her head with what looked like a salad fork holding it together. "There was something I had to deal with in Slidell, and since we're going to hang out tomorrow, I thought I could spend the night, and we could get an early start," Ben told her about Glenn Wilson and Tommy Huffman, and what he'd learned so far.

"That's horrible, the poor kid. Do you think he would talk to someone like you?"

"What does that mean? I can be nice."

"Oh, I know. It's just that you have that cop thing."

"What cop thing?"

Chevon deepened her voice and used a deadpan tone. "Just the facts ma'am. I have a fucking badge."

"Smarty pants, I was going to ask Rachel from the Agency to do it."

"I remember her… she's the hot brunette with the thing for Gabriel."

"I don't know about that. She has a boyfriend."

"Men are clueless. She may have moved on, but anyone can see she worships him."

"I didn't know that…maybe you should be the detective."

"And you'll play sax at the cafe?"

"I can try, but I think all the animals in the zoo might stampede."

She ran her finger over the scar on his shoulder. "How much does it hurt?"

"A bit."

She sat up and straddled him, "Then I'll have to do all the work."

CHAPTER THIRTY-ONE

The next morning Gabriel was having coffee in the kitchen and watching the local news on WLOX. His eyes were drawn to Mayor Baxter, who was being interviewed on the steps of City Hall. The interviewer was a young Latino woman. "Mr. Baxter, we understand you've released a statement about the explosion earlier this week on Travina. Can you share that with our viewers?"

Baxter, a tall man with thinning hair, dyed an unnatural color with Grecian Formula, flashed a wide smile at the camera. "Yes, I was happy to share what little I know about that tragic event with our fine police department. I told Acting Chief Murdock that I had known Mr. Friesen for a number of years, as my bank manager, and also from some committees and boards. I was able to shed some light on Mr. Friesen's frame of mind. He had recently become estranged from his wife, and this caused him a great deal of grief and self-doubt. On some occasions, I thought that he was slipping into a depression. Of course, I urged him to get professional help."

"Is it your opinion that Mr. Friesen might have deliber-ately caused the explosion?" asked the young reporter.

"I hope not, but I felt that it was my civic responsibility to inform the Chief about what I knew." Baxter again turned and smiled at the camera. "I should remind everyone that we will be having municipal elections in the fall. I appreciate having had the opportunity to represent the wonderful citi-zens of this community. We have made awesome progress fighting crime. Probably, I would say, the best progress any city has ever made. The development of our crime-fighting abilities has been exceptional. But because of mistakes made in the previous administration, we have attracted a bad element. Today, I have put in place the framework for a rapid response tactical team. This will be awesome, believe me. We'll be fighting crime bigly."

Jacqueline came into the kitchen carrying Benjamin and caught the tail end of the interview. She gave Gabriel a doubtful look. "What do you always say about coincidences?"

"There no such thing." Gabriel thought about the Mayor Baxter angle all the way into work. *Murdock confirmed that the explosion was deliberately set. Assuming that Friesen decided to stage his own death, what better endorsement could he get, than to have the esteemed Mayor suggest that he had been suicidal? But would the mayor risk his position by getting involved in such a crazy scheme? All for ten grand?*

When Gabriel got to work, he told Rachel about Mayor Baxter's interview on the local news.

"I know Mr. Friesen was a schemer, but did he seem suicidal to you?" asked Rachel, following Gabriel into the office.

"No, just the opposite actually. He was willing to go to

great lengths because he wanted to live. You know, if we had a client paying our expenses, I would look into what Friesen was up to at the bank, and what connection he might have to Baxter."

"What do you know about Mayor Baxter?" asked Rachel.

"Other than Ben not liking him, word on the street is that he's in bed with some pretty shady people wanting to turn Biloxi into some kind of Vegas of the south."

"There's something about this that doesn't make sense." Rachel sat in the chair in front of Gabriel's desk.

"What's that?"

"From what you said about the interview, it sounds like Baxter was suggesting that Friesen was depressed because his wife left him. In your experience Gabriel, do depressed men go out and sleep with other women?"

"When my wife dumped me for the guy that repaired her Pinto, I was depressed. But I didn't want to do anything other than run away."

"The other thing that doesn't fit is the suggestion that he blew up the house deliberately. Didn't Murdock say the remains found in the house were female?" Rachel sipped her coffee.

After a moment Gabriel snapped his fingers. "Baxter doesn't know they only found her bones."

———

LATER THAT MORNING Gabriel called Acting Chief Murdock to discuss their questions about the case, but had to leave a message as he was out of the office. It was after lunch before Murdock called back.

"Did you see that interview this morning with Mayor

Baxter on WLOX?" Gabriel asked, once he got the detective on the line.

"No, but I heard about it."

"Had you told Baxter about the ME's findings?"

"That the explosion was deliberately set?"

"That, and that they only found a female's remains."

"No, you asked me to sit on that for a couple of days."

"Then that makes me very suspicious of Baxter."

"How do you figure that?"

"Because if Friesen were going to fake his own death, he would want a credible person like the mayor coming out saying he was suicidal."

There was a pause on the line before Murdock said, "Ross, it doesn't matter anymore."

"What do you mean?"

Murdock took a deep breath, and Gabriel could imagine the man leaning back in his office with his feet on the desk. "Hey before I forget, I still need that girl from your office to come down to make a statement."

"Sure, she'll be over this afternoon, but why doesn't it matter anymore?"

"We've located Friesen. Or his body that is."

"I'm confused. Where did you find him?"

"He was found by the maid early this morning at a downtown fleabag. He hung himself."

CHAPTER THIRTY-TWO

Everything was happening so fast on the Friesen investigation. For that reason, Gabriel decided to pay a visit to the *Heritage Savings and Loan*. The bank was located in a two-story, yellow-colored brick building in the heart of downtown Biloxi. As he entered the building, Gabriel saw a beehive of activity. Some of the offices appeared to be occupied by employees busy with customers, while others had staff members hidden behind skyscrapers of reports, with only an arm and fingers visible, rapidly pecking on a huge calculator. He stepped up to the receptionist desk, where a middle-aged woman with the name Emily on her nametag was simultaneously typing something on an IBM Selectric while cradling a phone to her ear. As he waited, he noticed a plastic holder containing staff business cards. He selected a card that said 'William Friesen, Branch Manager.'

After a couple of moments, Emily put her call on hold and gave Gabriel a plastic smile that silently said, *I don't like interruptions.* "How can I direct you, sir?"

"I would like to speak to Mr. William Friesen," Gabriel announced, holding up the business card.

The question seemed to shake the woman. "I'm sorry sir. The Manager is not available. Would you like to speak to Mr. Huntley, he's the Assistant Manager?"

"I had my heart set on speaking to Mr. Friesen. Is he in a meeting?" The shook her head.

"Vacation?"

Headshake.

"On a call, visiting a client?"

Headshake.

"Off sick today?"

Headshake.

"I give up. Why don't you just tell me why he's not here?"

"I've been told to refer all inquiries to Mr. Huntley."

"Where is Mr. Huntley?"

"He's not here. If you want I can schedule an appointment for you."

Gabriel gave the woman a blank look and shook his head. "Listen, my name is Gabriel Ross, I'm a private investigator looking into an important matter. Emily, can't you just tell me where Mr. Friesen is?"

Headshake.

A few moments later, Gabriel walked away boiling with frustration, and an appointment to see Hollis Huntley at 4 p.m. later that day. He felt like a greyhound racing to catch up to a mechanical rabbit, only to discover the rabbit wasn't even real.

CHAPTER THIRTY-THREE

Once Gabriel got back from the bank, he asked Rachel if she could go see Acting Chief Murdock and make a statement on the Friesen adultery case. Since it appeared that Mrs. Friesen was dead, Gabriel said that there no longer was an issue with confidentiality. He warned her that Murdock figured himself to be a lady's man. "You might use your feminine charms to find out whether there are any other avenues of investigation."

Thirty minutes later, Rachel walked into the station house and was directed to the detective department on the second floor. She wore a tight clingy dress that accentuated her figure. When she got to the second floor, one of the policemen directed her to Acting Chief Murdock's office.

She discovered a middle-aged man with salt-and-pepper hair sitting behind a desk. He was listening to a Sony Walkman cassette player and humming like a wounded dog to whatever he was listening to. Rapping on the door frame didn't get his attention, so she walked into the office and sat down in the chair opposite him. He took off the headphones, and Rachel gave him her best smile. "I'm Rachel Henderson. Gabriel Ross told me that you wanted me to make an official statement."

"Well, hello there," said Murdock in full hound dog mode, giving her the once-over. "Can I get you anything - coke, coffee, Valentine's Day card?"

Rachel smiled, taking in the large office. "No. This used to be Chief Willis' office, right?"

"That's right. I'm the big Kahuna now." Murdock puffed out his chest and held out his hand. "Call me Ken."

"Nice to meet you, Ken." Rachel gave his hand a quick shake.

"Did you want to get down to it?"

"Sure, how do you want to do this?" Rachel smiled, crossing her legs seductively.

Murdock was mesmerized for a moment before he said, "I'll be the note taker. Once we're done, I'll get you to read it over. Then I'll get someone to type it up for you to sign. Maybe we could do lunch in the meantime."

Rachel smiled and said, "We'll see, no promises." She told him about the surveillance and how she'd caught Friesen with a different woman each night.

"What a hound!" Murdock said, feigning his disapproval. "Was Mrs. Friesen an attractive woman?"

Rachel paused for a moment, not understanding the relevance of the question.

Murdock elaborated. "I've only ever seen her bones."

"She was a lovely woman. I think at one point before he started cheating on her, she truly cared for him."

"Do you know the difference between love and marriage, Rachel?" When Rachel shook her head, he advised her,

"Love is like one long sweet dream, marriage is the alarm clock."

Rachel chuckled, "You sound like you have experience."

"I do, we're actually in a good place right now. We have an open marriage. If I meet someone, I'm attracted to..."

Rachel interrupted, "So there's not much more to tell you about the case. I met with Mrs. Friesen and gave her the photos, and she thanked me."

"I'd like to see those pictures." Rachel handed over a file folder, and Murdock took his time going through each one. At one point he shifted one photo 90 degrees and leaned back in his chair. "I might need to hold on to these...evidence you know."

Rachel nodded, "Gabriel told me about how you found her husband."

"Yes, it was pretty horrific. In this job, you have to deal with some pretty terrible things. The maid at the Belvedere came in to clean the room and was putting a pillow back into the closet when she found him. He was hanging in the closet."

"Really? How horrible for her." Rachel sat back and re-crossed her legs. "Was there a note?"

"No, just him, hanging in the closet. Must have given the maid quite the fright."

"I think it would be pretty hard to hang oneself in a closet. Mr. Friesen was a tall man. How tall was the closet?"

Murdock looked at his notepad as if he had somehow written down the answer to the question. "I guess it was tall enough."

"Hanging suggests a broken neck. For that, you would need the body to drop from a certain height. Maybe he smothered himself, you know, with a plastic bag?"

"Maybe, I'll know better when we get the Medical Examiner's report."

"What did you find in the room?"

"He must have been drinking heavily. We found a lot of alcohol."

"How many used glasses did you find?"

"I don't know. We also found a pizza, mostly uneaten," he said officiously.

"Really? Do you think he might have had company?"

"You mean like one of these dames you caught him with?" Rachel shrugged her shoulders. "Maybe, what's your next move, Ken?"

"Can't do much until the ME report comes in. But it's a bit of a formality. I've seen enough of these." His voice went self-important like he was verbally hitching up his pants.

"Does that wrap up everything Ken? The explosion, the wife, the letter carrier?"

"Yes, I guess it does. I figure Friesen killed his wife with the explosion then felt so bad about it, he decided to take his own life."

Rachel was just about to call 'bullshit' when a man walked into the office, noticed Rachel, and started to fumble his way back out. "Sorry boss, but the mayor is holding on line two. He says it's urgent. I didn't realize you had company."

"Give us a few minutes, Don," said Murdock.

Rachel looked up at the officer just as he was leaving. "Don? Dan? Or is it Drake?"

CHAPTER THIRTY-FOUR

Rachel and What's His Name walked to a place called *Jezzepis* just a block from the police station. After they were shown to a table, What's His Name started scanning the menu. "I'm thinking ravioli."

"Nah, I don't feel like having pasta."

"What were you doing with Murdock?"

"You said you would call me. Once again you didn't. No information until you come across with what the hell is going on."

"I don't know where to start."

"How about your real name?" *I'm guessing he's mid-to-late twenties. Tall with dark hair, brown eyes constantly flickering like blowing leaves. That dimple! Definitely in the ruggedly handsome category. Most important, no ring on his finger.*

"Don ...Green. I'm an undercover cop assigned to BPD to investigate a stolen car ring."

"Bullshit." Rachel shook her head in frustration. "What's with all the lies? You looked down at the green tablecloth before making up that last name. Not very convincing."

"Ok, it's Donald Candle..son," he replied, looking down at the candle flickering between them.

"That's so bad, it's funny." Rachel picked up the menu. "I'm going to order the most expensive thing on the menu. If I have to listen to your lies, I might as well eat well."

"Ok, ok ...it's Don... Mangina."

"Mangina?" Rachel laughed out loud.

"That's exactly the reaction I expected." He pointed his finger at her accusingly. "That's the reason I'm reluctant to tell people my real name. My family is second generation Italian from a small village in the Alps, called...."

"Mangina."

"I was going to say Locarno."

"Alright, never mind. Huedunit Painting. You're investigating the chop shop?"

"In a nutshell. Why were you there?"

"Getting my boss' car painted pink. Why haven't you raided that place? Any idiot can see what they do there." She took a sip from her water glass.

"I will, but I want to find out who's behind this. If we raid the place, they'll just reopen somewhere else. I need to be able to make a case against the guy in charge."

"What's with the name Drake?" Rachel asked.

"Drake? Your turn. Where did you hear that name?" Rachel gave him a cross look. "Okay, okay, on the arrest I didn't want to use the name Don because I was undercover, and I didn't want to use Dan which is my name at the Chop Shop, just in case they put two and two together."

"Does Acting Chief Murdock know about Huedunit?"

"I'm not sure what he knows. I don't work for him. He might suspect that I have something on the go, but I work for the Mississippi Bureau of Investigation."

"What's that?"

"Kind of like the FBI, but at the state level."

"Why wouldn't Murdock know?"

"I can't talk about that. I've already said way too much."

"Alright Mr. 'Mangina,' why was Jeffrey Motten arrested?"

"Is that what this is about? Are you related to that creep?"

"No, answer the question." Rachel grabbed a breadstick and threatened to bludgeon him.

"He was going to blow my cover. I thought Motten might recognize me from an arrest I made a while back. He used to ride with the Sons of Silence. I couldn't take a chance, so when he went on and on about wanting to have his wife killed, I made arrangements to meet him at a bar. I was already wearing the wire, all we had to do was have him arrested and put on ice until the operation is over."

"So, at some point, you're just going to drop the charges."

"Yeah, but for the record, he offered me a grand. Wait, do you work for his lawyer?"

Rachel chewed on the breadstick before replying. She was about to answer when a dark-haired waiter, wearing too much cologne and sporting a week's worth of stubble, approached the table and asked if they had decided what they would like.

Don spoke up. "I think we will both have the Rav...."

Rachel interrupted. "I have a craving for steak. How is the steak?"

"Is delizioso." The waiter kissed his fingertips and rolled his eyes towards the ceiling in rapture.

"Well then, Mr. Mangina here, and I, will both have that."

"Mangina? Parli Italiano?" asked the waiter. When Don didn't reply, he rambled on in Italian.

"That's okay, we're in a bit of a rush," said Don. Rachel looked at the undercover cop across from her and smiled. When the waiter had left, Don said. "Quite the little bundle, aren't you?"

"To answer your question. I work for a detective agency that's helping Mr. Motten's lawyer. That's why I was at the paint shop. I couldn't understand why an undercover cop would be interested in Motten."

"There you have it. That's also the reason I didn't call you back. It's easier if I don't complicate things. If the people who run the chop shop found out I was a cop, then I'd be dead meat."

After a moment, Rachel commented, "By not telling Murdock, it's like you're running an undercover operation on the BPD as well."

"Like I, said I can't talk about..."

"What's your next move then, Sherlock?"

"Yuri keeps a ledger in his desk in his office. I'd like to take a look at it. It might have a record of cars stolen and sold and who is behind this."

CHAPTER THIRTY-FIVE

Hollis Huntley was a thin, nervous man. As far as Gabriel could tell, he was middle-aged, although judging by his dowdy black tweed jacket and silver bow tie, he could have been older.

"All I can tell you is that Mr. Friesen is away from the office. Now Mr. Ross, what business would you like to discuss?" Huntley sat across the desk from Gabriel.

"I'd like to discuss the business of William Friesen."

Huntley gave Gabriel a blank look and then reshuffled some of the papers on his desk. "Well...what do you want to know?"

"What he was into? What would make him want to run away and hide? Why someone would want to hurt him?"

Judging by his open mouth and bulgy eyes, Hollis Huntley was clearly thrown by the questions. "All I can tell you is that he recently had some personal troubles, and on the advice of his doctor he decided to take some time. Now I've said more than I should have, so perhaps you could respect his privacy and leave."

"Listen, Huntley," Gabriel leaned towards the man, who was fidgeting with his pen. "You might not know this yet, but Friesen's dead. I'm looking into his death in conjunction with Acting Police Chief Murdock of the Biloxi PD." Gabriel realized he was stretching the truth, but he needed to shock Huntley into divulging what he knew.

"Dead? I don't understand," Huntley whined.

"What's not to understand? Dead. Checking out the grass from underneath. On the 'UNABLE TO BREATHE' list. His body was found in a closet in his motel room earlier today."

"Oh my God. Oh my, that's horrible. Oh my," Huntley repeated, standing up as if he had to do something, then looking around and sitting back down. His hand was shaking like a palm tree in a hurricane. "Maybe I should make an announcement...."

"Listen, Huntley, get a grip." Gabriel interrupted. "You're the top man now. This is pretty serious stuff. You heard about someone blowing up his house last week? Now they find him dead in his motel room. You'd better start explaining what he was into." Gabriel's voice was threatening. When Huntley didn't respond, he added. "Now I come here, and you're sitting in his chair. If you think my questions are hard, the authorities will be here shortly."

"I don't know; he was the manager. He did paperwork, approved loans, met with customers..."

"What customers?"

Huntley was about to say something, then bit his lip. Clearly, Gabriel hadn't shaken him enough because he replied, "That would be confidential."

CHAPTER THIRTY-SIX

B en and Chevon got up early and by 7 a.m. had hit Highway 10 across Lake Pontchartrain. They needed to be back in New Orleans by 11:30 so Chevon could get ready for her lunchtime set. As they drove, they watched the sunrise spilling light across the fields. The day promised to be another scorcher with temperatures expected to hit the mid-eighties by noon.

"Do you know the meaning of the name Picayune?" asked Chevon, trying to adjust the air conditioning in the truck. When Ben shrugged his shoulders, "It means something small and worthless. As in a worthless coin, sometimes called a Picayune. It can also mean, petty and worthless."

"Not very promising," replied Ben, wondering if he would have the courage to pop the question. He had worked up to it a couple of times the night before, but something always threw off his timing. He drove in silence for a few minutes, stealing glances at Chevon every couple of moments.

"I hear that they have a kick-ass teddy bear museum." Chevon was looking out the window but sensed his gaze.

"That's one of the things I thought we could check out."

After about ten minutes they were on the causeway. "Ben, was buying this pickup part of a plan to move out to the country?"

"Why do you ask that?"

"You don't seem like a guy who would drive a truck. Then, leaving the police force, spending the day out in Bumblefuck, Mississippi. I was just wondering."

"No plans, but I've been thinking about the future. I need to find out what comes next job-wise before I can make any firm decisions."

"Will you miss working for the department, or will they miss you so much that they ask you to come back?"

"I wouldn't go back while Mayor Baxter is still there. I'll miss it, but I think working at the Agency with Gabriel and his team will help."

They drove in silence for a few minutes before Chevon saw a large white bird flying over the water. "Pelican," she pointed to it.

Ben looked over. "I always thought they were kind of weird looking. Their mouths remind me of a urinal in a men's washroom."

"Hey, watch it." Chevon laughed. "Pelicans are Louisiana's state bird."

"Can you tell me the name of the state bird of Mississippi?"

"The mosquito?" she answered with a smile.

"Funny. No, it's the mockingbird."

Chevon started singing, *"Hush little baby don't say a word,*

Mama's gonna buy you a mockingbird, and if that mockingbird don't sing, Mama's gonna buy you a diamond ring."

"You have a beautiful voice, Chevon. You should sing more often."

"Were you a farm kid growing up?" Chevon deflected his praise.

"In Providence? No, we lived in an old part of the city called Federal Hill. It used to be all Irish families, but then things changed, now it's mostly Italians."

"No cows?" Chevon asked as they left the causeway and began passing fields, many with livestock.

"The closest I ever got would be when my older sister used to say, 'Ben settle down, don't have a cow.'"

"Kind of like I thought that causeway wasn't going to end until the cows came home."

Ben nodded, accepting the challenge, "The tolls they're charging to cross it, make it a big cash cow."

"Pretty good. Why buy the cow when you can get the milk for free?"

So true, Ben nodded silently, acknowledging that she had won the contest. He wondered if Chevon knew the struggle that he was having. A moment later she asked, "You've never mentioned a sister, will I one day find her half-dressed in your apartment?"

"She passed away from stomach cancer about 12 years ago. It was around the time my first wife left me."

"I'm sorry, Ben."

"My sister and I were close. She was the only person that understood me. When she died, and I got a call from Biloxi, I packed up and hit the road. It was just easier to start over. You know, wipe the slate clean?"

"That must have been rough Ben. I'm sorry to hear

about your sister." After a few moments, Chevon said, "I guess I've never been alone. My folks are still around, my uncle, my brother, lots of cousins. All within a few blocks of one another in New Orleans."

"That's nice for you Chevon."

"It is, I can't ever see myself moving away."

THEY ARRIVED in Picayune a little after 8:00 and spent time on some of the backcountry roads. There were lots of farms, all with long gravel lanes leading off the highway. "See that house on the left?" Ben asked. When Chevon nodded, "Do you remember the lawyer who died in the explosion last fall? That's where he lived."

"That was horrible. I can't believe everything that has happened to you, to Gabriel and Jacqueline. I sometimes wonder why you just don't get away from here."

"*Would you move with me?,* Ben almost asked. As they drove further into town, they both commented on the beautiful homes with sprawling front lawns and picturesque magnolia trees.

"Notice the houses all seem to have the battle flag flying in their yard," said Chevon.

"Do you see that as a racist thing?"

Chevon thought for a moment before answering, "Of course, don't you?"

"It might be just a link to the past. Folks in Mississippi are a little stubborn when it comes to change."

"Political answer," she answered. They passed a '*Welcome to Picayune,*' sign advertising Picayune as the birthplace of America's music.

Pointing at the sign, "Yeah, tell that to Nashville, Memphis or New Orleans," boasted Chevon.

"I've heard that before. Isn't Mississippi the home of the blues?"

"Oh, sure, Mississippi. BB King, Elvis, Bo Diddley, Jimmy Buffet, Sam Cooke, all kinds of great musicians came from Mississippi. But I can't think of anyone that came from Picayune."

Once they got into town, Ben pulled the truck into a parking space in front of Mayfield Creamery. According to McDiarmid, the dairy had the best ice cream in the county. A few minutes later they were enjoying their cones sitting on a bench out front of the store. Ben pointed to a church across the street. "Population is 10,000 people, and there are 78 churches. If you're a Baptist, there are 42 different churches you can attend."

"That's crazy! Are you religious?" Chevon took a large lick of her pistachio cone.

"Failed Catholic. You?"

"Same here. I go with my parents the odd time, just to make them happy."

Ben felt a shot of excitement that they'd found something in common. He was just about to ask about the future when he spied a Pearl River deputy sheriff making his way down the sidewalk towards them. He was an older white man with a paunch that suggested he liked his beer. He wore the blue uniform of the County Police and sported a pair of mirrored sunglasses. When the policeman noticed them, he stopped for a moment and then looked at Ben's truck with amusement. "That your truck sir?" he asked, not even looking in their direction.

"Yes, officer. Is there a problem?"

The deputy finally turned to face them and looked back and forth from Ben to Chevon before giving them a wide smile. "Good day for ice cream." There was something about his tone and smile that suggested to Ben that this wasn't about ice cream.

"Sure is, Deputy Cagle," Ben read the name tag on the man's uniform.

"Not from around, here are you?" The deputy pulled out a toothpick from his breast pocket and put it in his mouth before putting one foot on the bumper of Ben's truck.

Ben prepared himself for a comment about the color of the truck. "I'm from Biloxi and this gal here is visiting from New Orleans. We're just passing through."

"That so? Don't know what the rules are in Behluxie, but here we ask people to park between the white lines. Your vehicle is parked incorrectly."

Ben was surprised that the few inches would be worth mentioning. There was probably no point in explaining that had the truck beside him parked in the center of their space, he would have done likewise.

"Sheriff McDiarmid sure has some keen deputies," said Ben, standing up and approaching the man.

"I'd like to see some identification, sir," Cagle inched closer.

"That's your right I guess, Deputy Cagle." Ben pulled out his wallet and handed it to the deputy with the Mississippi driver's license open.

The deputy took his time looking at the identification and then glanced at the Biloxi PD ID before handing the wallet back. He chomped on his toothpick for a good minute, staring at Ben before saying, "Suggest you and your Missus here, finish your ice cream, and move your truck."

Ben nodded, and the deputy continued on down the sidewalk. Once he'd left, Chevon, who had finished her ice cream, said, "Ben let's just get out of here." Once they were back in the truck, she let loose. "That was all about a white man sitting with an African American woman in public."

"Maybe." Ben looked at her. She was clearly angry.

"Maybe? If I were a white woman, he'd have paid us no never mind. Ben, I haven't seen one African American person around. There something off about this place."

"There are quite a few blacks that live here, just not in this part of town." Ben didn't want to say they all lived on the other side of the highway. Instead, he smiled, "Hey, let's go check out that Teddy Bear Museum. That'll get our minds off that guy."

———

THE TEDDY BEAR MUSEUM was a one-story building off Memorial Blvd., just a few minutes away from downtown. Ben and Chevon spent the better part of an hour touring around over 15,000 teddy bears and Beanie Babies.

"Did you realize that teddy bears originated in Picayune?" asked Ben.

"Is this another one of those 'the birthplace of American music' bullshit stories?"

"No, I read it on that plaque over there, so it has to be true. It all started when Teddy Roosevelt, the President, went bear hunting near Picayune with some of his buddies. I guess the President's handlers caught a black bear and tied him to a tree and called the President to shoot him. The President refused to shoot the bear saying it was unsportsmanlike. The story found its way to the press, and in no time political cartoons started appearing showing the President with his pet bears."

Chevon gave Ben a skeptical look as they walked into the gift shop. Ben saw a teddy bear holding a saxophone and bought it for Chevon.

"That was pretty cool," said Chevon as they walked out of the museum. The incident with the deputy was forgotten. "Thanks for the bear, I love him. I'm going to call him Ben."

As they walked towards the parking lot, Ben contemplated popping the question. He took hold of Chevon and gently pulled her to him. "Chevon …I have something I wanted to ask you…" Just then he noticed the Pearl River County sheriff's cruiser. Deputy Cagle, still chewing his toothpick, was watching them.

CHAPTER THIRTY-SEVEN

B en looked in the rearview mirror. Deputy Cagle was following at a safe distance.

"What did you want to ask me, Ben?"

He didn't want to upset Chevon again by pointing out that they had picked up the tail after leaving left the museum. "Nothing important. I just wanted to ask if I could hear you sing again."

Chevon gave him an incredulous look before responding. "Sure, come to the club, and I'll see what I can do."

They had lots of time to get to New Orleans so Ben pulled into an Exxon gas station off Route 50, mainly to see what the deputy would do. As he pulled up to the pumps, he noticed in his mirror that the deputy had pulled into the lot and was sitting in his cruiser watching.

"Ben, what's going on? You keep looking at something in the rearview mirror," Chevon asked, turning around to look.

"Chevon, could you do me a favor?" Ben opened the driver's door.

"Ben?"

"When the attendant comes, tell him you want twenty dollars of regular. I have to go in and ...you know."

Ben hurried towards the station. Once in the building, he spied a pay phone. Putting in a quarter, he dialed the number he had for Sheriff McDiarmid.

"Pearl River County, Sheriff McDiarmid," came the answer.

"How many crullers have you had today Cliff?"

"Hey, Ben. I've turned over a new leaf. No more crullers for me. Lips that touch crullers will never touch mine."

"Is that right?"

"I've switched to salads, healthy boring salads. Listen, Ben, I was going to call you today. I had a chance to speak to one of the deputies who go back to Sheriff Harrigan's time. I asked him who the heavy hitters were in the drug trade back in '76-'77. His answer was that there were virtually no drugs in Pearl River County at that time. Sheriff Harrigan was tough on drugs."

"The deputy's name wouldn't be Cagle, would it? Old guy, kind of heavy?"

"Yeah, how'd you know?"

"Met him today. As a matter of fact, he's been my shadow since I left Picayune headed to New Orleans. Listen, I wonder if you could do me a favor...."

BEN LEFT by the back door and snuck around to the back of the deputy's cruiser. Thankfully he'd parked facing Ben's truck, so he didn't see Ben sneak up from behind. Ben just had to wait a few moments before a call on the police radio came through as expected. "Deputy Cagle, come in. We have a 133 in progress at the Exxon Gas station over on Highway 50. See the owner. Can you respond?"

"I'm on it, 10-4," Ben heard the deputy say. The next sound was the cruiser's door opening, and the car shifting and creaking as the heavy-set deputy climbed out. Ben watched as Cagle unsnapped his holster and walked purposefully to the gas station.

Ben moved quickly, walking to the cruiser's door and reaching in to move the seat up as far forward as it would go. He switched the emergency lights, siren, AM radio, wipers, air conditioning and turn signal to the 'on' position. Anything that would turn on when the ignition was engaged. He went to the back of the cruiser and used his penknife to make a slow leak in one of the back tires. Once done, he ran over to his truck where Chevon was waiting, enjoying the sunshine. "Okay, quick -get in, there's about to be some fireworks."

Ben had just started up the truck and driven back onto the highway when a flustered Deputy Cagle ran out of the station to his cruiser. Looking in the rearview mirror, he told Chevon to watch the action. Cagle got to his car and tried to climb into the front only to find that he couldn't. From the actions of the deputy, Ben could imagine his angry tirade. Once the deputy got the seat back far enough to get in, he started up the car, only to have everything turn on all at once. Ben saw the deputy put the car in gear, sirens blaring as he pulled out of the gas station. Cagle made it about ten feet before he realized that he had a flat.

"Oh, Ben! Was that the deputy?" Chevon looked back at the gas station, where the cop was running out into the highway and shaking his fist at Ben. She started laughing hysterically.

"Yeah, I decided to see if he had a sense of humor. We better hurry up and get over the causeway just in case he radios ahead to friends."

WHEN THEY GOT to the door leading to Chevon's apartment, Ben pulled her to him and kissed her. "I'm sorry, the day didn't quite work out the way I hoped."

"I had fun Ben, and I love my bear."

"I just thought... I don't know what I thought. I wanted it to be memorable."

"Well the sight of that deputy running down the highway after us isn't something I'll soon forget."

AFTER LEAVING Chevon to get changed for her next set, Ben drove downtown and parked his truck in a lot adjacent to the New Orleans Police Department. He had a former partner by the name of Rutledge who worked out of the station. For as long as he'd known the man, he'd known him only as Rutledge. He was well past normal retirement but kept working because he had nothing else in his life. Ben had known types like him before, and when they finally gave up the job, retirement usually didn't last long. Sometimes they looked for meaning by crawling into a bottle of Johnny Walker. In extreme cases, depression led to suicide.

Ben knew the layout of the building and found Rutledge buried behind a stack of files on the 2nd floor. "Hey old timer, remember me?" Ben walked into the man's office.

"Jesus on a cracker!" The large African American man

bellowed when he looked up and saw Ben. Wasting no time, he got up and extended a hand to his friend. "How you keeping, Ben?" he asked enthusiastically.

"I'm hanging in there. You look good, Rutledge. I thought you'd be long retired by now."

"Yeah, you and most of the people around here. I heard about the disability. It sounds like there might have been more to the story." Rutledge pointed to a chair.

"The mayor wanted to hang someone out to dry," Ben said, sitting down. "You know me. I've never been politically swift. I kind of took a dislike to his bullshit and dropped a hint or two that he was crooked. Maybe that got back to him. He told Chief Willis to fire me. Rather than do that, Willis told him to shove the job and walked out. I feel bad about that. Willis was a good man. It turned out to be all for naught anyway. I took a bullet in the shoulder and well, it's all over anyway."

"So how is the shoulder?"

"I'm in physio, but to be honest, it hurts like hell."

"So that's the end for you."

"I have that business on the side...the Eye on You Detective Agency. I guess I'll collect disability for as long as I can, then see what kind of trouble I can get into there."

"Right, I forgot about that. I met your associate a while back on that Mardi Gras serial killer case."

"Gabriel Ross. He's a good guy. He was an accountant at Ford Motor Company before I met him and convinced him to help open up the Agency."

"Great success story, I wish I had thought of it."

"Maybe we'll branch out ...open a New Orleans office."

"Yeah, you do that. Let me know if you need a good

paper pusher." Rutledge pointed to the files. "So, whatcha working on Ben? And how can I help?"

"Do you have anything on a couple of hoods by the name of Nantois? They might have been active in Mississippi at one time."

Rutledge leaned back in his chair and fixed Ben with a steely-eyed look. "Don't need to look them up. My memory's still pretty sharp. Kory and Kane Nantois. They're connected to Frankie Reznikov. Heard of him?"

"Yeah, he's a mobster."

Rutledge snapped his fingers and nodded his head. "They call him Frankie Fingers. The legend goes that one of his wise guys gave him the wrong answer and Frankie used tin snips on his fingers."

"What can you tell me about Reznikov's operations?"

"He has his fingers, pardon the pun, in all kinds of shady things. Massage parlors, tanning salons, I even heard something about him getting involved in the lobby to legalize gambling in Biloxi."

"That so? And the Nantois..."

"Local muscle. One, I guess has half a brain, the other is dumb as a fence post but a real psycho. I don't remember which one's which. We've busted them on assault charges, suspicion of arson, even a rape charge, but they always walk because a witness either disappeared or miraculously got amnesia."

"Any chance I can get a look at the booking sheet?"

"Sure, it will take a few minutes to get it from records, but before I do, are you going to tell me what this is about?"

"There was a case 7 years ago, a kid named Glenn Wilson was shot to death in the woods by his farm. There's a clearing perfect for a drug drop. I figure he saw something that he shouldn't have. The Sheriff at the time was Thad Harrigan, and he might have been caught up in this with those brothers."

"Sheriff Thaddeus Harrington. I remember him. It being in Mississippi, it wasn't my turf. But you hear things. Word was that Harrington was dirty."

———

BEN WENT to get coffees while Rutledge left to dig out the records on the Nantois brothers. Ben knew he could get a last known address and a mug shot of the brothers. As he left the building, he had no idea that Kory Nantois was watching him from across the street.

CHAPTER THIRTY-EIGHT

As Gabriel walked into the agency, he still felt frustrated. He had just wasted an hour talking to Hollis Huntley about a crime he wasn't being paid to look into, and gotten absolutely nowhere.

Rachel was sitting in his office talking to Arnie.

"Hey folks, hope you're having a better day than me." Gabriel settled into a chair. As soon as he'd entered the office, the conversation had stopped. He told them about his frustrating visit to the bank. "Because the ME said the woman's remains appeared to have been there a while, I have to think that Murdock's theory is partly correct. Friesen kills his wife because she found out he was having an affair; and because his partner was on his case about the money, he decides to cover up everything by blowing up his house. Somehow the partner found out where he was hiding and killed him. Does that make sense?"

Both Arnie and Rachel nodded. Rachel gave Gabriel a recap of what she had learned from Murdock. "The only difference in that theory, and what Murdock believes, is that

Friesen felt so bad about killing his wife that he killed himself."

"I like my theory better. Like you said Rachel, it's pretty much impossible to hang yourself in a closet."

Rachel told him about her lunch with Don Mangina. "I think Don wouldn't want anything shared with Murdock."

"So maybe the Mississippi Bureau of Investigation believes that Murdock is somehow involved in the stolen car ring?" asked Arnie.

"That would be the logical conclusion," replied Rachel.

"Murdock doesn't strike me as someone that ambitious," offered Gabriel. For a long moment, there was silence as they thought about the two cases. Finally, Gabriel spoke up. "Arnie, how about you stop by this Belvedere Motel. Ask them about visitors he might have had, who delivered the pizza, did anyone see anything? It's pretty clear Murdock is not going to do any investigating."

"Okay, Gabriel. I'll stop by on my way home. But Rachel has something to ask you to do. It was what we were discussing before you came in."

Gabriel looked back and forth between Rachel and Arnie, "Alright?"

"I guess your car is ready." Rachel bit her lip. "This Yuri guy wants it picked up. Arnie can't do it because he already met the man. And Don suggested someone else pick up the car because his boss, this Yuri guy, wants to get me alone. I just left a message to say that my fther, the real owner of the car, would be by to pay for it and pick it up."

"Father? I'm like two years older than you."

"I know, I just blurted it out on the message."

"Wait, wait, wait! You want me, your father to pick up my pink Volkswagen? And you want me to pay for it?"

"Yes," Rachel winced.

THE BELVEDERE WAS one of those motels where you drive up to your room. Arnie parked in front of Unit 16. This had to be where Friesen died, as the room had been sealed with yellow crime scene tape. The motel itself was a drab one-story building that had seen better days. The place was built in a "U" shape with a swimming pool that looked over-grown with algae in the middle.

Arnie noticed the maid's cleaning cart in front of Unit 11 and decided to have a word with her. Getting out of his van, he checked his watch. It was a little past 5 pm, and the sun showed no sign of cooling down. He knocked on the open door. "Hello, is someone in here?"

"Quien? What you want?" came a heavily accented reply from inside the room.

"I'm sorry. I didn't mean to interrupt. My name is Arnie Sims."

A short, heavy-set woman came out of the bathroom holding up a toilet brush like it was a weapon.

Arnie gave the woman a smile. "Were you by chance working when Mr. Friesen's body was discovered?

The woman, whose nametag identified her as Rosetta, nodded and then said something in Spanish. Arnie's Spanish was a little rusty, but from what he could gather, she said that it was her 15-year-old daughter Maria who had found him. "Do you speak English?"

"Un poco."

"I'm an investigator looking into Mr. Friesen's death. Can I ask you a few questions?" When the woman nodded, he asked, "First, how is Maria? That must have been terrible for her."

"She still screaming."

"Were you working the night before the body was discovered?"

Once again, the cleaning woman nodded and said she worked in lavanderia. She pointed to the office at the front of the building.

"Good, do you know if Mr. Friesen had any visitors?"

The woman paused for a moment, maybe considering how much she wanted to get involved. She finally said "Cicero."

"Cicero?"

"Pizza."

"Mr. Friesen had a pizza delivered from Cicero Pizza?" When the woman nodded, "Do you know what time the delivery was made?"

She held up seven fingers, which Arnie took to mean 7 o'clock. He had never heard of Cicero Pizza. "Were there other visitors, or anyone else you saw that looked suspicious?"

"Puta."

"A whore? Can you describe the woman?

She fired off a barrage of Spanish, flinging her arms in the air as if to make a point.

"Can you speak slower, or in English?"

In answer, the woman held her hands out in front of her as if she was holding a pair of huge breasts. "Okay, she had big breasts. What else do you remember?"

She searched for a word and then said, "Raincoat, but no raining. Big hat."

"She wore a poncho and a sombrero?"

The woman shook her head vehemently. "Raincoat and a big hat."

"Was she tall, was she white?"

"Muja blanca," she held her hand up to Arnie's chin, suggesting the woman was 5 foot and change.

"Why do you think she was a ...puta?"

"I see, she come here before ...same man. She big puta."

"What time did you see her?"

She shrugged her shoulder, "Later."

"Did you see anyone else go into the room?

She shook her head and repeated "lavanderia," making a gesture that she was washing clothes by hand.

"What about your daughter Maria, did she see anything?"

"No, Maria work," she held up five fingers.

Arnie thanked the woman and got her contact information.

He went to the motel office where a black man with cornrows and wearing a Hawaiian shirt watched *Hill Street Blues* on a small black and white portable. There was a marijuana smell in the office. Arnie gave the man his business card and said he was there about William Friesen.

"Who's that?" the man asked without taking his eyes from the screen.

"The dead guy."

The clerk looked bored and only reluctantly tore his eyes from the screen to nod at Arnie.

"Were you working in the office the night before Mr. Friesen was discovered?"

"Always work nights. I go to school during the day."

"The maid told me that Friesen had company...a pizza delivery guy and then a woman."

"Might have, I'm having a problem remembering clearly."

Arnie nodded, pulled out a twenty and laid it on the counter.

The man's eyes bulged like a lizard's as he snatched the bill and put it in his pocket. He closed his eyes as if he was trying to visualize. "There was a pizza guy and then a woman."

"I already know that, but I think there was someone else, maybe later."

The man took a deep breath and closed his eyes again, "Everything is getting cloudy again man."

"Buddy, have the cops been around asking these questions?"

"Nope, not since I came on. I heard they were here this morning when they found the stiff."

"Listen to me. I have no more money. If you know anything else, you better speak up, or I'll call the cops and tell them you're smoking pot."

"I didn't see anyone else, but I did see a blue car parked out there. I don't think it belonged to any of the guests. I figured someone had a visitor. But before you ask me, I was in the can so I didn't see what room they went into."

"What about when they came out?"

The man shook his head, "No, I was in the can again. Stomach thing."

"What kind of blue car?"

"I don't know, something sporty." He turned back to *Hill Street Blues*.

CHAPTER THIRTY-NINE

Chevon called Jacqueline early the next morning. "Hey Jacqueline, how's my godson?

"Oh Chevon, I was going to call you today. I saw Jerry Seinfeld on *Carson* last night; he said having an 18-month-old was kind of like having a blender but not having a top for it."

"Ha-ha, that's funny."

"To answer your question, he's doing well, but he is soooo busy now that he can pull himself up on things. He's been saying, Dada a lot, but still no Mommy."

"It'll come, don't worry."

"So how was your romantic weekend with Ben?"

"Good. No, mostly weird. Weirdly good."

"Spill it, babe."

"On the positive side, Ben surprised me by showing up unannounced on Friday night. My brother Tray has been staying with me. He answered Ben's knock because I was taking a shower. Anyway, Ben saw a young, muscular black man wearing only pajama bottoms, and, well, he jumped to a pretty huge conclusion."

"Oh my, I can just picture Ben's look. Did things improve?"

"Sure, he came to my show, bought me dinner and then spent the night."

"....and then what?"

"We got up early and headed to Picayune. Nice day but I don't think Picayune and I are a good match."

"Really, why's that?"

"There are no black people there, the cops are racists, and the place gives me the creeps."

"Wow, I think Ben was hoping that you would like Picayune."

"Really? He didn't seem to like it any better than me."

"Get to the good stuff Chevon, what happened next?"

"Oh Ben, played a trick on some dumb cop that was tailing us," Chevon told Jacqueline about Ben's prank and how the deputy had chased them down the highway, shaking his fist in the air.

"That sounds like something Ben would do. I guess you really can't go back there now. Did Ben give you anything, Chevon?"

"I forgot. We went to the Teddy Bear Museum, and he bought me this little bear that comes with a saxophone. Really cute. I'm going to call the bear Ben."

Jacqueline was stymied that she wasn't getting the answer she was looking for. "Was there anything else Chevon?" she asked slowly, her tone betraying her expectations.

"Like, did he ......pop the question?"

"Did he?"

"No, was he supposed to?"

"Gabriel said he was going to. That he had picked out Picayune as a place halfway in between New Orleans and Biloxi."

"I wish I had known."

"I was sworn to secrecy. I wonder why Ben didn't ask, you guys are so right for each other."

"I have to admit that my intuition was telling me that he had something on the tip of his tongue. I hope I didn't throw him off by saying I hated Picayune."

"He probably just got gun shy, or maybe that deputy threw him off his game."

"Or maybe he reconsidered. I'm half his age, and I don't think interracial marriages have been invented in Mississippi."

"Chevon, would you have said yes if he had asked?"

There was a pause on the line. "I don't know. I just want him to be happy."

"I'll pump Gabriel for information tonight. Chances are he's spoken to Ben. Anything else going on?"

"There is one thing. Probably just a holdover from being followed on Saturday, but ever since we got back from there, I've felt like someone is watching me."

"Should you call Ben?"

"Nah, I'm just being silly."

CHAPTER FORTY

Rachel dropped Gabriel off a block away from Huedunit Painting and wished him good luck. On the walk to the shop, Gabriel sweated under the hot sun and grumbled at the injustice of what Rachel had foisted on him. He had himself worked up into a lather as he crossed the dusty parking lot.

Opening the door to the paint shop, he found a heavy-set man bent over looking at a magazine at the cash register. The guy had "Yuri" on his overalls. "Good evening, I'm here to pick up my car."

Without looking up, the man said, "Name?"

"My name is Gabriel Ross. It's a Volkswagon Beetle."

The man finally looked up and eyed Gabriel suspiciously. "Where is girl?" The man had a huge head and a bad case of body odor.

"She couldn't come so she asked me. It's my car anyway." Gabriel showed his ownership to the man.

"She left message, say her father would be picking up car."

"That would be me."

"You not Father."

"Yes, I am. And I am here for my car."

"Car, piece of shit."

"Yeah, but that's beside the point."

"You want little pink car?" he winked at Gabriel.

"Yeah."

"Say you want, little pink car."

"I want the pink car." Gabriel picked up his vehicle regis-
tration.

"Say pretty please, I want my pink pussy car."

"No, I'm not going to say that."

"You want party in little pink car?" Yuri asked with a
lecherous wink.

"No. Just give me the keys."

"It is $600 for paint job."

"This just gets better and better," Gabriel said under his
breath. Gabriel handed the man his MasterCard.

Yuri processed the payment, all the while alternating
between blowing him a kiss and winking at him. "I get
someone to drive it up front."

"I don't mind going back myself," Gabriel said, turning
to go into the hangar.

"No customer go back there."

Gabriel had little choice but to wait outside for his car to
be driven up. He waited about five minutes, feeling Yuri's
eyes bore into him from the office.

Finally, the Bug was driven around the front. A young
dark-haired man got out and smiled at Gabriel. They
exchanged looks as the young man flipped him the keys. His
name tag said "Dan."

CHAPTER FORTY-ONE

It was Saturday night, and Arnie was getting ready to go out to a house party. One of his cousins was having a BBQ and had invited many of the family to stop by. While he was putting on his shoes, there was a knock at the apartment door. As superintendent, Arnie's first thought was that one of the tenants had locked themselves out of their apartment. When he opened the door, he was surprised to see Bernice Cross wearing a brown velour lounging outfit. He couldn't help notice the top's zipper was pulled halfway down, revealing her generous cleavage.

"Oh, Bernice. What brings you out tonight?" Arnie heard a noise coming from the kitchen. It sounded like a metal bowl being pushed across the floor.

"I hope I'm not disturbing you, Arnie," Bernice craned her neck to see past Arnie in the doorway. "Do you have company? I think I heard something."

"That's just Bourbon," he said without thinking. Suddenly he remembered the little white lie he had told Bernice.

"Bourbon, that's your girlfriend. Is she here? I'd like to meet my competition."

"She's in the bedroom. What's up, Bernice?" Arnie asked again.

"Aren't you going to invite an old friend in?" Bernice played with the zipper of her top.

"This isn't a good time. She's..., you know, not er...decent."

"Oh, I understand," Bernice whispered conspiratorially. "I'm just a little jealous." Arnie looked at her, and for a moment there was an awkward silence. Finally, she said tearfully. "Harold threw me out. I have nowhere to go."

"Oh, I'm sorry Bernice, why don't we step out into the hall and talk about it?" Arnie grabbed her elbow and tried to escort her out of the apartment. From the back of the apartment, came a "MMEEEOOOWW," louder and longer than he'd ever heard.

Bernice stopped in her tracks. "What was that?"

"That's Bourbon. She gets like that, when you know, she's a little impatient."

"Horny?" Bernice's eyes bulged wide with shock.

"Yeah, I'm sorry." Arnie pulled her out into the hall and shut the door behind him.

"Don't be sorry Arnie. I get like that sometimes too. Sometimes I get so excited I could howl at the moon."

"She can be tiring. You know," he said, making a piston motion with his arm.

"I don't want to keep you, Arnie. You get in there man, and take care of that poor girl."

"But what did you want, Bernice?"

"I was just looking for an apartment to rent. Nothing

special, maybe something on this floor, something close to you," she said hopefully.

"Why don't you call the rental office in the morning?" He looked back at the apartment. "I had better, like you said, take care of things."

Bernice made the same pumping motion with her arm as she said goodbye and walked down the hallway.

CHAPTER FORTY-TWO

On Monday morning Gabriel drove into the Agency's parking lot as Ben was just getting out his truck. Ben took one look at the VW and gave Gabriel a big smile. "I like it! You could sell cosmetics with that car."

"Funny... Rachel had them paint it at that paint shop they're investigating."

"Why?"

"Long story, but take a good look because it won't last. I'm going shopping this week." The two men walked together to the Agency. Finally, Gabriel asked, "Well don't keep me in suspense, what did Chevon say?"

"I wimped out. If you knew how many times I was about to ask her, only to have something spoil the mood..." Ben filled him in on what had happened in Picayune on Saturday, including the prank he'd played on the deputy.

"I wish I had seen that! What do you think is going on?"

"Did you know that Picayune means petty?"

"No, I just thought it was the name of a town."

"That's what it means, and I think at first the deputy was

just petty. Later though, I think he realized who I was and that might have been why he was tailing me."

"Sounds like you should talk to your friend the sheriff. Getting back to Chevon, are you still going to propose?"

"I don't know. We definitely won't be living in Picayune, or as Chevon calls it, Bumblefuck. She pretty much hated everything about the place."

Gabriel unlocked the door and followed Ben into his office. "Are you and Rachel still planning on going to Slidell today?"

"Yep, if it's still okay with her. It can't hurt. I got a call from the Flowers' on Sunday. That's Tommy's aunt and uncle. They're the people that took him in when his parents were murdered. They moved to Louisiana, and I went to visit them. They have two sons of their own around Tommy's age, who are away at Ole Miss. They checked with them to see if Tommy might have shared something. Basil, one of the boys, said that one time they were riding with some older boys, spending the day in New Orleans. Their car was pulled over by a St. Tammany Parish deputy. You can imagine the stress that four Negro boys would be feeling, coming back from Mardi Gras, and getting pulled over. The driver of the car started arguing with the deputy, and things got tense, a little rough. It all died down as quickly as it had started, but Basil told his mother that Tommy was shaking with fear. When Basil's brother Aster tried to make fun of it, Tommy apparently said, 'Tell that to Glenn Wilson.'"

"That might validate your theory, but hearsay evidence isn't going to mean much."

"I know, I think I have a lead on a couple of brothers who might have been in on it. Sounds like a drug deal out of New Orleans."

They were interrupted by Rachel, who came into the office all bright smiles. "Gabriel, I'm so sorry! I saw your car out there, and well, I'm just sorry."

"It cost me $600 and a date with Yuri."

"Nooooo, say it ain't so? Did he hit on you? He must have thought you were, you know," she made a limp hand gesture and started laughing.

"Hardy-har-har young lady!" answered Gabriel.

"It actually looks good next to Ben's truck." Arnie walked in the door, holding Bourbon.

GABRIEL INVITED everyone to grab a coffee while he got a can of tuna for Bourbon. They all reconvened in his office to bring each other up to date.

Arnie recounted his discussion with Rosetta at the Belvedere Motel. "I was thinking about this...what if I go back with the pictures Rachel took of the women she saw Friesen with, and see if she recognizes one?"

"That's a good idea, Arnie," said Gabriel. "Do you think this woman might have killed him?"

"No, but maybe she's friends with this mysterious business partner. Friesen calls her from the Belvedere where he's been hiding since the explosion. He wants to party. She, in turn, tells the mystery man where he is."

"That plays," said Gabriel.

"To make it even better, the guy in the office said he saw a blue sports car parked in the lot that night. He didn't see what unit the person might have gone into. The guy in the blue car might be the mystery guy."

"Do the motel's calls route through the office?" asked Ben.

"I don't know, but I'll find out."

"If the calls go through the office we might be able to get a number for the woman," said Rachel.

"I'll go back this afternoon and show Rosetta the pictures and then talk to the guy in the office."

"Ben, there's something else that I told Gabriel and Arnie yesterday." Rachel picked up Bourbon, who had finished his tuna. "Technically, it's related to the Huedunit case, but while I was at the police station, I saw the guy that has been working undercover at the paint shop. You know, Drake or Dan? Anyway, we went for lunch, and he works for the Mississippi Bureau of Investigation. His name is Don, Don Mangina."

"Don Mangina," laughed Ben, "That's the worst under-cover name I've ever heard."

Everyone laughed, and then Rachel continued, "I guess I understand the undercover part, but Acting Chief Murdock has no idea what Don is really doing. And while I was there, Mayor Baxter called, and he told me the call was urgent."

"Obviously, Murdock and Baxter are close," said Ben. "But to conduct an undercover operation right under his nose would mean that the MBI thinks Murdock or Baxter might be involved in the stolen car ring."

"Anyway, Don said he was going to try to copy a ledger that the boss has in his desk; it might include the cars, the sales, maybe who is behind the whole operation."

"Seems to me that Baxter might be implicated in both the Friesen murder and also in what's going on at the chop shop," said Gabriel.

"That would be so fitting, I would love to see that man behind bars," said Ben.

There was a pause in the conversation before Gabriel spoke up. "You're up Ben, what's new in Slidell? "

"I'm hopeful that Rachel will miraculously get through to Tommy Huffman, whom I believe saw who killed his friend in the woods that day. While the sheriff at the time - a man named Harrigan - is dead, I have a pretty good line on a couple of guys who might also have been involved. When, and if, Rachel thinks it's appropriate, I have pictures of the suspects we can show him."

CHAPTER FORTY-THREE

Kane Nantois was sitting on the couch in the apartment he shared with his brother. To his left was a case of Budweiser, on his right were half-eaten and day-old cartons of what he called "Chink" food.

"Would you quit playing that fucking game?" Kory yelled from the kitchen. Kane had bought a Commodore 64 and was playing *Texas Chainsaw Massacre*. *Perfect game for a fucktard* thought Kory. He couldn't bear to watch anymore as Kane navigated *Leatherface* through the program, using a chainsaw to shred various women. It wasn't so much a game to Kane, more of a fantasy. Kory thought his half-brother was seriously deranged, and the acid Kane was dropping on a near daily basis was turning him into something even worse.

Kory was the one that had to keep an eye on this cop from Mississippi. The one with the fruity truck and the nigger girlfriend. He had watched him go into the cop shop yesterday.

Kory had gotten a call to say that the cop was hanging around Picayune asking questions about Harrigan and that thing that happened seven years ago. *I thought that was all ancient fucking history.* With a little help from Harrigan, Kory had been pretty successful in dealing with the fallout from the thing in the woods. He was sure Reznikov had known about what happened, but as Frankie liked to say, 'Shit happens, the real question is whether you're smart enough to handle it.'

Kory thought back to that fateful day in the woods, *Harrigan had been the one who'd first spotted the Wilson kid sitting in the tree watching them. The plane had been late, and Kane was talking his normal shit about some crazy heavy metal band when Harrigan said under his breath, "Don't look now, but some kid is watching us from a tree over to my right." Ignoring Harrigan, Kane had snuck a quick look, then taken off, sprinting through the trees like he was some kind of Carl Fuckin' Lewis. When the others caught up to him, Kane had the kid on the ground and was wailing on him.*

"Settle the fuck down," I'd screamed at him as I tried to pull him off the kid. The kid hadn't seen shit. The plane hadn't even come. A story could have been spun, but Harrigan didn't even try. The kid, maybe sensing an opportunity, bit Kane on the hand, which of course led to one of Kane's psycho rages. He was banging the kid's head into the ground. I pulled him off, but when the kid started to get up, Kane hit him with a branch. The kid was out cold.

What happened next had seemed to pass in slow motion. I'd looked over at Harrigan, who nodded. Kane was breathing heavily, out of control. His eyes were clouded with anger, like the sky before a hurricane. He pulled out his revolver.

I shook my head and said "No."

Harrigan started yelling, "DO IT, DO IT!," like he was cheering on a mob.

Kane put one point-blank in the kid's temple.

CHAPTER FORTY-FOUR

"Buenas tardes, Rosetta," Arnie practiced his Spanish. The woman, still holding the toilet brush, gave him a wide smile.

"Buenas tardes, Senor."

"How is Maria?" Arnie asked, concern in his tone.

"She no open closets." Rosetta waved her finger.

Arnie nodded. "I have some photographs of a woman that I would like you to look at, would that be okay? It will only take a minute or two."

"Puta?"

Arnie made the big breast motion. "Si, puta." He went over to the bed which had yet to be made, and spread a half-dozen photos showing Friesen with the women Rachel had caught him with. Maria took no time in nodding her head.

The picture she pointed to was of a woman sitting on Friesen's lap. Her back was to him. His hands were holding her breasts.

"Are you sure?" asked Arnie.

Maria nodded, then picked up the picture of the brunette and said, "Puta."

The picture had been taken through a window and showed Friesen and a large-breasted brunette naked on the bed. Friesen, as they used to say in the neighborhood, was 'stuffing the turkey.'

"Was this woman here that night too?"

Rosetta shook her head and made a gesture with her hand, suggesting to Arnie that she recognized her from a previous encounter.

"Gracias, Rosetta!"

THE SAME USELESS desk clerk was on duty when Arnie opened the Belvedere Motel office door. This time he was watching what looked like *Barnaby Jones* on television. Arnie walked up to the counter, reached over and turned the TV off.

"Hey, you can't do that!"

"Listen, buddy; I was here the other day. I have $20 already invested in you, and I don't want any more bullshit. I want to know if there were any calls placed by Mr. Friesen that night."

"Mr. Friesen?"

"The dead guy," Arnie said, his tone showing how stupid he thought the kid was. "Just how many times does your maid find a man hanging in one of your closets?" The kid shrugged his shoulders as if the number might be too high to estimate. "The phone calls."

The kid held out his hand and said that his memory wasn't what it used to be.

"Forget it kid. I have no other money. You can either answer my question, or, I'm going to call the cops."

The kid rolled his eyes and went to a file cabinet to pull out a folder. He looked down at a sheet of paper, "Listen, are you going to pay these charges, that would only be fair?"

"How much are the charges?"

"$20 which includes three outgoing calls. On television, the cops have to get a warrant for this kind of confidential information."

"There's no confidentiality if the guy is dead," Arnie said. Losing the staring contest, he forked over the twenty. The kid handed over the sheet. The bill showed three calls. *Oh-Oh*, he thought when he realized that he recognized one of the numbers.

CHAPTER FORTY-FIVE

"Dr. Marcotte, thank you for meeting with us today. This is Rachel Henderson; she has extensive experience in working with severely traumatized patients at the Gulf Oaks Psychiatric Center in Gulfport. In one case, in particular, she worked with one of my associates to uncover evidence that led to the conviction of a public official. The witness had been severely injured and up to that point unable to communicate," Ben explained, looking over at Rachel. She was dressed in a simple print dress, brown hair curling onto her shoulders.

Dr. Marcotte allowed Ben to finish before interjecting. "Ms. Henderson, thank you for faxing me your resume and the letter from your previous manager. It says on your resume that you were employed at the hospital as a nurse. Is that correct?"

"Yes, I had responsibilities to tend to some of the patients."

"How old are you, Ms. Henderson?"

"I'm 24 years old," Rachel replied.

"And you were employed at the hospital from 1978 to 1983, and then you went to work for this Agency in Biloxi?"

"That's correct."

"Were you hired to be a nurse when you were 18?"

"I was originally hired to work in the laundromat. The supervisor suggested that I apply for the nursing position."

"Your resume says you went to St Mary's High School in Biloxi." When Rachel nodded, Dr. Marcotte continued, "Then you took a couple of post-secondary courses. Might I ask what subjects?"

"American History and Law."

"Do you have any formal medical or nursing education?"

"Just what she learned from working at the hospital," Ben jumped in, seeing that the meeting wasn't going the way he had hoped.

Dr. Marcotte turned to face Ben, "Mr. O'Shea, I truly understand your desire to speak to Tommy Huffman. In our last conversation, you told me that Miss Henderson had unique qualifications that would help Tommy."

"Dr. Marcotte, I would like your permission to have Miss Henderson talk to Tommy and, at the appropriate time, show him some pictures of the men we suspect might have been involved in the killing of his friend." Before he could answer, Ben continued, "Prior to coming here Rachel and I met with Mr. and Mrs. Flowers, Tommy's legal guardians. They signed this letter giving their blessing to this." Ben handed the letter to the Doctor.

Dr. Marcotte examined it. "You've spoken to Bert and Agnes Flowers?"

"Yes, they were very complimentary about you and your team."

"Showing Tommy pictures of these men might cause him

to withdraw further into himself. You have to realize that Tommy isn't making a choice here not to speak. He literally can't."

"I understand the risk, but I wouldn't ask if it hadn't been one of the most heinous of crimes to have happened in the past ten years. Further, it stands to reason that the individuals who killed Glenn Wilson, have killed others including Tommy's own parents. I believe they are still operating in the area and may have hurt others."

"You've made good arguments, but you know as well as I that whatever comes from a meeting with Tommy would never be permitted in a court of law."

"That is true, but it certainly wouldn't be the only evidence we would use to convict these men. I also have a letter here signed by Mr. and Mrs. Wilson. They are the parents of the boy that was murdered. Mr. Wilson, in particular, is not well. He doesn't have much time left. It would mean a lot to them to gain closure for their son."

Ben had a staring contest with the doctor, not knowing which way she was leaning. It was Rachel who broke it up by saying, "I have a suggestion. How about you give me an hour a day with Tommy, and we try it for a week, under the supervision of yourself or someone on your team? If it doesn't work, then we agree to drop it and not pursue this further."

Ben saw the first crack in Dr. Marcotte's foundation as a smile flashed across her face. "Miss Henderson, I want you to wear a proper uniform, and you are not permitted to bring up what happened or show pictures unless I give you the go-ahead."

TOMMY WAS SITTING in a chair looking out the window. He was slim with short dark hair. His room was a sterile off-white square box with a single bed and end table. The room had a faint smell of bleach; the floor was faded gray linoleum. Rachel understood why people brought flowers to hospital rooms. Despite all the advances in medicine, there was something about the human spirit that required natural beauty as part of the healing process. She was happy to see that someone had brought some fresh cut flowers for the room. Some hospitals treated patients like robots in for repairs. Just seeing a poster on the wall could lift a person's mood.

Rachel looked at Tommy; his unflinching eyes stared out the window. He was dressed in a plaid shirt and a flowery quilt covered his legs.

"Tommy, this is Rachel, she's a new member of my team," said Dr. Marcotte, leaning down so that she was in his line of vision. Tommy gave no sign of understanding. Rachel looked at the black youth and thought that he appeared much older than his 21 years.

Taking a spot to the right of him, Rachel said, "Hello Tommy, I know you don't speak much. That's okay; you don't need to. I'd like to sit with you a spell." Dr. Marcotte brought in a chair from the hallway for Rachel.

"It's a beautiful scene out your window, Tommy. I really like the tall trees. There a gentle springtime breeze blowing through those pines. There is that earthy smell in the air. If you go out to those trees, you can hear the mockingbirds. Maybe you and I could go for a walk someday."

Rachel sat in silence for a while, not wanting to put pressure on him. Finally, she said, "I heard from your aunt and uncle that you're doing better. That's great to hear. They care a lot about you and send their love. They're very proud of you and all the progress you've been making." She looked over and caught the Doctor's eye, who slowly nodded.

"I understand you grew up on a farm. That must have been fun. I did too. We had cows and chickens and a couple of old mules that were always too stubborn to work with. My job was to help Daddy with the cows. I had to get up early before sunrise, but every day Daddy would be there with me so we could work together. He would always have a silly joke for me. He'd ask, 'Rachel, why do you think the cows laugh so hard at my jokes?' And I'd say 'They ain't laughing Daddy,' and he'd say 'Because they found them amooooozing.'"

There was no reaction, except a smile Rachel saw on Dr. Marcotte's face. "I'll try to remember another one for tomorrow." Rachel continued to talk about growing up on a farm, careful not to ask Tommy a question. "Say, Tommy, I bet you like music, if it's all right with Dr. Marcotte, I'd like to get them to turn off the elevator music and bring in a cassette recorder. Maybe we can listen to a little music when I come back tomorrow." Rachel was conscious of not going over an hour and thanked Tommy for letting her visit before promising to return on Tuesday.

When they walked out in the hall, Dr. Marcotte said, "Okay, that was better than I expected. What was your strategy?"

"I don't want to pressure him by asking questions. I just want him to see me, smell my perfume and hear my voice. I think the music will help a bit. I used to tell the man in Gulf Oaks a joke every day. Corny, I know, but I think it helped."

"I was getting worried when you brought up growing up on the farm. You know the way his parents died."

"It might have been a bit of a risk. But I figure he has some images playing over and over in his mind like a broken record. If he's hearing me, maybe we can substitute those images with happier ones from growing up on the farm."

Dr. Marcotte seemed to weigh her response before saying "I'll see you tomorrow."

CHAPTER FORTY-SIX

G abriel was getting frustrated. He was sitting at
Rachel's desk trying to get through some of the
reference checks but was constantly being interrupted by
people looking to speak to Arnie. Bourbon wasn't helping. If he wasn't complaining, he was lying right on top
of the reference checks. *If Rachel is going to be in Slidell for
any length of time, we'll have to work out something.* Gabriel
had no sooner finished one call when the phone
rang again.

"Eye on you Detective Agency, when you really need to
know, Gabriel Ross speaking."

"That's quite the mouthful," said a voice that sounded
familiar. "Of course, that's what she said last night."

Only one person would make that crack. "Murdock?"

"Yeah, of course. Listen, Gabriel, I really liked your gal
Rachel. I think I might take her out to dinner."

"No, I don't think so."

"Oh, I think she liked me. If we hadn't been interrupted,
we would have gone on our first date."

"Don't waste your time Murdock. She doesn't date married guys."

"I think she might make an exception for me. Besides, wifey and I have an understanding."

"Yeah, she understands that you're a perv?"

"Now, now Gabriel, I was actually calling to say something nice to you."

"That right?"

"Yeah, I got the Medical Examiner's report. It turns out that William Friesen was strangled with his tie. You were right; it was a homicide."

"Brilliant! Tell me, was his tie still around his neck?"

"Yeah, of course, where else would it be? The ME also said the autopsy showed he had a powerful sedative in his bloodstream. The kind they give to horses."

"Ketamine?"

"Yeah, something like that."

"Now that you realize it's a homicide, what are you going to do?"

"Don't know yet. I have a bunch of other cases. I'm pretty swamped, and the mayor wants me to set up the new Rapid Response team."

"It was murder. It happened right under your nose, Murdock. Don't you think you should be investigating?"

"Oh, I will. I'll be sending one of the new guys to look into this. Just as soon as I can find him."

AFTER THE INTERVIEW at the Belvedere, Arnie drove back to the

Agency hoping to catch Gabriel before he left for home.

He opened the door to the Agency only to find Gabriel sitting at Rachel's desk, phone cradled to his ear, shuffling a bunch of faxes in front of him. He listened for a moment.

"I'm sorry Mrs. Cross, I know Arnie normally works on Mondays but," Gabriel looked up at Arnie who was shaking his head, "He's out on a call at the moment...can I take a message?"

When Gabriel finished the call, he let out a sigh, "Don't tell Rachel, but I wouldn't do this job for twice what I'm paying her. There are a half-dozen messages, all from people wanting you to call back. The last call was a lady by the name of Bernice Cross. You remember the lady last fall that came in unscheduled at the same time as her husband, both accusing each other of cheating on one another? That was quite the scene," Gabriel laughed. "I can still picture her swinging her purse at her husband."

"Believe me; I haven't forgotten. Did she happen to say what she wanted?"

"She said to tell you that she rented an apartment at the Trade Winds. Then she said something weird. I might have misheard...I thought she said that she hoped her meowing doesn't keep you up. What's she talking about?"

"It is a long story. One best shared over a couple of beers."

"I'm glad you're back. The call before Bernice was Chief Murdock. He said the medical examiner has ruled that Friesen was murdered. Someone strangled him with his own tie."

"Big surprise. You know, you'd have to be pretty strong to strangle someone, and then hang the body in the closet."

"The ME also found a powerful sedative in his bloodstream."

"Well then, maybe a woman, but I still don't see it."

"How did you make out at the *Belvedere*?"

"I think we might be able to give Murdock a leg up in his investigation. I showed Rachel's surveillance pics to the maid, and she positively identified one of the women as the one she saw go into Friesen's room."

"That's great, so we have a suspect."

"It gets better. I paid the desk clerk $20 to get Friesen's phone calls." Arnie put the invoice in front of Gabriel. "It looks like there were three outbound calls made from Friesen's room the day he died. One of those numbers, the one at 6:15 p.m., was to Cicero's Pizza. I've already checked. The other one at 7:02 p.m., I figured, was to the blonde inviting her to the motel. But look at the one earlier, the one I circled at 4:15 p.m."

"435-6254?"

"Maybe because I spent my whole life in Biloxi, I know that's the main number for city hall."

"I CALLED the other number on the statement, and it's been disconnected," said Arnie, coming into Gabriel's office. "I called my cousin who works for the phone company. The number used to belong to someone named Dixie Furlong. According to my cousin, the latest bills were returned, so the service was disconnected."

"That must have just happened. It's a little suspicious. So, the theory goes, Friesen calls someone and tells them where he is hiding. It would have to be someone he trusts. That person tells Friesen's partner, and this person goes to the motel and kills him."

Arnie nodded. "That makes sense, and unless Cicero's is in the habit of killing off their customers, then it's either this blonde or the person he called at City Hall."

The Agency door opened and in walked Rachel and Ben, back from Slidell.

"Hi guys, how did you make out?" asked Gabriel.

"Pretty good," said Ben. "It was all Rachel. Doc wouldn't even let me in the room."

"I spent about an hour with him, and it's too early to tell. I think if I don't see anything after going every day for a week then we should drop it."

"You're going to be in Slidell all week?" Gabriel groaned.

"I can work the mornings and then head out. Ben doesn't even need to come with me."

"Okay, we might need your help on something, Ben." Gabriel and Arnie took turns filling Ben and Rachel in on the ME report, the identification of the blonde and then the phone numbers found on the invoice. "We need to find this Dixie Furlong."

"It sounds like she's a working girl. I still know a few people that might know her," responded Ben.

"What about the call to City Hall?" asked Rachel.

"That is going to be tricky," said Ben. "They can probably identify which extension the call went to, but they won't tell us without a court order."

"Let's think on that overnight." Gabriel got up from his desk. "Jacqueline started back to work today, and I'm running late to pick up Benjamin at her parents."

CHAPTER FORTY-SEVEN

They had gone over the plan a dozen times. Jacqueline drops off Benjamin at her parents on her way to work at the Art Gallery. That's every second Tuesday and Thursday. On the off week, it's Wednesday and Friday. Gabriel picks Benjamin up no later than 5:30 and they meet at home to make supper. Of course, of course, I have it. No need to repeat it again, he'd said. Was it the dazed look on his face that prompted her to tape little reminders around the house? Did his wife have no confidence in him?

Gabriel checked his Casio and saw that it was just past 6 p.m. as he drove into the parking lot adjacent to the Chen's apartment. The apartment was in a heritage building that dated back to the Civil War. When his in-laws had moved down from Chicago, Mrs. Chen had fallen in love with the quaintness of the old building, its oak trim and moldings. He scrambled up the stairs and knocked on the door to their apartment.

While waiting in the hall, he remembered the argument they'd gotten into about Jacqueline unilaterally deciding to return to work and foisting their son on her parents. He'd soon discovered that a simple "Calm down" in a soothing voice, made matters worse. The door was opened by Mr. Chen, a retired math teacher who prided himself on his precise manner. He was holding Benjamin in his arms while simultaneously looking at Gabriel and checking his watch.

"I'm so sorry for being late Mr. Chen. I hope I didn't inconvenience you."

"Jacqueline warned us that you have a problem with deadlines. In college, we call these people non-finishers."

Gabriel heard Mrs. Chen's voice coming out of the kitchen, "Oh Gabriel, we have had a wonderful day with Benjamin."

"Hello, Mrs. Chen." Gabriel took his son in his arms, not sure how he felt about being called a non-finisher.

Mrs. Chen called out from the kitchen, "I know my daughter has you on a tight schedule, but I just brewed some tea. Please stay and visit with us."

"Well alright, just as long as you don't tell her I was late." Gabriel noticed their living room floor was covered in Lego blocks and toy cars.

"She already knows," Mr. Chen said, sitting in an easy chair. "She called at precisely 5:30." He nodded for Gabriel to sit down on the couch.

Benjamin sat on Gabriel's lap facing him, busy trying to explore his father's nose. "Looks like you had a busy day. Why don't I help get this picked up..."?

Mrs. Chen interrupted from the kitchen. "Don't bother Gabriel. I tried picking up a couple of times, but it's like raking leaves during a hurricane." She came into the living room and put a tray of Chinese tea and cookies on the coffee table.

"How do you feel about Jacqueline returning to work?"

asked Mrs. Chen as she poured the tea. Benjamin was doing the stiff bend back routine, wanting to be put on the floor to play with his toys. Mrs. Chen smiled and said, "Just let him play."

Gabriel let his son down and watched as Benjamin beetled over to his favorite toy cars. "In answer to your question, I'm okay with it. It gives her something to do that she's interested in."

"You need not worry about Benjamin with us. We like taking care of him. You and our daughter are doing a wonderful job," said Mrs. Chen.

The phone rang, and Mrs. Chen rolled her eyes at her husband. "That would be Jacqueline; she's been calling every ten minutes."

While Mrs. Chen went to answer the phone in the kitchen, Mr. Chen asked whether there had been any developments in the Glenn Wilson case. Gabriel told him about Rachel's attempts to help Tommy Huffman. Mr. Chen was saying something about the laws of probability of Tommy ever speaking again when there was a knock on the door.

Mr. Chen went to the door, and Gabriel was surprised to see Mabel and Maven, two older women who lived in an apartment on the same floor. Gabriel remembered that Jacqueline had said her mother had let her fiery French-Canadian temper show over one of the women's overt flirting with her husband.

"Well hello, Dong," one of the women said. "I hope we're not interrupting anything." Gabriel saw the one with blue eyeshadow craning her neck to see into the apartment.

"I was visiting with my son in law, Gabriel Ross," said Mr. Chen.

"Oh yes," the woman pushed past Mr. Chen. "I

remember meeting this little cutie last year. Mabel, ain't that so?" Maven meanwhile went over to Gabriel and kissed him on the cheek. Mabel, the one with green eyeshadow, barreled by Mr. Chen and did the other cheek.

"Look, Maven, he has an almost perfect imprint of my lips on his cheek," said Mabel, a touch of pride in her voice.

"Mine's better," replied Maven. She twisted Gabriel's face to show off her imprint.

"Mine's darker," replied Mabel, twisting Gabriel's face back.

"That's because you insist on wearing that hooker lipstick," suggested her sister.

"Nice to see you ladies, again," interrupted Gabriel, pulling a handkerchief from his pocket.

"Really nice to see you too Gabriel," said Maven in a provocative voice. Both she and her sister were wearing matching flannel nighties along with black executive socks.

"Is there something I can do for you ladies?" asked Mr. Chen.

"Well, Dong, we've come to borrow you. We have a little competition going in our apartment, and we want you and your fantastic intellect to be the judge."

"His name is Hong, not Dong, and what kind of competition would that be?" asked Mrs. Chen, rejoining them from the kitchen.

"Maven and I made cherry pies, and we want the Dong, I mean Hong, to tell us whose cherry pie tastes the best." Mabel gave an exaggerated wink at Mr. Chen.

For a moment it looked to Gabriel like Mrs. Chen was about to blow a gasket. The moment passed, and she smiled at the two women. "Mr. Chen and I would be happy to help.

Let's have all the tarts over, and we will be happy to judge them."

This clearly wasn't what the women had in mind, and Mabel blurted out that they were still in the oven. But maybe later. There was tension in the air until Gabriel steered the ladies out of the apartment and said, "I have a question for you ladies...."

CHAPTER FORTY-EIGHT

T he muggy heat pressed down on them even though it was barely 10 a.m. Ben and Gabriel were standing by his truck looking at Dixie Furlong's apartment building. "How was Jackie's first day back to work?" asked Ben.

"She said it was alright. It must have been a little stressful. She seemed a little angry when I got home."

"Tell me again how you got Dixie's address."

"You remember those women that live on the same floor as the Chens?"

Ben grunted and rolled his eyes, "Mabel, Mabel get off the table..."

"The two bucks is for the beer," Gabriel finished. "I was picking up Benjamin and ran into them. I thought since they were kind of in the same profession they might know Dixie. Mabel said that everyone knew Dixie Furlong, and she knew where Dixie lived. She said that Dixie did the wrong address scam any time she didn't want to pay her bills."

"Good work, Gabriel."

"It's still early. Someone in her profession might still be sleeping," said Gabriel.

"Tough, she'll just have to get up. Let me see that picture again. Hmm. I should have checked to see if she had a record. I'm slipping in my old age."

"So how do you want to play this?" Gabriel mopped the sweat from his brow.

Ben took off his rose-colored blazer and put it in the truck. He was wearing a red shirt, a western string tie, and blue jeans. "Just play it by ear."

"She's probably not going to cooperate." Gabriel got out of the truck. "Too bad you still don't have your police identification."

"I do. I've been using it all week."

"What happens if she calls to check you out?"

"Depends on who answers, most likely Murdock would say that I'm on leave." Ben looked up at the three-story apartment building.

"Friesen's been all over the news, so she might have already skipped."

"That would be a little incriminating. Let's just go in there and have a chat with her." Ben pulled his 38 out of its holster and checked the ammo.

"Do you really think that's necessary?" asked Gabriel.

"The last time I went on a call with you, I got shot in the shoulder, remember?"

After 4 knocks on Dixie's door, they heard a sleepy voice coming from inside the apartment. "Go away. I don't want any."

"Dixie Furlong, open up. Biloxi PD," yelled Ben, banging on the door loud enough to wake the neighbors.

Gabriel heard some shuffling from inside the apartment.

"How do I know you're a cop?" The woman's voice sounded like she had a mouthful of marbles.

"I'm going to hold up my Biloxi PD identification up to the little spy hole so you can see it."

After about a minute and more shuffling, the voice from behind the door said, "You don't look like a cop. You going to the rodeo or something?"

Ben flashed an amused smile at Gabriel. "We're here about William Friesen. You heard he was murdered, right?"

"I don't know any William...what did you say his name was? And who's that little guy with you? Jesus, is this take your kid to work day?"

"This is Gabriel Ross. He's a private detective, consulting on the case. Listen, do you want to have this conversation out here in the hallway? Open the door and let us in."

"I said, I don't know any William what's-his-name."

Ben took the picture of Dixie at the bar and slid it under the door.

After a moment, "Okay, okay! That guy. His name is William? He told me his name was Chuck, Chuck Pimplebutt."

Gabriel heard a chain being rattled and then the door opened. They weren't prepared for the sight of the woman standing in front of them wearing a ragged terry cloth robe. Her hair looked like porcupine quills, and her eyes were like two holes burned in a blanket. She was a cross between Phyllis Diller and Dolly Parton. Just to be sure, he asked, "Are you Dixie Furlong?"

She turned to the mirror in the hall as if she needed to check. Her reflection made her jump, "I've looked better."

Dixie turned and trudged into the living room and sat on a chair.

"You knew William Friesen?" Gabriel noticed the morning *Herald* open on the table. The headline was blasting the news of Friesen's death.

"I met him at that bar, the one in that picture. He bought me a few drinks. I thanked him... a lot."

"I understand that you knew him well, and had other dates with him," Gabriel asked, looking around the small apartment. The place needed a year's worth of cleaning.

"No, as I said, I just met him once."

Gabriel shot Ben a look and then turned back to Dixie. "We have an eyewitness that says you were seen with him more than once."

"Let me look at that picture again." She looked at it, then pulled out a pair of glasses from her robe. At first, she put them on upside down, then fumbled with them and finally got them on right. "Okay, okay, I got it. I had him confused with another guy. This guy is Spanky, Spanky Fuzzynuts." She started to laugh, which was more of cackle. "So, we went out a few times. Big deal."

"Did you happen to see him this past Saturday night?" asked Ben.

"Nope, had the girl flu. Slept most of the weekend."

"The reason we're here Dixie, is that there was a call from Friesen's motel room to your number here the day he died. Now just tell us the truth, please," said Ben.

Dixie reached over to a black rotary dial phone and pressed the receiver button down a couple of times. "Impossible, Tex - assholes at the phone company disconnected my phone."

"It was working last Saturday when you took a call from William Friesen." Ben was growing frustrated.

Dixie slapped her head as if she had just remembered. "Okay, okay, I forgot. But I didn't lie, I never saw him."

"But you went to his motel room. I have a witness who recognized you going into his room at 9 p.m.," said Gabriel.

"Jesus Christ, who are all these witnesses? Like why don't they mind their own beeswax?" Dixie cackled and then lit a cigarette butt that she retrieved from the over-flowing ashtray beside her chair. "I went there because he left a message on my machine asking for a party. I went over there, but like I said he wasn't there."

"But you were seen going into his room," said Gabriel.

Dixie let out a sigh and flashed him an irritated look. "I knocked, there was no answer. The door was open, so I figured the guy was in the can. I went in and lay on the bed all seductive like. But he wasn't there, so, I left."

"Did you look in the closet?" asked Ben.

"Why would I look in the closet? You think he was playing hide and seek? We weren't into those kinds of games."

Gabriel pulled another photo out of his coat pocket. This one was of the brunette taken by Rachel. He flashed the picture at her. "Dixie, one last question: then you're free to go back to bed. Do you recognize the woman in this photo?"

Dixie glanced at the photo and then looked in turn at Gabriel and then Ben. She let out a staccato laugh, "Is this some kind of a joke? You guys work for the city, and you don't recognize the mayor's wife?"

CHAPTER FORTY-NINE

Tommy was in the exact same position he'd been in when Rachel left on Monday. "Hi Tommy, it's Rachel again, I was hoping I could sit with you and visit." Once again there was no apparent reaction. Dr. Marcotte left for another meeting, but reminded Rachel not to bring up what had happened to his parents.

Rachel sat down in a chair beside Tommy. "A little cloudy today Tommy, but still really nice. The air has that spring smell, where everything comes back to life again." After a couple of minutes, she said, "I watched Rocky last night. You know the original, they've made sequels, but they're not as good. My favorite part was when Rocky ran up those steps. He was so happy that he had come so far and was ready to compete. Boy that was a great moment," she laughed softly. "It makes me want to take on the world." Mr. and Mrs. Flowers had told her that Rocky had been Tommy's favorite movie.

They sat in silence for a few more minutes before Rachel pulled out a cassette recorder from her bag and put it on the nightstand. She pressed play, and the voice of Eric Burden took over, singing about a house in New Orleans. Once again, Mr. Flowers had told her that Tommy liked the song. They listened to the music for a while with Rachel humming along to the lyrics.

"Oh, I almost forgot, I said I would try to remember another one of Dad's corny jokes from the farm. One day," she started to laugh. "It was a spring day like today. I remember talking to him about school while we were looking after the cows. 'What subjects do you think our cows would do well in?' he asked me. When I said, I didn't know he said, 'mooooosic, psycowlogy and cowwwwculus.' I thought that was pretty funny," Rachel laughed to herself.

Dr. Marcotte joined them after about fifty minutes. "So how are you two making out today?"

"Pretty good. I almost had Tommy laughing when I told him a corny joke." The doctor asked if Rachel planned to return on Wednesday. "Absolutely, I thought this room could use a little personality. Tommy likes the movie Rocky; would you have any objection if I brought some pictures for him?"

"As long as you think it'll help."

When Rachel walked back to the car, she felt she'd had a good session with Tommy. She was so preoccupied with what she was going to do tomorrow she didn't notice the man in the powder blue Barracuda.

RACHEL GOT BACK to the Agency just before 5 and found Gabriel and Ben talking in the office.

Gabriel waved her in. "How did you make out today, Rachel?"

"I think we had a good day, but he's a tough audience. Still no reaction to anything. I tried jokes, music, movies and no response. Tomorrow we'll listen to more music and look at some photos from happier times. Any luck finding Dixie Furlong?"

Ben looked over at Gabriel and said, "Yes, Gabriel was able to source an address...but, she wasn't very cooperative. She said that Friesen - or Spanky Fuzzynuts - as she called him, wasn't in the motel room. But she didn't look in the closet, so maybe he was already dead."

"Spanky Fuzzynuts? She called him Spanky Fuzzy Nuts? She sounds like quite the character." Rachel laughed.

"Here's the other piece," said Gabriel "I showed her the other photo you took. The one of the brunette. Get this: she claims that the brunette is Mayor Baxter's wife."

"What!!!!!"

"Exactly, the mayor. I believe he lives on Shorecrest Drive. Do you remember the address you followed Friesen to that night?" asked Ben.

After a moment Rachel's eyes came alive. "Oh my God, it was Shorecrest."

"WHAT DO WE DO NOW?" Rachel started to pace the floor in front of Gabriel's desk.

Ben shook his head. "If I still had my badge I'd go down to City Hall and get that slimy Mayor Baxter to fess up."

"I'm not sure you have any proof that the good mayor has done anything wrong," said Gabriel. "It's not a crime for your wife to have an affair. As for the phone call to City Hall, if it was in fact to him, it could have been for any number of reasons."

"Here's a thought," said Rachel. "What about if we leak this whole business to the press? They arrange for an exclusive one-on-one interview with Baxter, and then instead of talking about the new Rapid Response Team, they ask him about his wife's affair?"

"I like it, but it probably wouldn't get us anywhere," responded Ben. "This is a smooth politician skilled in the art of flinging bullshit. As Gabriel said, it's not a crime for your wife to have an affair."

"What about approaching that Mangina guy? We lay out what we know and see what he says." Gabriel looked up at Rachel.

"It would be worth a try. Don was going to try for the ledger tonight. I'll see if he needs any help."

CHAPTER FIFTY

It was eerily quiet. The kind of cool evening that Rachel would have found relaxing, even calming, if she hadn't been so terrified. It was just after 4 a.m. and the streets were deserted, the businesses long shuttered. Everyone had left Huedunit Painting, and Rachel and Don were sitting in his Camaro arguing.

"Listen, Rachel, I gave in and said you could come, but no one said anything about you coming in with me. Just sit tight and if someone comes, honk the horn."

"No, I'm coming in with you."

"This is official police business."

"Two sets of eyes are better than one. We'll be out of there in half the time. Quit arguing with me Mangina; I've already made up my mind."

"You're a piece of work." Don was clearly frustrated as he got out of the car. He'd brought a flashlight, and Rachel slipped on Gabriel's night vision goggles. "Where'd you get those?"

"I'm a detective, tools of the trade." Rachel wore tight black jeans and a dark navy-blue blouse.

Don was wearing denim jeans and a black golf shirt. "You look good in those jeans, by the way," whispered Don as they made their way to the chain link fence.

"Keep your mind on the task at hand. Do you have the key?"

"Yeah, I made copies of both the gate and front door keys." Don shone his flashlight on the padlock.

"You sure there's no night watchman, right?"

"Nightwatchman?" Don repeated, trying to imitate Yuri's voice, "We don't need no stinkin night watchman...we have fuckin' fence."

"So no alarms?"

Don let out a sigh, then whispered, "Think that through, Rachel. The alarms bring the cops. If you were running a stolen car ring, would you have alarms?"

"Seems too easy," replied Rachel, as Don got the lock open and then swung the fence door open a crack. "So what have you learned so far about this place?" she asked as they crept towards the office door.

"They have a bunch of guys whose job it is to steal the cars. They bring them here. Sometimes they paint the car a different color, and then they change the VIN numbers. Later that night or early the next morning, they drive the car down to the dock where it's put with other cars into a shipping container. That's why they like Biloxi with its port access. The container gets loaded onto a ship and then - bada boom, bada bing - off to Europe, and to another contact who will move the cars."

The first sign of trouble came when Rachel stopped short

in her tracks, causing Don to bump into her." I thought I heard a noise coming from the back of the property!" she whispered frantically.

Don cocked his head, trying to listen. After a moment, "It's just your nerves. If you want, you can go wait in the car."

"Shut-up...there it is again." Rachel did a sweep of the hangar area with the night vision goggles but came up empty. "It sounded like someone snoring."

"Snoring? I told you they don't have a night watchman."

They made it to the office door, and Don shone his light on a key ring, looking for the copy he had made of the office door.

"Don, Don, DON, they may not have a night watchman, but they have a dog!" Rachel screamed grabbing his shoulder. With the night vision goggles, she could see a green Doberman racing around the side of the building.

"Shit!" Don fumbled with the keys then dropped them on the ground.

The dog was advancing quickly. Rachel could hear it snarl. "Shit, shit Don, hurry up. HURRY THE FUCK UP!"

Don couldn't see the dog but could hear the growl. He started going through his keys again, trying one and then another.

"Why the fuck do you have so many keys?" Rachel asked in frustration. She looked around desperately for something to use as a weapon. The dog was coming full speed. She spied a push broom to the right of the door and held it up, wielding it like a medieval mace at the oncoming dog. "Hurry, Don." The dog was close enough for Rachel to smell its breath. It lunged, foam flying from its mouth. Rachel swung the broom as if she was Babe Ruth. "Thwack!" The broom hit the dog hard on its front shoulder, the impact causing both the broom and the dog to fall to the ground. "Booyah!" yelled Rachel, turning to gloat. "Did you see me nail that big boy?"

Don was still fumbling with the keys while trying to shine his flashlight at his key ring. He took a look behind him. "Oh, Rachel, you just pissed him off." Don nodded at the dog which was now up again, snarling and showing its teeth. The dog started to advance.

"Shit," yelled Rachel again. She looked around desperately for a place to run. The dog would be on them in seconds.

"Got it," said Don, opening the office door and reaching back to grab Rachel's blouse. He pulled her in just as the Doberman leaped again. Quickly, he slammed the door closed. They could hear the dog growling through the door.

"Don't you know the difference between snoring and growling?" Don felt pleased that he'd been able to save the day.

Rachel muttered, "I don't need no stinking watchman."

"Dog, not a watchman. You didn't ask me if there was a dog."

"I'm too tired to argue, where's this ledger?"

"Yuri keeps it in his desk, behind the cash."

Rachel walked over and pulled the drawer open and started rifling through the papers.

"Hey, be careful, we don't want him to know we've been here."

Ignoring him, Rachel continued to sort through the mess in the drawer. "I don't know Don. I don't think you guys are going to get the cleanliness award from Popular Mechanics." They could hear the Doberman letting out a low howling noise like he was summoning the dead. "Don, I'm sorry, there's no ledger in here. Just a bunch of papers and stuff."

"Okay let me look through them, you check the side drawers."

As Rachel started looking through the first side drawer, she pulled out a dog-eared magazine. "Ugh...Yuri likes *Playboy*. It's the one with Bo Derek hugging a gorilla. Does that do anything for you Don?"

Don took a quick peek, "She was Miss Ape-ril!

"Hardy-har-har, funny man. Hey, is that Geoffrey Motten's application form that you're looking at?"

"Yep, I see here that he put down an interesting reference."

"Who's that?

"Bruce Gale Richardson. He's one the originals of the most notorious motorcycle gangs in America. He and a bunch of others were just sent to prison for kidnapping. Kind of a funny choice for a reference."

Don abandoned his search and got on his hands and knees.

"What the hell are you doing?" asked Rachel, discarding the *Playboy*.

"Just looking," came the reply. Don crawled under the desk and after a minute yelled out, "There's a little shelf under here. Eureka." He stood up, holding an eight by ten notebook. He opened it on the desk and shone his light on the first page. The first column bore dates going back three years; the second was the make and model of the car followed by a year. The next column was the car's color, followed by a dollar amount. Don presumed that the last column was the date shipped and the purchaser. "Look, Rachel; a 1982 red Ford Mustang went to a guy named Keith Jagger. I wonder if that's Mick's brother?"

"Not likely," Rachel replied. "It looks like 90% of the cars all went to an outfit called the Louisiana Trading Company. Who owns that company?"

"Good question. Yuri has a photocopier in the lunch-room. I'm going to take this back there and copy it. In the meantime, try to figure out what to do about the dog."

After ten minutes, Don came back out and carefully put the notebook back where he had found it. "What have you come up with?"

"Is there a back door to this place?"

"Yeah, you want to lure the dog in the back while we go out the front, right?"

"Something like that, but what will Yuri do when he finds that Devil Dog is in his hangar?"

"He'd be suspicious and would know someone was snooping."

"Right, so I'll go out the back door and lure him back there, while you go out the front to the gate. Open the gate wide and drive your car up to the door. Once I know the dog is in the back, I'll race through the place, lock the door and get into the car."

Don looked at her with new admiration. "You're a piece of work."

THE PLAN WORKED BEAUTIFULLY; Rachel almost felt sorry for the dog. When she came out of the hangar, she took the time to pick up the broom. Even though her plan went off without a hitch, her heart didn't stop doing the tango until they were miles away.

They pulled into a 24-hour Waffle House and ordered an early breakfast. It was already 5 a.m. and the sun would be coming up soon. The waitress came by and brought them coffee and took their order.

"Thanks for your help back there, Rachel. I would never have made it without you."

Rachel rolled her hand to tell him she wanted more praise.

"Like you were great, I wish I had a picture of you and the broom."

"You owe me one. What are you going to do with the photocopies?"

"Evidence, my boss will want to find out who owns the Louisiana Trading Company. If it's who I think it is, then I would say we're pretty much done. We raid the place and pick up the bad guys."

"You think you know who it is?"

"This is confidential, but since you've been so helpful... it's a theory my boss has. There's a guy; his name is Frank Reznikov. His base is in New Orleans, but he's involved in a lot of crooked businesses here in Biloxi. On the surface, he's a respectable businessman lobbying for legalized gambling for the Gulf coast. We know he's also involved in the drug trade. Lots of his reputable businesses are a front for illegal activity. He has hookers working out of massage parlors, gambling places in the back of taverns; he even owns a Cicero's pizzeria as a way to peddle drugs."

"Not a Waffle House?" Rachel looked around them.

Don ignored the comment. "I had to go check out a couple of his massage parlors when I first got here."

"You did, did you?" Rachel took a sip of her coffee.

"Had to. It's all part of the job."

"Were they any good?"

"No, not really, but I got the job at Huedunit by going in there."

The waitress brought their blueberry pancakes and left.

"Okay, payback time," Rachel said.

"What? You want my sausage?" Don asked with a smile.

"Nothing that small. I want your help." As they ate their breakfast, Rachel filled him in on the William Friesen case, right from the day he'd walked into the office, to the discovery that Friesen was boinking the mayor's wife.

"Is this all true?"

"Absolutely, how could I make up a story like that?"

"Your boss, the little guy I met the other day, thinks Mayor Baxter's a killer? He killed this Friesen guy because of an affair?"

"To be honest, we don't know what to believe. Both Friesen and his wife are dead. We have a connection to the mayor as well as a possible motive."

"Pretty skimpy. For any allegation you make there might be a perfectly valid explanation."

"What would you do if you were investigating this?"

Don gave Rachel a serious look. "Let the police look after this. It's our job, not yours. Do you guys even have a client? Who's paying you?"

"We're taking this on because of the injustice of someone getting away with murder."

"Fine, if the cops need you, they'll shine a bat-light in the sky."

"You owe me."

"Rachel, the best I can do is speak to my boss. This is a pretty big investigation. Tonight was only the tip of the iceberg. If there is some way to help you, then I will. But I can't say any more."

CHAPTER FIFTY-ONE

Rachel had a lot on her mind as she made the drive to Slidell. It took her a while to recover from the clandestine visit to Huedunit. She knew she was developing strong feelings for Don. They worked well together. He was handsome, athletic, funny and close to her age. She tried to dampen her growing attraction by addressing her reflection in the rear-view mirror. "Girl, you don't know squat about that man. Do you really think his name is Mangina? Seriously, he's just using you. Don't you be thinking about getting involved with him."

She forced herself to think of Tommy. *It was Wednesday, hump day. Will this be the day when Tommy shows a sign?* "Maybe he'll laugh at one of my corny jokes." Rachel had spent the early part of last evening at the public library copying scenes from the Rocky movie. Hopefully, they'd trigger a happy memory.

Because it had been such a late night, Gabriel had said she could sleep in and go straight to Slidell for her afternoon appointment. Rachel parked her car in the hospital parking lot and went into the hospital. She was surprised to see Dr. Marcotte waiting for her. "Hello, Dr. Marcotte. A beautiful day isn't it?"

Dr. Marcotte ignored Rachel's question. "Miss Henderson, to my office, please."

Rachel could sense there was something wrong. She followed along as Marcotte led the way into her office. Once they were seated, the doctor began, "Miss Henderson, as the person in charge of the welfare of our patients, something has recently come to my attention that I find very disturbing."

"What is it, Dr. Marcotte? I think I've been making progress with Tommy."

The doctor responded by pressing a button on her phone and saying, "Please send in Ms. Gilling."

A moment later a woman with a thick waist, small beady eyes, and a snub nose walked in. Marcotte gestured for the woman to have a seat. "April Gilling is an employee of the hospital. She works in the cafeteria. Miss Gilling, this is Rachel Henderson."

At first, Rachel had thought the woman was in her thirties, but when she woman turned to face her, she decided Gilling was more likely in her twenties.

"April, please repeat what you told me earlier."

April breathed a big sigh and then turned to address Rachel. "I went to a bar last night. A place called Kappy's. It's a place where a bunch of nurses and doctors hang out. It's kind of a pickup bar if you know what I mean. I was telling the doctor here, that I was up at the bar when some guy dressed like a cowboy came and sat beside me. Like, he had the black hat, the black fringe jacket, cowboy boots. The whole package. The guy told me his name was Kody or something, and that he was passing through. He was pretty friendly. I find most of the men around here just want to talk about themselves," April rolled her eyes. "Anyway, this guy, Kody, was different, he was nice. He took an interest in me. You know, where I lived; did I have a boyfriend; what I did to earn a living; what it's like to work at the hospital? The whole thing. He bought me this drink I never heard of it before, called a slippery nipple. I loved it." A serious look washed across her face, "I think I might have had too many."

April took a deep breath and continued, "That's why it didn't strike me as odd when he asked about Tommy Huffman. He said that he had met Tommy's parents up in Greensville, Mississippi and since he was passing through, he promised them that he'd stop by and visit. I didn't think I was doing anything wrong by confirming that Tommy was one of our patients; like, he already knew that."

At the mention of the man knowing Tommy's parents in Greensville, Rachel let out a gasp and gave Dr. Marcotte a panicky look.

"April, there are all kinds of warnings on Tommy's chart about giving out information," Dr. Marcotte reproached.

April looked at the doctor, and said indignantly, "And I would know that how? I work in the cafeteria."

"Wait a minute," said Rachel. "How would you even know there's a patient named Tommy Huffman? I don't imagine he goes to the cafeteria."

"I often have to bring his food to his room. I feed him."

Rachel's pulse picked up with concern. "Did the man ask about Tommy's condition?"

"Yeah, I told him I wasn't a doctor, but that I had heard

that Dr. Marcotte was working with him to get over a traumatic experience."

"Did the man ask what room Tommy was in?" Rachel asked quickly.

"No, but I think I told him that he was in the long-term care ward."

"Is there anything else you haven't told us, April?" asked Dr. Marcotte.

April was about to say no when she caught herself. "There is one other thing. I'm still a little blitzed from the booze. Anyway, I must have left the house this morning without my key card. When I got to the hospital, I had to ring to get let in."

Rachel seized on something and reached for an envelope in her purse. "April, this is very important. Did the man happen to look like either of these two men?

She pointed out Kory Nantois right away. "That's Kody."

Rachel jumped up right away and spoke frantically to Dr. Marcotte as she opened the office door. "Scramble your security team right now! She just identified one of the men that killed Tommy's parents!"

CHAPTER FIFTY-TWO

Mayor Baxter grabbed the files he was working on and slid them in his briefcase. It was 7:15 p.m., and he was dog-tired. *One boring meeting after another. Budget meetings, town planning meetings, staffing meetings, meetings to plan for meetings, meetings to debrief meetings. Things would go a hell of a lot smoother if other people would just shut the fuck up. On top of everything, there's this shit going on down at the bank. Government pencil pushers looking at things, asking questions. I no longer have Friesen to play interference. Yeah, Friesen, he would have been the perfect patsy. I feel a little sad about that. Now that his death has been ruled a homicide, wifey's on my case.*

"I was fucking... a dead man," she'd screamed at him over breakfast earlier.

Baxter had looked at her across the table. Flowing tears had caused her eyeshadow to run and made her look like a raccoon. "Not to put too fine a point on it Madge, but he was alive when you were fucking him."

She'd given him her bitch face, "What did you do Bill? Was this all about me fucking him?"

"Don't flatter yourself, Madge. I had nothing to do with what happened to Bill." *It had started innocently enough, two couples drinking a little too much red wine, and getting too comfortable with one another. A little kiss, a little grope, then before I knew it, I was following Bonnie Friesen around like a lost puppy.*

He pressed the button in the elevator for the 1st floor. Taking a deep breath he thought, *I promised I'd be home for dinner. By the time I get to Shorecrest, Madge will be pissed. Maybe I should just call and tell her that I have to work late.* Before the elevator doors could close, a man with pork chop sideburns and long greasy dark hair got on. Baxter could feel his heart start to race. The hairs on his arms were standing at attention, a parade of chills marched down his spine. *There's no way this guy works in the building.*

"What floor do you want?" Baxter forced himself to ask, looking at the floor buttons, not wanting to make eye contact.

"Hehe, let's take a ride to the parking garage, Dad."

Baxter ignored the comment and pressed the button for the parking garage. The man pulled a switchblade from his black leather car coat and started picking at his fingernails. As the elevator started its descent, the mayor silently berated himself for staying late in the building by himself. Over the speakers, he heard the *Muzak* playing an instrumental, butchering a classic old rock song.

The hood next to him started to sing the lyrics, *"Oh, won't you gimme three steps, gimme three steps, mister. Gimme three steps toward the door? Gimme three steps, gimme three steps, mister..."*

The man's voice along with the terrible Muzak was bad enough, but then he started to do a little dance step. Baxter inched further into a corner.

Thankfully the elevator was almost on the ground floor. Baxter moved closer to the door, ready to make a run for it. The man stepped forward, blocking the mayor's exit from the elevator. "Ride's not over, Dad."

This guy aims to kill me. Frank must have sent him to get rid of all the loose ends. First Friesen than me. As soon as the door opens, I'll swing my briefcase at his head, and then run like hell. Maybe there will be someone down there.

As if sensing his thoughts, the guy turned and faced Baxter. The elevator opened to an almost deserted parking garage. Baxter tightened his grip on the attache case. "There's someone who wants to talk to you. Get in the car," the hood said, gesturing to a dark tinted limousine. Baxter let out a sigh. There was only one car on this level. He'd walked up to the rear door when Pork Chop said, "No Dad, you sit in the front, in the passenger seat."

No point arguing with the man pointing a knife at me. Baxter opened up the front door and got in. The hood got into the back and sat behind him. *Just like in the Godfather. He's going to pull out a garotte and strangle me.* The mayor glanced nervously behind himself, ready to beg for his life when he saw the other man sitting in the dark behind the driver's seat. *Frankie Reznikov.*

"What's this about Frankie? I have an important meeting," Baxter said impatiently, looking over at him.

"Hello, Opey." Frankie used Baxter's given name, likely because he knew how much it irritated him. The mayor preferred to use John, his middle name. "Something's going on at the bank, Opey," said Frankie with a Russian accent.

"Oh yeah? I hadn't heard that," Baxter lied.

"Fuck, Opey. You haven't noticed all the suits walking around?"

"I've been busy…"

Frankie cut him off, "I'm paying you to keep an eye on things, Opey." Baxter heard the sound of a lighter and saw that Reznikov had lit a cigar. "Now that Friesen's gone, we need to promote someone who'll play along."

"Maybe we should lie low for a spell. Let me concentrate on the elections." Baxter looked at Frank in the vanity mirror.

"Wrong answer, Opey." Baxter sensed Frank lean forward and then felt the heat of the cigar near his neck, "I don't want to do that. We've got a good thing going. There's lots of money at stake."

"I don't know who we can get to replace Friesen."

"Friesen was a coward. And you got too friendly with him." Then after a long draw from his cigar, Frankie asked, "So did your wife like fucking him?"

"I…don't know."

"Now his wife. That Bonnie!" Reznikov let out a whistle. "Bonnie, Bonnie, Bo-onnie, Banana -fana-fo fonnie, fee-fi-fo monnie, Bonnie. Like that little song, Opey?"

Baxter felt his chest tighten. *Fuck, I could have a heart attack right here.*

"Bonnie was pretty hot but in the end such a BITCH," Reznikov said angrily. "You should have seen what she was threatening to do." Baxter bristled at the comment about Bonnie. "She was trying to blackmail me. Threatened to go to the cops if we didn't pay her off."

"I don't know anything about that."

"Say, what about Hollis Huntley…you know, that nervous little weasel at the Bank. Isn't he next in line?"

"Hollis? He's a goody two shoes. Not sure he would play ball."

"Maybe you might need to persuade him. Maybe you kick up some dirt that just happens to have his fingerprints all over it. Make him an offer he can't refuse."

I don't want to get Hollis involved. But if I know anything about Frank, he isn't asking me to help him decide. One nod from Frank and Pork Chop will shove his switchblade in the back of my neck.

"Now Opey, I want you to arrange a new line of credit for us. I'll need $500,000 by the end of the week."

"Is that wise? You know, without having Friesen to push things through?"

"You ain't fuckin listening, Opey." Frank's voice went up a couple of octaves. "I need the cash, and I want it by Friday. Use the Louisiana Trading Company."

Baxter reluctantly nodded, his mind racing. "I'll start the process tomorrow."

"That's the attitude, Mr. Mayor." Frank passed over a thick envelope of cash. "Here's your cut. It's a little thicker than usual because you get William's cut too. That only seems fair."

Baxter took the envelope and quickly put it in his briefcase. "I'll talk to Hollis."

Reznikov leaned forward so that he was breathing in Baxter's ear. The man smelled of garlic and Cuban cigars. "You'll do more than talk about it, Opey. Otherwise, we might need to find a closet for you."

CHAPTER FIFTY-THREE

Arnie was sitting at Rachel's desk. Gabriel had called him and asked him to watch the store while he went to Slidell to deal with an emergency. Gabriel's instructions had been to try to get ahold of Ben and to have him join him at the hospital. *Did this mean that Rachel was in trouble? Or maybe she had a breakthrough?*

Bourbon jumped up on his desk, looking to distract him. "Bourbon, Bourbon, Bourbon...boy you got me into a lot of trouble last night my friend."

Arnie had been chatting up this beautiful, young black woman he'd met at the YMCA. Last night was going to be the night. Grace Kennelly had agreed to come over to Arnie's apartment and sample Arnie's culinary expertise. The night had started off well with a little Isaac Hayes on the stereo, a little white wine and the wonderful scent of Arnie's lasagna in the oven.

They'd just been getting comfortable, sitting on the couch when there was a knock on the apartment door. Arnie got up and looked through the spy hole in the door to see

Bernice Cross standing in the hallway. Shaking his head in despair, Arnie raced back to the couch where Grace, who looked fantastic in a beige leisure suit, was relaxing. "Listen, Grace," he whispered, "Would you do me a huge favor? There's a woman at the door who has a kind of a thing for me. So much so, that she moved into an apartment down the hall. To get rid of her I told her I already had a girlfriend."

"You want me to help you get rid of her by acting like your girlfriend?" Grace asked incredulously.

"Please. There's just one thing. Her name is Bernice, and she wanted to know the name of my girlfriend. In a moment of weakness, I said that I was getting all the pussy I wanted and that my girlfriend's name was Bourbon."

"You said your girlfriend was your cat?"

"No, not exactly. She doesn't even know I have a cat. She thinks my girlfriend's name is Bourbon."

"I don't know Arnie; this sounds pretty weird." There was another knock on the door, and the doorknob rattled.

"Please," begged Arnie.

"I'm not a very good liar, Arnie."

"Please just play along. It won't take long, and then I'll make you the most wonderful dinner."

There was more rattling of the doorknob. "Arnie, I know you'se in there. I saw your shagging wagon in the parking lot. Open up; I have something hot for you. Meowwww."

"Oh my God Arnie. Who is this woman? I'm getting scared."

"She's very persistent," he whispered. "Can I open the door?"

Grace shrugged her shoulders and grabbed a pillow off

the couch, holding it to her chest as protection. Arnie opened the door and feigned surprise as Bernice walked in.

"It's about time, Arnie. Now, what were you up to? Were you thinking of me?" Bernice handed him a casserole dish and pushed her way into the apartment hallway. "I don't know if you take the time to eat, I made this tuna casserole myself." Bernice walked into the living room and stopped cold when she saw Grace sitting on the couch, drinking a glass of wine.

Before Bernice could form words, Grace stood up and extended her hand, "Hello, my name is...Bourbon."

"Well, slap my head and call me silly! Arnie, I didn't know you'se was entertaining. Oh, and this is your lady friend, well let's have a look see. My oh my, you'se somethin pretty, Angel."

"Thank you, won't you sit down and have some wine with us?" asked Grace, despite seeing Arnie shaking his head desperately at her from behind Bernice.

"I don't mind if I do."

Arnie took the casserole and put it in the kitchen, returning with a wine glass. "This is one of my oldest friends, Bernice Cross."

"Don't say it like that Arnie. It makes it sound like I'm just about the oldest person on earth."

"Okay, sorry. Bernice and I went to school together."

"Since kindergarten, I reckon. Remember when I let you kiss me in the closet?" Bernice turned her attention to Bourbon, "I just love your name. Do you mind me asking if your Mama was a big boozer?"

"Boozer?"

"Drunk, alcoholic."

"It's an interesting story; my Daddy worked for a

whiskey company up in Jackson. I guess he thought my complexion reminded him of Kentucky bourbon."

"Well, well, that's quite the story. What was the name of the company?"

"It was called ...Cathead."

"Cathead?"

"Yes, Cathead," Grace nodded. Arnie was impressed with Grace's ability to bullshit.

"I think I've heard of them."

Arnie poured another round, while Bernice continued the attack. "What's your last name, Bourbon?"

"Well you probably won't believe this, but it's Walker."

"Bourbon Walker?" Doubt was creeping into Bernice's voice.

"Yes, and my Daddy's first name is Johnny."

"Johnny Walker and Bourbon Walker?" Bernice asked, her face questioning. All of a sudden she cracked a smile and started laughing. She looked at Arnie. "That's precious. Her daddy's name is Johnny Walker, and her name is Bourbon!"

Both Grace and Arnie laughed along with her. Arnie breathed a sigh of relief but worried that Grace had carried the story too far.

A loud crash came from the kitchen. Arnie moved quickly, followed closely by both women. What they found was the tuna casserole on the floor and the cat going to town.

"Oh my God, Bourbon, you bad kitty," said Arnie.

"Wait, I don't understand," said Bernice. "The cat?" Then turning to look at Grace, "Bourbon?"

"I told you I was getting a lot of pussy," said Arnie.

CHAPTER FIFTY-FOUR

Rachel ran as fast as she could, yelling, "Get out of the way," to those in front of her. While the hospital was all on one floor, Tommy's room was at the end of another wing. *My God, don't let me be too late.* Even though Tommy had shown no signs of trying to communicate, she felt a desire to protect him. She finally reached Tommy's room and grew alarmed. The door, which had been open on her previous visits, was closed.

Rachel pushed open the door and found a man dressed as a cowboy with his back towards her. At the sound of the door opening, he turned, revealing that he had something around Tommy's neck. "Ahhhh!" Rachel screamed. She threw herself wildly at the man, hands flailing, trying to scratch his eyes out. She was able to scratch his cheek and draw blood before he got hold of her wrists. She used her knee on his midsection and heard him groan. He recovered quickly, and they wrestled. He was too strong and threw her off. Rachel slammed into the end table by the bed and fell to the floor.

"Bitch," the man hissed at her.

Rachel saw Tommy had slumped from his chair to the floor. The man abandoned Tommy and headed for the hospital door. She summoned everything she had and threw herself at the man's legs, causing him to stumble and lose his balance. One of his cowboy boots hit her in the face, momentarily stunning her.

"Bitch," he repeated. The man had now regained his balance and was opening the door.

Rachel screamed, "Nooooo." But by the time she'd recovered from the boot kick, he was halfway out of the room. She looked over at Tommy. He was lying unmoving under the window.

Rachel moved quickly and knelt beside him. There was a thin wire around his neck. She frantically pulled at it, loosening it. He gasped, trying to breathe. She tried to gauge his pulse rate. At the sound of footsteps in the hall, Rachel yelled, "Help! I need help here!"

Moments later the door to the room opened, and 2 security guards ran into the room. "He ran down the hall. Tall guy, black fringe jacket, cowboy hat. The two guards looked at each other, not moving. Rachel screamed, "Go. Shut the hospital down. Find him, for Christ's sake."

The guards ran out of the room while Rachel continued to hold Tommy's hand. She was shaking with the realization that had she arrived a few minutes later, Tommy would be dead.

Dr. Marcotte raced into the room. "Oh my God!" She knelt down and put her fingers to Tommy's neck.

"There was a man here trying to hurt Tommy," Rachel blurted out.

Dr. Marcotte forced Tommy's eyes open and used a small

penlight to look into his eyes. She loosened his shirt and then looked over at Rachel, "He'll be okay, but we need to get him to a medical hospital. Tell me what happened."

"This man, I think it was one of the men Ben is looking for, had his hands around Tommy's neck. I went batshit on him, and he threw me off."

A siren went off somewhere in the hospital, and for the first time, Rachel felt a throb of pain on the right side of her face. She instinctively put her hand to her face.

"Did he punch you? You'll need a compress."

"Actually, I think I tried to tackle him with my face. I caught a cowboy boot trying to stop him."

Dr. Marcotte spoke to a couple of nurses who were standing in the doorway watching. "Help me get Tommy into bed."

———

FORTY MINUTES LATER, Rachel was sitting in Dr. Marcotte's office holding a bag of frozen peas to her face, when Gabriel burst into the room. "Oh! Rachel, what happened.?"

Rachel almost started to cry as he knelt in front of her. "I'm sorry I had to call, Gabriel. Thank you for coming. This is Dr. Marcotte, Tommy's doctor. She's been very helpful. Dr. Marcotte, Gabriel is my boss along with Ben, they own the agency."

Dr. Marcotte and Gabriel shook hands, and Rachel proceeded to tell Gabriel about the man she'd interrupted who was hurting Tommy.

"It's a good thing Rachel was there," added Dr. Marcotte. "She no doubt saved Tommy's life."

Gabriel gave Rachel a hug, "Is Tommy going to be alright?" he asked the doctor.

"He was taken by ambulance to a proper medical facility as a precaution. But I think he'll be physically able to recover. How this experience might affect his mental condition is another thing."

Gabriel gave Rachel another hug. "Did the guy punch you?"

"Not exactly." Rachel started to cry again. "I'm sorry he got away."

Dr. Marcotte jumped in, "He was able to run out the side door, which caused the alarms to go off. In all of the confusion, he got away. It was no one's fault, except maybe for the woman who lost her pass card. We've already confirmed that this animal used her card to get into the Long-Term Care ward. One of the security guards saw him get into a powder blue Barracuda and drive off."

"Don't suppose he was able to get the license tags?"

"No, the local cops asked the same thing," replied Marcotte.

"It was the man in the mug shot. I'm positive, Gabriel."

"So the local police have been here?"

"Yes, they've taken our statements, and they're interviewing the security guards."

Gabriel knelt in front of Rachel again and shook his head. "I'd better go talk to the police, tell them what we know. You're a very brave girl Rachel. I'm proud of you. Are you up to calling the Agency and talking to Arnie? I'm sure he must be beside himself with worry."

Rachel nodded, and Gabriel went to find the local cops.

CHAPTER FIFTY-FIVE

Ben needed a fallback plan. The work that Rachel was doing with Tommy was worthwhile but might not pay dividends. And as Dr. Marcotte had said, nothing that Tommy might ever say would hold up in court.

Ben decided to drive to Poplarville and compare notes with Sheriff McDiarmid. The sheriff had sounded guarded on the phone and suggested they meet at the coffee shop. As Ben walked into the building, he was amused to see the younger man sitting in a booth, a plate of donuts in front of him. "Hey Cliff, I thought you were going to lay off the crullers." Ben slid into the booth.

"I was going to, but I guess I'm just a cruller man. Salads just aren't my thing. Somebody should invent a salad with bits of cruller in it."

Ben smiled and waved the waitress over to order a coffee.

"So I heard about that prank you played on Cagle. You'd better hope he doesn't see your truck."

"He told you about it?" Ben asked in a surprised tone.

"I heard about it, but I suspect there might be a stretching of the truth."

"Yeah, well I already forgot about it." The waitress came by with his coffee.

"Seriously, Ben I'd be careful driving around these parts just the same. I'd be surprised if Cagle has forgotten about it. He told the guys that you did that business with his cruiser because he ran you and your girlfriend out of town."

"That so?" Ben took a sip of his coffee.

"Said you were mouthing off and that your nig....I mean girlfriend spit on him."

"Cliff, that's bullshit. If anyone was out of line, it was your deputy."

"Do you want to file an official complaint, Ben? I might be able to use it to get him to retire a little earlier."

"No, like I said it's forgotten. Where I come from, cops don't file against other cops."

Sheriff McDiarmid nodded and then lowered his voice. "How's that thing working out in Slidell?"

"My gal said she's making progress, but we should face the reality that this could take months."

"It was worth a try. What's Plan B?" asked the sheriff before devouring a donut.

"That's why I stopped by. Earlier in the week, an ex-partner of mine, guy by the name of Rutledge, recognized a name that Harrigan's widow gave me. She told me she remembered her late husband meeting with two brothers named Nantois. Tough looking thugs." Ben took another sip of his coffee and then continued. "Rutledge knew them right away. He said they used to be active this way, and that they worked for a man from New Orleans named Reznikov. Ever heard that name?"

"No, can't say that I have."

"Rutledge even got me pictures of the brothers." Ben pulled a sheet of paper from his jacket and put it in front of McDiarmid. "Look familiar?"

The sheriff took his time studying the mug shots, then shook his head. "Where are you headed with this, partner?"

"Putting two and two together." Ben counted on his fingers, "Reznikov was active out here back in 1977; Reznikov is big in the drug smuggling business; the Nantois boys were identified by the sheriff's widow, and they work for Reznikov."

"So, you want to ask them if they remember shooting some kid in the woods 7 years ago?"

Ben gave him a 'wise guy' look. "I know what they look like; I know who they work for, their last known address, and what kind of car they drive. I think we should start by tailing them and see what we can pick up."

———

BOTH KORY and Kane Nantois had given an apartment on Decatur Street as their address on the arrest record. The same address had come up when Rutledge did a motor vehicle search. Kory was the registered owner of a blue Barracuda. No car had come up for the other brother. Decatur Street was in the old part of New Orleans and ran parallel to the river.

Ben parked his truck by the curb, a half block down the street from a gray clapboard house. There was no sign of the Barracuda. Of course, there was no reason to believe the brothers still lived there, so Ben got out of the car and climbed the metal stairs to the front door. There were three separate mailboxes, and Ben figured the place had been divided into 3 separate residences. Opening the mailbox for apartment #2, he found a hydro bill as well as a magazine; both addressed to Mr. K Nantois. The magazine was in a plain brown wrapper. Leaving the hydro bill, Ben took the magazine back to the truck and settled in to wait and watch. He ripped open the wrapping to find a copy of *Juggs Magazine* featuring a naked African-American woman holding up her two humongous headlights. As he looked through the magazine, he found pretty much the same throughout. He threw it disgustedly onto the floor of the truck.

As gross as the magazine was, it reminded Ben of the previous weekend and his trip to Picayune with Chevon. *Fuck that trip. It couldn't have gone more wrong. So much for the dream of living the country life. Am I being fair to her? I'm twice her age, overweight with a gimpy shoulder. All I know is being a cop. That's what has kept me going all these years. Now I won't have that anymore. Sure, I can be a private detective but am I ready for that? What should I do?*

It was like he had a good angel on one shoulder and an evil one on the other. *Fuck it! said the good angel.* Even good angels swear sometimes. *You should quit being a pussy and just go ahead and ask her. You've been together, off and on, for a few years. You get along well. Let's not make this complicated. Why don't we go down to City Hall and get hitched?*

The evil angel jumped in. But what if she wants the whole church wedding? What about her parents? After all this time, the only member of her family you've met was half naked and wearing dinosaur PJs. Is she embarrassed to have you meet them? I think so, honky. Will they disapprove of the mixed-race relationship? How do you feel being called a nigger lover? Don't think they won't be calling you that!

Ben's thoughts were interrupted when he saw a man with pork chop sideburns, greasy hair and a black leather coat walking down the street. Ben held up the mug shot of Kane Nantois. "Bingo, scumbag."

He watched as Kane ambled down the street towards the apartment house, smoking a cigarette. The guy was looking at his feet pretty much the whole time, so Ben was confident that he had not seen his truck. Keeping an eye on him, he saw him flick his cigarette butt into the street and climb up to the front door. Ben observed as Kane opened the mailbox and pulled out the hydro bill. Taking another look in the mailbox, Kane looked disappointed. *Looking for your magazine? It's right here, scumbag.*

Ben watched as Kane went into the building.

———

BEN WAITED ALMOST AN HOUR. It was 11:30 when finally he noticed Kane coming out of the house. Ben watched to see what direction Kane headed before getting out of the truck and following him on foot. Kane went west on Decatur towards the French Quarter. Ben kept a respectable distance behind, but Kane seemed impervious that someone might be following him. He crossed Franklin and then some side streets. When he got to the corner of Frenchmen and Decatur, Kane stopped and looked north at something on Frenchman. The hair on the back of Ben's neck went up when he realized that *Trois Muses*, the cafe where Chevon performed, was a mere stone's throw away. He continued to watch as Kane lit another cigarette, still

253

standing on the street corner. Taking cover in the entranceway of a flower shop, Ben saw Chevon turn the corner and walk towards the cafe. *This can't be a coincidence.* Kane took a final puff of his cigarette and again flicked it into the street. He then proceeded to cross at the traffic light so that he was walking behind Chevon.

CHAPTER FIFTY-SIX

A rnie called Sheriff McDiarmid on the chance that Ben might have decided to work the Glenn Wilson case.

"Deputy Cagle, Pearl River County sheriff."

"Good morning Sir, I was wondering if a Mr. Ben O'Shea might be there today." There was a pause on the line. Arnie figured that the deputy might be checking with someone.

"Who is this?" Cagle replied.

"I'm sorry. My name is Arnie Sims. I work with Ben O'Shea. I'm trying to get an important message to him."

"There's no Ben O'Shea here. You want, you can give me the message for the sheriff."

"Do you know if he's expected today?"

"No, so just give me the message."

"Can I speak to the sheriff?"

"No, he's off today."

Arnie took a deep breath before saying, "He's to call Arnie at the Agency right away. Something big has happened at the hospital. Rachel might be in trouble. He should meet Gabriel there as soon as possible."

Deputy Cagle repeated the message as he wrote it down on a scrap of paper. "Okay, I'll surely get this over to him."

Once Cagle hung-up, Sheriff McDiarmid, who was sitting in the next office, walked by and asked, "Anything important?"

"No, nothing." Cagle crumbled up the piece of paper and threw it in the garbage.

CHAPTER FIFTY-SEVEN

Ben watched Chevon walk into the cafe. A couple of minutes later Kane followed. Ben was frantic, realizing that Kane was stalking her. He walked into the restaurant and saw Chevon with her back towards him, setting up her saxophone. Kane had been shown to a table at the back of the room.

One of the waiters approached him. "Lunch for one, Messieurs?"

"I'm meeting someone. I see they're already seated at a table at the back." The waiter made a welcoming gesture and invited Ben to join his friend and have a nice lunch. Ben made his way to the back, pulled out a chair next to Kane's, and sat down.

"What the fuck, Dad? I'm not looking for any...," Kane paused to take in Ben's attire of lime green seersucker jacket and plaid shirt, "homo action."

Kane had beady eyes and smelled like he'd bathed in *Hai Karate*. Ben gave him a smile, noticing that he had letters tattooed on each of his knuckles. It spelled something rude.

"Did you hear me fucktard? Get lost."

The restaurant was about half full. Chevon hadn't noticed Ben yet but would most certainly see him in the small room. "Relax. The waiter said they were expecting a big crowd, so he said he had to sit someone here." Ben gave him a smile. Kane's right hand moved quickly, and he popped a switchblade out of nowhere.

"Go eat at another restaurant then, Numbnuts."

Ben moved equally quickly. With his good shoulder, he slipped his hand behind Kane's head and smashed the man's face hard into the table. Kane's face made a crunching sound, and he let out a little groan. Ben looked around and repeated the maneuver. The noise and action had caught the attention of the other diners and people were looking back at the scene. He took advantage of Kane's shock to snag the switchblade out of his hand. He pointed it at the man's testicles. "Careful now young fellow, I don't think scumbag testicles are on the menu."

The waiter who had spoken to Ben as he came in, approached the table. "Messieurs, is everything all right?"

"Oh yes, my friend is just a little under the weather." Ben looked over at Kane. Blood was dripping down his face. "Maybe I should help him outside. Some fresh air will do him good." Ben noticed Chevon looking at him as he escorted Kane out to the entrance, the switchblade digging into his side under his coat.

"Ben?" she called out.

"I just have to take care of something, Chevon. I'll be right back."

Ben grabbed Kane by the collar and dragged him to an alley adjacent to the cafe. "Now you were saying something about eating somewhere else?"

"Fuck you, I think you broke my nose," Kane whined.

Ben held Kane's head up using the blade of the switch-blade. "Let's take a look. No, I don't think it's broken. Do you have trouble breathing?" Before Kane could say anything, Ben punched him hard in the nose. The blow knocked Kane backward into a bunch of garbage cans. "There, now it's broken."

Ben moved quickly to pull Kane up by his collar. "Listen, Kane; I know who you are. I know where you live. Stay away from the girl you were following or next time I'll do more than break your nose." Ben let the man slump back down into the garbage. "And hey, way too much *Hai Karate!*"

When Ben walked back into the *Trois Muses*, Chevon came right over to him. "Ben, what was that all about?"

"Long story, minor disagreement over what was on the menu. Would you be okay if I hung around for a bit? Listened to your set?"

"I would love that."

Ben wondered when Kane and his brother would be back to even the score.

———

WHEN CHEVON FINISHED her lunchtime set, Ben walked with her back to her apartment. On the way, he watched for someone who might jump out of an alley at them.

Chevon finally stopped, "What really happened back there at the restaurant, and why are you looking around when I'm talking to you?"

"There's a guy, on that case I told you about. He might be involved in what happened to that boy in the woods. I'm not sure, but when I came to New Orleans this morning, I noticed that he was following you. I watched him follow you into the restaurant and then take a table at the back. I sat down at the table and was just going to warn him off when he pulled this switchblade on me. I didn't want to disrupt your act, so I took him into the alley next door and had a conversation with him."

"A conversation."

"I made it clear that he should stay clear of you."

"But why me?"

"That is a really good question. Someone who knows I'm looking into the murder must have fingered me and then followed me to your place."

"Who would that be, and am I in danger?"

"I don't know. As for danger, I'd like to stick around for a while."

Chevon put her arm through his. "Well, that guy better not come near us, or I'll do more than have a conversation with him."

WHEN THEY ARRIVED at Chevon's apartment, Ben checked the operation of the locks on the door. He went around and made sure the windows were all locked, especially the one that led to the fire escape. "Is Tray still living with you?"

"Yes and no. He has a new girlfriend. He's spending a lot of time at her place."

"Alright, I'm going to be your shadow, but in the meantime, it might be a good idea to get you some protection."

"You're not referring to condoms, right?"

Ben smiled, "I was thinking a gun and then teaching you how to use it."

"I'm scared of guns, Ben. With my luck, I'm going to end up shooting myself."

Ben gave her a hug. "I'll stay as long as you want."

"Really, like forever?"

Ben looked into her eyes and kissed her. "If that's what you want." Before Chevon could respond, Ben asked if he could call the agency.

"Sure, make yourself at home." Chevon walked into the bedroom and looked out on Treme Street, trying to find something out of place. She overheard Ben speaking to someone on the phone.

"I met with the sheriff this morning. No, I didn't get a message, when did you call him?"

"Oh? To the deputy. His name wouldn't have been Cagle, would it?" Chevon heard Ben's voice grow animated and she came and put her arms around him. "Okay Arnie, I got it. When did all this happen?" Ben looked at his watch. Holding the phone and turning to Chevon, "Can you come for a little drive, if I promise that we'll be back by your next set?" She nodded but gave him a concerned look. "Okay, Arnie hang tight. If Gabriel calls back then tell him that I'll be there in thirty minutes."

BEN HAD LEFT his truck on Decatur Street, so they had to hoof it a few blocks. Chevon could sense that Ben was angry. She could almost hear his teeth grinding as they walked down the street. When they got to the truck, she climbed into the passenger seat and saw a magazine on the floor. Before he could say anything, Chevon picked up the magazine and looked at the cover image of a black woman with large breasts. "Seriously Ben?" she asked, giving him a quizzical look. "Is this what you like?"

"It's not like that Chevon..."

"My God, I need to arrange for a boob job to compete with this," she leafed through the pages.

"That guy I said I was following, his name is Nantois. I wanted to make sure I was after the right guy, so I took that magazine out of his mailbox. Just check the address label."

"Kane Nantois," she read off the label.

As Ben turned the truck onto the highway leading to Slidell, he said, "And by the way, no boob job, I love you just the way you are."

Chevon seemed satisfied with the explanation, but she continued to hold onto the magazine. "This guy scares me, Ben." After a few minutes of speed on the highway, she gripped the dashboard in fear. "Shouldn't you slow down, Cowboy?"

"I remember hearing somewhere that fear was wisdom in the face of danger. It's a good thing to be tuned in enough to feel fear and figure what to do about it, that's called bravery."

"Are you going to tell me what I should be scared of?"

"Arnie has been looking for me all day. He said he left a message with that jackass deputy we met, to have me call him right away."

"What's wrong, Ben?'

"Do you remember that girl Rachel from the Agency?"

"Of course, we talked about her the other day."

"She's been working with Tommy Huffman at the hospital, and she interrupted a man trying to strangle him."

"Oh my God, Ben!"

"Tommy's alive because of her. Rachel is going to be okay, but apparently, she got a black eye trying to stop the guy."

WHEN THEY GOT to the hospital, Gabriel was sitting talking to Rachel and Dr. Marcotte.

"I'm sorry, I just got the message about this." Ben quickly introduced Chevon to Dr. Marcotte. "Rachel, are you alright?"

"Yes except, I let that bastard get away. It was Kory Nantois. The guy in the mug shot."

"Really...I had a run in with Kane Nantois today. I caught him following Chevon to her restaurant. He came out with the worst of it."

"How did these guys know about Chevon and Tommy?" asked Gabriel.

"There has to be an inside man. My money is on that deputy up in the Pearl River County Sheriff's Department. The day that we drove back from Picayune, he followed us. He could have got word to the Nantois brothers and had me tailed. That would have led them here and to Chevon's."

"What do we do now?" Rachel asked.

Dr. Marcotte spoke up. "First, young lady, I want you back here tomorrow to pick up where you left off. We can't let these people intimidate us. Slidell Police are going to post a patrolman outside Tommy's room."

"Thank you," said Rachel, still holding the frozen peas to her face.

"I'm going to call Sheriff McDiarmid and see what can be

done about the deputy," said Ben. "Meanwhile I'll be staying at Chevon's apartment."

Gabriel spoke up, "I told the local cops all about the Nantois brothers. They have their address and details on their car. They'll find them. Meanwhile, I want to take Rachel home."

Dr. Marcotte's phone rang. She answered it and listened for a few moments, then said, "Put him through." She handed the phone to Ben. "It's someone named Arnie Simms."

"Hi Arnie, everything is going to be alright here." Ben listened for a minute, everyone watching his expression. "That's a surprise. Did he say anything else?"

When Ben hung up, "Two things; one, Arnie's glad you're okay Rachel, but he wants you to know you can have your job back. Way too stressful." Everyone laughed,

"What was the second thing?" asked Gabriel.

"Chief Willis wants me to call ASAP."

CHAPTER FIFTY-EIGHT

They decided to leave Rachel's car in the parking lot and drive back to Gulfport in Gabriel's pink bug. "Not sure how I feel about you spending the night alone," said Gabriel, pulling out of the parking lot. "You can stay with us tonight."

"Thanks, Gabriel. I don't want to put you out."

"You wouldn't be. Jacqueline, Jelly Bean and I would be happy to have you. And if you don't, I won't be able to sleep worrying about you."

"I'll think about it."

"What's going on with that Dan guy?"

"You mean Dan as in Drake, as in Don Mangina?"

Gabriel laughed and turned onto Highway 10. "Yes, that's who I mean, the guy who works for the MBI."

"I like him, maybe a lot." Gabriel looked over at her as she rested her bruised face against the window. "But, I'm not sure how he feels about me. Maybe because he's lied to me so much, I'm not sure what's real. I couldn't believe that after risking my life to help him get that ledger, he wouldn't even confide in me about the investigation." They drove in silence for a while and then Rachel sat up. "So how is the pink car thing working out for you, Gabriel?"

"I kind of blank it out, but I keep finding these little messages under my windshield like, 'My daughter wants her Barbies back', or 'Does this car match your undies?'"

"How did you like the one about, 'When are you delivering my cosmetics?" Rachel laughed.

Gabriel's eyes narrowed. "Was that you leaving little notes for me?"

"Yeah, I couldn't help myself. But it was Jacqueline's idea. She thought you needed a little extra push to get a new car."

"You are horrible, conniving people."

"Are you guys going to get a new car?"

"Ben used to say, even before you had the car painted, that it was too noticeable for surveillance. I can just imagine what he thinks now."

"Have you seen his truck? He's one to talk."

ONCE THEY GOT to Gabriel's house, Jacqueline started crying when she saw Rachel's face. "Oh, Rachel! What happened?"

Gabriel made a pot of tea as Rachel told Jacqueline about what had happened. They sat around the kitchen table talking about Tommy Huffman, the attempt on his life, and whether there would ever be a breakthrough.

"You're a very brave woman, Rachel. I really admire what you are doing. Tommy may never be able to help convict these men, but you are going to help him regain his life. I think you've found your calling," Jacqueline said.

Gabriel went into the bedroom and came out with Benjamin, who had woken up and started to fuss. As soon as the toddler saw Rachel, he extended his hands to her.

Rachel held him on her lap facing her. He was moving up and down on his knees, laughing, when all of a sudden, he stopped and gave her a serious look. Benjamin touched her bruised face with his little fingers.

"Jacqueline, some idiot has been leaving these little notes under my car windshield. I thought it had to be someone who works at the strip mall, but then I found one when I went to get in my car this morning. It was particularly crude, something about taking my balls out of my purse and getting a new car. I think it's our neighbor, Mr. Kennessey. I saw him watching with a big grin on his face. He's such an old coot. I'm going to go over and talk to him about it."

Jacqueline looked over at Rachel, and they both broke up laughing. "Alright, it was us. But it was Rachel's idea."

"Funny, she said it was yours."

CHAPTER FIFTY-NINE

When Ben and Chevon got back to her apartment, he put Kane's switchblade on the night table. He'd been surprised to hear from ex-Chief Willis. While Ben felt they'd had a solid working relationship, it wasn't the kind of connection that crossed retirement borders.

Once he had gotten Willis on the phone, they talked about retirement. "I'm filling in time at my cottage near Ocean Springs. Most days I sit on the beach, drinking beer and reading the latest Grisham. I get a little drunk sometimes and then stagger back to the cottage." Willis was a widower, having lost his wife a decade earlier from breast cancer. As far as Ben knew, there was no significant other in his life - although in the past he'd suspected Willis of dating a *Herald* reporter.

"How long did it take you to wind down?" asked Ben. Willis had a ridiculous temper and had been known for his outbursts and throwing staplers across a room.

"The beer and the sun are helping. I even occasionally walk down to the pier and drop a rod. You should stop by."

"Things are pretty busy for me right now. I'm looking into a cold case involving a kid that was murdered in Picayune seven years ago."

"The Wilson case. Getting anywhere?"

"I will. You know me, I'm not going to give up," said Ben.

"You should stop by. My cottage is on Front Beach Drive, number 4220. See you no later than 10 tomorrow morning, O'Shea."

Willis was making it pretty clear. He was still in boss mode and had summoned Ben to his cottage. Agreeing to drive to Ocean Springs meant that Ben was still in employee mode.

———

THE FOLLOWING MORNING, Ben got to Ocean Springs a little after 9 a.m. He was early and had time to stop and make a call to Picayune. Sheriff Cliff McDiarmid answered his phone right away. "Cliff, it's Ben. Something came up yesterday, and I think you need to know about it."

"What's that, Ben?"

"Let's start off by saying one of my associates, Arnie Sims, called there looking for me yesterday. He ended up leaving a message with Cagle. I don't suppose Cagle gave you the message?"

"No, this is the first I heard of it. I went by his office at one point during the day, because I thought I heard him on the phone mentioning your name. But when I asked him, he said it was nothing. Did something bad happen?"

"We have a leak. Someone sent the Nantois boys, first after my girlfriend, and second, after Tommy Huffman.

There is no way anyone would have known where to find them."

"Is everyone alright?"

"Pretty much. My associate, the girl working with Tommy, got knocked around pretty bad, but she saved Tommy from being strangled. As for my girlfriend, Kane Nantois might need to get his nose fixed."

"Shit, I'm sorry if one of my deputies is responsible for any of this. Hold on a sec, Ben." There was about a minute of dead air before Cliff came back on the line. "Jesus Ben. I found a crumpled-up piece of paper in Cagle's garbage can. It's all right here, urgent message from Arnie Sims. For Ben O'Shea. Fuck! Ben, I'm going to suspend this asshole right away. If he gets the union involved I may need that statement from you."

There was a pause on the line then Ben said, "Don't do that. This is what I want you to do..."

CHAPTER SIXTY

Gabriel received a call from the Slidell Police in the morning. It was Detective Harper, who had taken Gabriel's statement at the hospital the previous day.

"We got a hit on the Barracuda late last night. A car matching the description was torched in the Bayou. We can send a team out, but there's not much point."

"I'd like to check it out anyway. They're going to need another car. How many car thefts in New Orleans last night?"

"About 50 or so. This is the stolen car capital of America."

Gabriel thought of Huedunit Painting and the car ring in Biloxi. "Alright, where does that leave us?"

"We checked out that apartment on Decatur and got a friendly landlord to let us in. But other than a huge supply of porn, we didn't find anything that might help us. We're running a check on phones. We might get lucky. Other than that, we have a uniformed cop outside of Tommy's door

24/7, or until the Nantois brothers are apprehended. He'd be pretty stupid to try it again."

As Gabriel thanked Harper for the update, he noticed that Rachel had walked into the kitchen wearing a pair of Jacqueline's PJs.

"Good morning Rachel," said Gabriel as he hung up the phone. Her black eye had turned into a collage of yellows and purples. "Hope you slept well."

"I slept like a baby." She wiped the sleep gingerly from her one good eye.

Gabriel poured her a cup of coffee as she sat at the kitchen table. "Jacqueline took Benjamin for a stroll; she should be back in a bit."

"You were on the phone, anything new?"

Gabriel gave her an update on the hunt for the Nantois brothers. "I think until they're caught we should make sure there is someone with you all the time."

"Thank you, Gabriel, but I need to go to my apartment and get some clothes."

"Why don't I make you some breakfast, then when you're ready, I can take you to your apartment, and you can get some stuff?" Rachel didn't get a chance to respond, as the kitchen phone rang. Gabriel answered and then mouthed to Rachel that it was Ben. When Gabriel eventually hung up, he rolled his eyes. "This is just getting more bizarre by the minute. Ben's seeing Chief Willis at 10 at his cottage in Ocean Springs. He'll be in the office to give us an update after that. Ben thinks that it has something to do with what we're working on. He also spoke to the sheriff in Pearl River, and they've agreed on a plan. This is what he wants to do..."

SHERIFF McDIARMID WALKED into the station house and saw Deputy Cagle in the lunchroom talking to one of the volunteer helpers. "Hey folks, gonna be a great day! Oh, Cagle, when the coffee's ready, let's get together in my office. I have exciting news."

A few minutes later the two men were sitting in Cliff's office. "Thanks for the coffee, Cagle. Listen, you know that detective, the one you had the run-in with last weekend?"

"Yeah, don't remember the name. But he was a real piece of work."

"Right." Cliff smiled. "I think I mentioned that he was looking into that Glenn Wilson case. Remember I asked you about drug dealing going on at that time?"

"I remember. But I don't think there was any drug problem back then."

"That's what you said, and you'd know. I was in high school back then."

"Boinking all the cheerleaders."

McDiarmid smiled. "Here's the deal, they've discovered that there was a witness to everything, a kid named Tommy Huffman. This kid has been holed up in a hospital refusing to talk. This O'Shea guy, that's the detective, is working with him and the kid is opening up big time. Now that he's talking, he's been moved to his Uncle and Aunt's place in Slidell. So, get this, the kid saw everything on account of him being in the woods that day. I think we'll finally get a resolution to all of this. Isn't that great news? I know you're one of the few deputies that were active back then, and would want to hear about it. I only wish Sheriff Harrigan was still alive to see this resolved."

Deputy Cagle gave a silent nod, but had preoccupation written on his face.

"Anything wrong, Deputy?"

"No, not at all. Great news. Let's celebrate! Donuts are on me. I'll just mosey on down to the coffee shop and be right back."

"Make mine a cruller."

CHAPTER SIXTY-ONE

Ben pulled his truck up to the small yellow cottage. He was getting out of the truck when the screen door to the cottage opened, and Willis appeared holding two Budweiser's.

"O'Shea, still dressing like a male hooker I see." He didn't wait for a response and nodded to the beach, "Come on."

Ben looked down at his outfit. Unlike Willis, who was wearing Bermuda shorts, Ben was wearing polyester plaid slacks and his mauve oxford button down. He followed Willis down to the beach where an umbrella and a couple of lounge chairs were set up. A woman and a young boy were building a sand castle nearby. As he let his body settle into a lounger, Ben looked up and saw the jewel-blue waters of the Gulf. On the horizon, the sea merged with a light blue sky, accentuated by white fluffy clouds. A gentle breeze blew the salt air across the beach. Waves gently lapped the shore dragging clumps of seaweed onto the beach. It was all very peaceful. He could see how this would help a person to relax.

Ben clinked his beer bottle with Willis. "Beautiful spot Chief. Seems funny though, meeting with you out here."

"It's very relaxing. Sometimes I just sit here for hours, meditating. What's in the bag, Ben?" Willis pointed at the shopping bag Ben had brought with him.

"We never had a chance to say goodbye. I was in the hospital when you had the retirement party. I meant to give you something to remember me by." Ben pulled out a trophy out of the bag. The inscription on the base said, "I'm not like a boss, I AM THE FUCKING BOSS." On top of the wooden stand was a gold stapler.

"That's pretty fucking precious, O'Shea." Willis held up the trophy. He was still chuckling when he asked, "How's the shoulder?"

"Fine, pretty good," Ben lied.

"You're looking into the Picayune thing. Harrigan is dead, isn't he?"

Ben looked over at his former boss. "Yeah, he died a couple of years ago. But I think there's more to this than Harrigan."

"Good luck with that. I don't need to tell you to be careful. Harrigan was protecting someone. That person is still there." A couple of gulls landed near them, then proceeded to have a squawk fight over something that had washed ashore.

"I think you know that I wanted to talk to you about something but it's not about the Picayune case." A beach ball bounced into Willis' lap, and the young boy who was building the sand castle came running over. Willis laughed and tossed the ball to the kid.

Maybe retirement, the beach, and the sun have mellowed him, Ben thought.

Willis turned back to Ben, "I'm going to do the talking, and you're going to listen. There's stuff that I kept from you, Ben. Maybe I shouldn't have, but I made a call. Let's just say you're not the most politically astute cop I've ever worked with."

Ben began to say something to his defense, before seeing a scowl wipe across Willis' face.

"Shut the fuck up O'Shea. I'm trying to help you." Just then the boy threw the ball again, and it hit Willis in the back of the head. This time Willis grabbed the ball and kicked it into the ocean. The little boy ran back to his mother crying.

Same old Willis. Ben took a swig from his Bud and waited for Willis to continue.

"I had a relationship with Debbie Sheehan."

"Kind of knew that. You were constantly busting my chops about passing inside information in return for sex. And to think all the time you were slipping the salami to her." Ben shook his head in disapproval.

"Fuck off O'Shea. Not that kind of relationship."

"You weren't having sex with her?"

"No. I wasn't. We were working on a story together. I was very concerned about my name and number being in her address book because the story involved Mayor Baxter."

"Mayor Baxter?"

"Are you going to repeat everything I say? Debbie had a source at the Heritage Savings and Loan bank. This source gave her information about bad loans, false contracts, money laundering, and bribes. My sources tell me the guy you're investigating, William Friesen, was part of a scheme to defraud the bank of millions."

"I knew Baxter was dirty."

"You have no idea, but beyond Baxter, there's a man named Frank Reznikov. Part of the Russian Mafia, or Brotherhood as they like to call themselves. This crook was treating the S & L like his own personal piggy bank. Baxter's role was to look the other way on the money laundering and fraudulent loans. In return, Baxter received a six-figure bonus."

"And you have proof of all this?"

"We're getting there. When Debbie died, I took everything to a man I knew at the Mississippi Bureau of Investigation. By then the writing was on the wall. The mayor swept in and hired Murdock as the new Chief, who let's just say if he had an idea it would die of loneliness. There are people from the Mississippi Department of Banking and Consumer Finance in the bank now, doing an audit."

"I thought you were retired?"

"If you remember I walked out when Baxter started to get on my case about you. Since I started the investigation with Debbie, I'd like to see it through."

Ben let the information sink in. "Gabriel's been looking into Friesen's death. He's thinking that this was all about Friesen and Baxter's wife having an affair."

"Nah, he and Baxter were friends, and that includes a little hanky-panky with each other's wives. The MBI believes that Frank Reznikov had Friesen's wife killed because she was threatening to go to the cops. Friesen freaked out and went to see Gabriel when he couldn't get ahold of his wife. We have a lot of this on tape. The judge denied the bugging of the mayor's office, but not his main residence."

"This is huge. Frank Reznikov has also been implicated in that murder case in Picayune."

"That's interesting, but not surprising."

"What should we do?"

"Nothing, we've been able to get a copy of a ledger that implicates Frankie Reznikov in a car theft ring. We're just waiting for some more stuff from the audit in the bank before we arrest everyone."

"I'd like to be there when they arrest Baxter."

"Figured you would."

CHAPTER SIXTY-TWO

Ben arrived back at the Agency, his head about to explode with everything that was happening.

Rachel, Gabriel, and Arnie were all seated around Gabriel's desk in his office. Travis Franklin, a young man whom Gabriel had befriended a few years ago, was sitting in Gabriel's chair with his feet up on his desk.

"Good morning folks. The gang's all here. Nice to see you again, Travis. What's brings you in today?"

"Gabriel gave me a call, said you had a tough case and needed my expertise. Kind of a consultation."

"We've brought Travis up to date on everything. I thought he could help watch the office so that we can make sure both Rachel and Chevon are not left alone," explained Gabriel.

"Thanks, Gabriel. Good thought." Ben stopped for a moment, noticing the bruising on Rachel's face. "That looks painful, I've had plenty of shiners, and they run their course in about a week. For now, it gives you character."

"How did you make out with Chief Willis?" Gabriel

changed the subject.

Ben recapped the discussion with his former boss.

Halfway through the story Rachel got up and started pacing the floor. "You were right all along, Ben. Talk about corrupt, and to think I voted for Baxter!"

"I didn't see the Debbie Sheehan thing coming." Gabriel picked up Bourbon, who was swishing about, rubbing up against his leg.

"Neither did I." Ben turned to Rachel. "I have to think that your guy Dan arranged for Willis to call me."

"Drake?" Arnie asked.

"I thought it was Don...Don Mangina," said Gabriel.

Everyone had a good laugh before Rachel took charge. "So, we just sit back and wait for the cavalry to swoop in and arrest everyone?"

"I'd like to catch the guy that hurt you, that's why we're going to use the Flowers' as a decoy," said Ben.

"Have they agreed to this?" Arnie asked.

"Absolutely," said Ben, "When they heard about what happened at the hospital, and that we're pretty sure the same people are responsible for killing Tommy's parents, they were enthusiastically onside. Bert Flowers' last words to me were that he was going to get his shotgun."

"So how is this all going to work?" asked Travis.

Ben smiled and nodded his head at Travis. "For today I thought Arnie could be Rachel's bodyguard. There's supposed to be a uniformed Slidell cop outside Tommy's room. Now that we have you minding the store Travis, maybe Gabriel and I can take turns watching the Flowers' house, with the other watching Chevon."

"Okay makes sense. So, this is the command center...." said Travis.

CHAPTER SIXTY-THREE

K ane was sitting up on the bed drinking a six-pack. His breathing was labored and his nose crudely bandaged with black hockey tape. He was watching *Magnum P.I.* on the Motel 6 TV. "I'm cheering for the bad guy," he wheezed. "Just once I'd love to see Magnum get his ass kicked."

Kory was looking out the window at the stolen Toyota Celica in the parking lot. He was pissed at having had to torch his beloved Barracuda. He looked over at his brother, who was writing something in the motel Bible. "What the fuck are you writing, numbnuts?"

"I'm autographing. 'Hope you enjoy the story, signed Jesus K. Christ."

"You're an idiot. There's no middle initial K."

"Yes, there is. Mom said I was named after him. Jesus Kane Christ." Kane drained his beer and crushed the can.

"Mother was a fucking liar."

"You're a fucking liar."

Kory looked at his younger brother. He'd always taken

care of him, even though he knew the kid was a psycho. "You sure it was this Biloxi cop?"

"Yeah. Fuck, how many times do I have to tell you? The fucker got me from behind. One minute I'm fantasizing about what I'm gonna do to his nigger, then wham, he hits me from behind. Fuckin' broke my nose."

"You're an idiot for letting him get the drop on you. You should have seen him coming."

"Fuck you. How come the fucking witness isn't dead, huh? Huh? At least I didn't get my ass kicked by a girl!"

Kory lit a Marlborough and shook his head. "She didn't kick my ass."

"Yes, she did."

"No, she didn't."

"Did."

Kory pulled the Enforcer and aimed it at Kane. "Fuck off. I'm just pissed enough to put a fuckin' bullet in your head." They stared at each other for a couple of moments, and then Kory holstered his gun.

"I win," Kane gloated over winning the staring contest. "What are we going to do now?"

"Lie low. Frankie will call us back, and he'll take care of everything." As if on cue, the phone in the room rang.

Kane jumped off the bed to answer the call.

Kory told him to back off. "I'll get it," Kory said, picking up the receiver. "Yeah?' He listened for a few minutes, then cradling the receiver he picked up the hotel pencil and scribbled something on the notepad.

When he hung up the phone, Kory said, "Plans have changed, the kid's blabbing about that day in the woods. Apparently, he was there all along. He's probably telling them that he saw you put a bullet in that kid's head."

"Fuck! Too bad that girl kicked your ass," said Kane, his eyes fixed on the TV screen.

"At least I'm not the one with hockey tape on my nose. I'll take care of it. Big brother always takes care of every-thing. It'll be easier this time. They moved him back to his uncle and aunt's house in Slidell."

CHAPTER SIXTY-FOUR

Rachel and Arnie arrived at the hospital at 2 p.m. after having spent the whole way discussing the case. As they walked through the entrance, a security guard directed them to Dr. Marcotte's office.

Once there, Rachel introduced Arnie. Marcotte shook his hand but then took a look at Rachel's face and almost cried. She gave Rachel a hug and handed her a present that had been hastily wrapped. "For what you did yesterday."

Rachel opened the present and found a heavy brass object with a series of four holes. "Brass knuckles?" She looked at Arnie.

"A former boyfriend gave me those as a gift ten years ago. I've been using it as a paperweight."

"Thank you, Dr. Marcotte."

"Adrienne, please. What's in the bag, Rachel?" The doctor pointed at the Piggly Wiggly shopping bag Rachel was holding.

"The Flowers' gave me some of Tommy's stuff. Just

things he had on him when they brought him here. I thought maybe it might help." Rachel replied.

"There's something else that I think you should know," said Arnie.

"What's that?" Dr. Marcotte asked.

Arnie explained the plan for using the Flowers' as a decoy.

"That seems so dangerous, why don't you folks just let the police handle it?"

"That's a good question. After what happened yesterday it's become personal." Arnie looked over at Rachel.

RACHEL AND ARNIE walked to Tommy's room and showed their identification to the policeman standing guard.

"If you guys are gonna be here, do you mind if I take a quick break?"

"No, you go ahead. I'll keep your seat warm," answered Arnie.

Rachel walked into Tommy's room and saw that Tommy was not sitting in a chair. He was lying on his bed with his eyes closed. She pulled out a chair and watched his face for a sign of movement. Finally, she grasped Tommy's hand and whispered softly, "I'm back Tommy. It's Rachel." When there was no response, "I'm sorry about yesterday, we missed our meeting so if it's okay with you, I can stay a little longer today."

She set up the cassette and pressed play. Once again, the sound of Eric Burden filled the room. "I just love this song. Oh! I have another joke that my Daddy used to tell. I remember being up with him late one night as we had a cow that was giving birth. I stayed awake just so I could be there to see the calf. Daddy asked me, 'What did the mommy cow say to the baby cow?' When I told him I didn't know, he said, 'It's pasture bedtime!' Corny, I know. You don't have to laugh." She continued to hold his hand, alternating different pressure, receiving no response.

"I brought some pictures that I got out of the library. I wish you would open your eyes and look at them. But until you do, I'll describe them to you. Here is a picture of my favorite scene from Rocky where he ran up all those stairs. What a great scene. Sometimes when I'm having a tough day, like yesterday, I think of that scene."

Rachel then pulled out another picture, "I don't know if you remember this scene, but it's the first morning where Rocky is getting up in the dark to start running in the streets. I think about him eating the raw eggs, and it reminds me that nothing worth doing in life is easy."

"Remember that scene in the meat locker where he was punching the beef?" Rachel laughed. She sat back and watched Tommy's face a bit more. *At least on Tuesday, his eyes had been open.*

"Your uncle and aunt gave me some things of yours. I thought they might be important to you." She reached into the shopping bag and pulled out a black and white photo. "Here's a picture of you and your cousins Aster and Basil. It's got you in the middle with your arms around them. Three handsome boys, I bet a lot of the girls up there had their eye on you."

"Here's a baseball glove. Your Uncle Bert told me that you used to be a pretty good Little League player when you lived in Picayune." Rachel slapped the pocket a couple of times, making a loud whack. "Next, we have a baseball card.

It's autographed by Lou Brock. Your Uncle told me that you went on a school trip to St. Louis and you asked him to sign it. That must have been a special moment."

Rachel reached into the bag again and felt something metal. She pulled it out and looked at it. It was a Zippo lighter. She hadn't noticed it before when Mr. Flowers gave her the bag. *Why would a kid have a lighter?* She was about to say something when she turned it over and saw the initials, 'KN.' *Kory or Kane Nantois? Could Tommy have found this when he discovered his parent's bodies?*

Sadness flowed through her veins and deadened her mind as she held the lighter. It was like a poison to her spirit; a link to something so horrific, it had robbed Tommy of his ability to communicate. Superstitiously, she quickly put the lighter down. A tear ran down her cheek. She was so choked up she hadn't realized that Tommy had opened his eyes.

CHAPTER SIXTY-FIVE

Ben and Gabriel drove to the Flowers' house together in Ben's truck. When Gabriel got in, he noticed a magazine on the floor. Picking it up, he started to laugh. "Seriously Ben, *Juggs?*"

"Long story, but I pulled it out of Nantois' mailbox. I probably should have gotten rid of it before Chevon saw."

"She saw it?"

"She gave me quite the look. Luckily for me, the wrapper still had Nantois' address on it." Wanting to change the subject, "Want to hear some good news, Gabriel?"

"What's that?"

"You know how you were concerned that there was no one to invoice for the time spent looking into the Friesen case?" Gabriel nodded, although so much had happened in the case, he didn't care anymore.

"Well Cliff, the sheriff up in Pearl County, said there's still a pretty hefty reward leading to the closing of the Wilson case."

"Really? How much is hefty?"

"$20,000. I told you there was lots of publicity surrounding the case, with Mrs. Wilson making numerous appeals to people with information to come forward. Some felt so bad for the Wilsons that they raised the money for a reward. Sheriff Harrigan actually put in a claim on the reward, saying that he had solved the case by ruling that it was suicide."

"Really, that's pretty ballsy."

"Mrs. Wilson told him to get stuffed."

"If the Agency gets any money, it'll be a bonus."

They drove into Slidell and Ben pull the truck to the curb on a quiet residential street one block from the Flowers' bungalow. "Check your gun, make sure it's loaded. Don't hesitate; these guys are proven, killers. Let's work in 8-hour shifts. I'll be back to relieve you at 11 p.m. If the Nantois' take the bait, they'll likely come at night. Let's go, and I'll introduce you to the Flowers."

They walked the short distance to the small gray bunga-low, vigilant that there might be someone watching. Agnes Flowers was sitting on the porch while her husband Bert was inside having a nap.

"Mrs. Flowers, thanks again for doing this." Ben walked up the front steps.

"Bert is pretty excited to get his hands on these guys, that's all he talks about. I hope this plan works. Otherwise, he'll be mighty disappointed."

"This is my partner Gabriel Ross. He's a private detective and has the first shift. I'll be back to relieve him at 11 tonight."

When Ben left, Mrs. Flowers looked at Gabriel. "You know you are just about the same height as my two boys,

Astor and Basil." Then as she walked in the door, she added, "When they were twelve."

Gabriel was sitting in the Flowers' living room leafing through a *Home and Garden* magazine when Bert got up from his nap. After introducing himself, Bert sat down on the couch across from Gabriel. "You're the tough guy that's going to protect us from these killers?" Bert was an older man with the wiry physique of someone used to hard work.

"Yep, that's me." Gabriel pulled out his .38 and put it on the coffee table.

Bert responded by reaching behind him, taking a double barrel shotgun out, and putting it on the table. Gabriel nodded. Then Bert pulled out a Colt revolver from the magazine rack and put it on the table next to the shotgun. Gabriel raised an eyebrow showing he was impressed. As if that wasn't enough, Bert bent over and pulled out a Colt Mustang from an ankle holster and put that on the table too. Speaking to no one in particular, "Bring it on, you fuckers. If they mess with us Gabriel, they'll be wishing they'd stayed home."

Mrs. Flowers joined them in the living room wearing a WWII army helmet and announced that dinner was ready. They ate off TV trays so they could watch Doris Day in *Please Don't Eat the Daisies.*

Gabriel broke up the monotony by getting up and peeking out the window. Every slow-moving car coming down the street looked suspicious. *So what kind of car are you driving now Nantois?*

"What do you know about our enemy?" Bert got up from the couch to join him at the window.

"Two brothers, Kane and Kory Nantois. Apparently, one looks like a greasy-haired punk and the other dresses like a cowboy. Both are tall and thin, mid to late thirties." Gabriel pulled out the mugshots which he had in his coat pocket. "They're killers and will no doubt be well armed."

"Bert, Mr. Ross, you should come back and sit down, you're going to miss the ending," said Agnes. "*The Ugly Dachshund* is coming on next. That's a really good one!"

They watched the second movie and Gabriel actually thought it was funny. At around 10:30 they heard a car door slam. Gabriel picked up his gun and went to the front window while Bert selected his shotgun and went to cover the back door. There were a few people on the street, but no cowboys or greasy-haired punks. *Maybe Ben's plan with the deputy isn't going to pan out.*

At a couple of minutes before eleven, Bert started to nod off. He'd snore, and then after a couple of moments he'd startle himself and jolt awake, reaching for his shotgun.

"You were in the war Mrs. Flowers?" Gabriel gestured at her helmet, thinking a little levity might help distill the tense atmosphere.

Agnes laughed. "Bert served in Sicily. He says he saw more than his share of combat, but he doesn't like talking about it much."

They were interrupted by a soft knock on the front door. Gabriel nudged Bert, who nodded and grabbed his shotgun.

"I'll watch the back door," whispered Bert.

The front window didn't afford a view of who might be at the door, and there was no spy hole. Gabriel whispered to Agnes that she should hide behind the couch. "I'm going to count to five and then open the door." He got to four when he heard a clanging noise coming from the back that made him jump. "Bert," he called out. "You alright?"

"I think the neighbor's cat jumped up on the garbage cans."

Another knock on the front door, this time louder. Adrenaline was kicking in. He was about to yank the door open, with his .38 at the ready when he heard, "Gabriel, it's me, Ben."

Gabriel opened the door, and his face betrayed his relief at seeing his partner. "Agnes, Bert, it's Ben. Maybe we should agree on a secret knock like two quick and then one single."

"Everyone alright here?" Ben smiled at Agnes, who had come out from behind the couch.

"Yeah, we're fine," replied Gabriel, as Bert came back into the front room. "Everything alright with your gal?"

"Her brother is with her. But she'll be happy to see you, Gabriel."

"Then I'm off. Good luck."

"Here are the keys. I parked the truck in the same spot. Be back here at 7 am, and we'll go for breakfast." Once Gabriel left, Ben sat in the easy chair and chatted with Bert about the army.

"Did you serve?" Bert asked, putting his shotgun back on the table.

"Korea, 2nd infantry division. Corporal."

"That makes me feel better; your partner was pretty jumpy, not sure how much good he'd be in a firefight."

"Gabriel? Wow, he's shown me more courage than anyone I have ever served with. I've seen him kill 3 men in the past three years and heard about another. All 4 deserved to die. No, Bert. I wish I had as much heart as Gabriel Ross."

"I heard you hurt your shoulder?" asked Agnes.

"Last fall we went into a hanger down by the docks. A mafia guy had a man tied to a chair with a gun to his head. Gabriel yelled at him to take his focus off the hostage. The man turned, shot at Gabriel and missed. I took the bullet in the shoulder. He would have finished me off if it wasn't for Gabriel emptying his revolver into him."

"Good story," said Bert. After a few minutes, he added, "I'm going to grab a few hours of sleep. Otherwise, I won't be of much use. I'll be down at 2 p.m. to relieve you, Ben."

"I've not tired Bert. Not to worry."

"Do as you're ordered, Corporal. Holler if you hear something, and I'll come running."

As Bert and Agnes went down the hall to their bedroom, Ben looked out the window. He was hoping the Nantois' would come.

CHAPTER SIXTY-SIX

The car rolled to a stop a few houses down from the bungalow. It was just after midnight. There was only a sliver of a moon, so they had to let their eyes adjust. A porch light illuminated the small house. "Bedrooms and kitchen in the back," said Kory, lighting a Marlborough. They could see a yellow glow in the front room.

"Someone's watching T.V.," said Kane. "I wonder what they're watching."

"Who gives a fuck? Alright, so let's go over the plan."

Kane spoke as if he had memorized his English test. "I go to the door. I ring the bell. I wait until they answer. Whoever comes, I ask to use their phone..."

"Wait, numbnuts, they're not going to let a hood like you use their phone."

"Oh, I forgot. My car, that piece of shit you stole, broke down and I need them to let me in so that I can kill them."

"Come on, be serious."

"As soon as they let me in, you follow with your big gun."

"Alright genius, what if they say no?"

Kane made like he was Ralph Kramden with a swinging fist. "Oh, oh, oh, kapow, Alice, right to the moon."

"Alright, let's rock."

BEN WAS SITTING in Bert's chair when he heard a noise outside. It was faint, someone trying to be quiet. He crawled over to the front window but couldn't see anything. He was sure he'd heard a shuffling noise. He crawled out into the hall and called out softly, "Bert, I think we have company."

He heard a knock on the front door. Ben waited on his hands and knees to give Bert a bit more time. He crawled over to the TV and turned it off, plunging the room in darkness.

Ben heard the knock a second time. Grasping his revolver in his right hand, he yanked the front door open. What he saw was the same punk whose nose he'd broken yesterday. The guy was surprised speechless to see him, obviously expecting Mr. Flowers.

Ben sensed movement to his right, and something heavy came down on his gun hand causing his gun to fire as it fell to the ground. A moment later the guy with the bandage on his nose charged him and hit him with something hard.

Ben fell to the ground and Kane jumped on top of him. They wrestled, the younger man trying to get his hands around Ben's neck. Ben could feel pressure on his windpipe as Kane pushed his thumbs into his Adam's apple. Ben tried to push him off, but his left shoulder didn't have the strength.

The next sound Ben heard was Bert. "Get off him you fuckin Nazi!"

Out of the corner of his eye, Ben saw the old man standing in the hall pointing the shotgun. He noticed movement to his right and then heard a loud gunshot. Bert fell, the chest of his flower-patterned nightshirt exploding in red. Ben watched helplessly as Bert landed next to him, blood bubbling from his mouth.

Thankfully Kane was distracted and loosened the pressure on Ben's throat. Ben took advantage and was able to get his right fist loose. He gave the punch all he had. He heard a crunching noise and saw the younger man's head snap backward.

Kory stepped into the doorway, leveling his gun at Ben. A smile washed across his face. "You're the fucker Cagle told me about. Where's Tommy Huffman, dipshit?"

Ben was staring down the barrel of Kory's gun. "Go to hell."

My number is up. In a nanosecond, Ben's memory flashed back to a surreal collage of growing up in Providence; his first day as a cop; his wedding to his wife; getting divorced; moving to Biloxi; setting up the Agency; Gabriel; Jelly Bean, and lastly Chevon. *Fuck I should have asked her.*

Another loud bang came from behind him. Standing in the hallway was Agnes, wearing that WWII helmet and holding a huge handgun in her quivering hands. Ben looked over just in time to see Kory fall backward in the doorway.

Mrs. Flowers then fell to the floor crying, trying to cradle her husband's head. Ben looked up but didn't see Kane. He crawled over to Bert and took his pulse, already sure that he was gone. "I'm so sorry, Agnes. You made things right for Tommy," he said, holding her frail body.

"Is that bastard dead?" she gestured to Kory's body in the doorway.

"Yeah, I think so." Ben suddenly realized that Kane couldn't have gone far. He got up and ran outside. He was about thirty seconds too late, judging by the squeal of tires and disappearing taillights going towards the highway.

CHAPTER SIXTY-SEVEN

K ane ran to the car. *What the fuck just happened? Kory's dead. Kory's plans always worked. What the fuck?* The whole side of Kane's face was on fire from where the cop had punched him.

Getting in the driver's seat, he found that Kory had left the keys in the ignition. Kane hadn't driven for a couple of years, ever since he'd had his driver's license permanently revoked for about ten DUIs. Kory gunned the Toyota and then had to control the skid as the car fishtailed down the street. He had white knuckles from clenching his fist too hard. He gritted his teeth in anger, hatred like acid burning inside of him. He heard the sound of sirens as he took the first left, trying to find a road leading out of Slidell. A little voice in the back of his mind told him to lay low and let all this blow over.

After a few frustrating dead ends, Kory drove into a gas station and pulled up to the payphone. Taking out a piece of paper out of his wallet, he dialed a number. The phone rang and rang. "Jesus K Christ, answer the fuckin phone!"

Finally, a sleepy voice answered the call. "Yeah... who the fuck is calling me so late?"

"It's Kane. Kory is dead." There was a pause on the phone. "KERRY, DID YOU FUCKING HEAR ME? OUR BROTHER IS DEAD."

"FUCK, WHAT HAPPENED?" The voice mirrored Kane's outrage.

"Too long a story, but some fuckin' cop is responsible. We need to take care of this. FOR KORY."

"FOR KORY, YEAH RIGHT MAN! WE GOTTA GET THIS FUCKING COP."

"So, you're in?"

"Yeah, FUCK, YEAH!"

"Wake up Keifer, and the two of you meet me at ...." Kane read out Chevon's address on Treme Street. "And bring the tools."

THE POLICE ARRIVED, having been alerted by the neighbors about five minutes after Kane took off. It took a while for Ben and Agnes to tell the story and to alert them that Kane had gotten away. The cops confirmed that both Bert Flowers and Kory Nantois were dead.

"Alright Detective O'Shea, you know this guy. Where do you think he might go?" asked the Slidell detective named Harper.

"He has an apartment on Decatur in the city."

"We checked that out earlier today, but I'll have the NOPD send out another unit."

Ben nodded, then a thought came to him. "I have to use the phone." He went into the living room looking for the phone. The Flowers' had camouflaged their beige rotary dial phone with flower stickers. He dialed a number he knew well. Chevon answered, and Ben breathed a sigh of relief. "Chevon it's me, is everything alright there?"

"Sure, Gabriel and I are playing cards. Everything alright? You sound stressed?"

"I'll tell you about it later, for now, better let me talk to Gabriel."

Gabriel got on the phone. "What's going on Ben?"

"We were hit, Bert is dead, so is Kory Nantois."

"Oh, my God." Gabriel gave Chevon a serious look.

"Listen, Gabriel, Kane got away and may be coming to you."

"Thanks for the heads up. We'll be ready. Is Agnes okay?"

"She's upset, not only about her husband, but she was the one that killed Kory. I'm on my way with a Slidell detective, and we're going to radio ahead to the NOPD and have them send the cavalry."

Detective Harper had listened to Ben's conversation. "We can take my cruiser, and I'll radio ahead and have them scramble a unit."

───────

GABRIEL HUNG up the phone and told Chevon what had happened in Slidell.

"I'll wake Tray up." She had no sooner started down the hall when they heard a car door slam out in the street.

Gabriel went to the front window. It was almost 1 a.m., but the street was still alive with partiers. In amongst the crowd, there were 3 men. One had black electrical tape on his nose, and he was pointing in the direction of the apartment. All 3 men wore black leather jackets and had greasy black hair and ridiculous mutton chop sideburns.

Tray got up, still wearing the dinosaur PJ bottoms. Gabriel spoke quickly, "There's three of them out in the street, likely with guns. We only have my .38. The cavalry is coming, but we're on our own for twenty minutes or so. It won't take them long to figure out which apartment we're in." Looking down again, he saw the three men had dispersed. Moments later, he heard a noise coming from the other bedroom. It was the fire escape.

"I have an idea," said Tray.

CHAPTER SIXTY-EIGHT

Kerry had a .38 while Kane carried a Glock. Kane wondered how much time they had before the cops showed up. *Do I have time for a little fun with the cop's nigger? That would make revenge that much sweeter. That would be like, chocolate icing on a fucking chocolate cake. How do you like that, Mr. Cop?*

Keifer, following Kane's directions, had circled around the back of the building. A rickety old fire escape ladder went up to a 2nd-floor window. He jumped and grasped the bottom rung of the ladder, pulling it down.

Meanwhile, Kane and Kerry had gone through the front door and were checking the mailboxes, looking for the right apartment. "Okay, what's her name?" asked Kerry.

"I don't know; she's a nigger. There's a Marshawn and Shaniqua Williams in apartment 1A. That must be it," replied Kane confidently.

"Wait a minute. There's Demarcus and Lacuanda Cackleduck." Kerry laughed pointing to the names on the mailbox for 1B. "Sounds pretty black to me."

"Fuck, look at this, there's a Chevon Knight in apartment 2. You know, like Gladys Knight and the Pimps."

"I think it was Gladys Knight and the Pips," corrected Kerry.

"Yeah well, I think I remember hearing the cop call her Chevon."

They took their time going up the stairs to the second floor, "Fuck, these stairs creak like an old whore," whispered Kerry.

When they got to the second-floor landing, Kane peered down the hall and saw that there were only two doors on the floor. One said garbage, so the other one must be the girlfriend's apartment. He heard a crashing sound, like a window breaking from inside the apartment. *Could Kiefer already be in there?* He and Kerry ran down the hall to the apartment. Finding the door locked, Kane stepped back into the hall. He leveled a hellish karate kick at the door. The solid oak door didn't budge. "Fuck, fuck, fuck," Kane yelled as he hobbled around the hall on one leg. *Broken nose, black eye, and now a gimpy leg.*

Kerry was about to kick the door himself when it opened.

CHEVON HAD LED the way to the garbage room. Once they were in, Tray looked at the garbage chute. "You've got to be kidding Chevy. I can't fit into that thing. Maybe you and Gabriel should just go. I'll try to hold them off with Gabriel's gun."

"I'm not leaving anyone here," said Gabriel.

"Relax guys. There's an attic," said Chevon. "You just

pull that rope behind you Gabriel, and a set of stairs comes down. We'll head up into the attic and hide until Ben, and the good guys get here."

They heard the floor in the hall creaking. Gabriel put a finger to his lips, signaling that someone was in the hallway. He jumped for the rope, landing at least a foot short. After a couple of tries, Tray walked over and jumped, easily pulling the rope down, "Show off," whispered Gabriel. They pulled the staircase down just as they heard a loud thump and someone saying, "Fuck, fuck, fuck" in the hallway. Tray helped Chevon up the attic stairs, Gabriel following on their heels.

The attic was small, maybe ten by twelve feet, and loaded with things tenants had left behind. Tray pulled the stairs back up and managed to pull the drawcord up into the attic as well. They all breathed a sigh of relief. The room was pitch black; the only light was a sliver coming from an air vent at the front of the attic facing Treme Street. After a couple of minutes, they heard voices from the hall.

"Fuck, they're not here. What do we do now genius?" asked a voice.

"I never said I was no genius," replied another.

Then yet another voice, "The burner was still hot on the gas stove, so they can't have gone far."

"We came up the stairs and didn't see them come down."

"You sure they're not hiding in the apartment?"

"I looked. No one is hiding in the closets or under the bed."

"Fuck, where could they have gone?"

"If we didn't pass them on the stairs, or the fire escape,

and they're not in the apartment, then there must be one of those bookcases that hides like a secret passage."

"Shut the fuck up, numbnuts!"

They didn't hear anything for a few moments, and then they heard the door to the garbage room open. "Hey, guys check this out." The metal door of the garbage chute clanged open. "Do you think?"

"Kiefer you're the smallest, I'll give you a boost."

"I don't want to go down that...what if I get stuck?" Kiefer whined.

"You won't get stuck, they build these big, so you can dump those big green garbage bags."

"I'm gonna land in a pile of shit," Kiefer complained again.

"Ain't gonna make much of a difference, you already smell worse than my feet."

"Not like you, Mr. *Hai Karate.*"

Chevon smiled at Gabriel, who rolled his eyes. There were some scuffling sounds from below; then they heard the garbage chute door open. "Fuck you guys. I'm doing this for Kory." The next sound they heard was "Wheee," followed by a scream.

CHAPTER SIXTY-NINE

Detective Harper radioed his dispatch, gave Chevon's address and said there was a possible 207 in progress. "Proceed with caution. Armed and dangerous. The suspect is wanted for multiple murders."

The drive to Chevon's apartment was agonizingly slow.

Despite the lights and sirens, there were still too many partiers out on the street, some too drunk to move out of the way. *God, I promise, if you help me get there in time, I will do anything you want. I'll become a nun,* thought Ben. There was no doubt in his mind that the man who'd had his hands around his neck minutes ago had meant to kill him.

"Wow! Where did he go?" asked Kerry.

"He's probably lying in a pile of garbage in the basement," answered Kane.

"Hey what the fuck is that?" Kerry pointed up at the ceiling.

Just then they heard a scream coming from above, "What the fuck was that?" asked Kerry.

"They're up in there. Must be an attic."

CHEVON, who'd been sitting on an old trunk, felt something run across her foot. "Ahhhhh," her scream tore through the attic like an air raid siren. She kicked out wildly with her feet long after whatever it was had scurried away. A mental image of a long-tailed, beady-eyed rat made her shiver uncontrollably.

Gabriel whispered, "It's okay Chevon. It's gone." He pointed to the attic vent at the far end of the room. They crab-walked as silently as they could towards it. Before they could make it to the vent, they heard a gunshot from below. A bullet came through the floor where they had just been sitting. A narrow stream of light pierced through the bullet hole in the floor.

Gabriel used his foot to kick out the vent, leaving a small space that was too small for Tray to fit through. Gabriel could make out the others in the shadows. Before either of them had a chance to say anything, Gabriel whispered, "I'm not leaving Tray." More gunshots, this time closer to their new position. "But Chevon, you could probably fit. There's about a ten-foot drop to a narrow roof. Here I can give you a hand..."

"No. No. No, and No. Not only do I not like heights, but I'm not leaving you guys here," said Chevon, defiance in her tone.

"Alright, let's see, see how they like it," whispered

Gabriel. He was able to stand up in the attic. He fired his revolver three times down at the men.

"Fuck, they're up there. Keep shooting," yelled a voice.

Gabriel gestured for Tray and Chevon to go back the way they'd come.

"Chevon, stand on that trunk," Tray said. The bullet-ridden floorboards in the attic creaked with every step. The men below were concentrating on the spot where Gabriel had fired the shots from, and a new volley of shots rang out.

Gabriel, who was moving quickly from the front of the attic, started yelling, "Fuck I 'm hit, oh it hurts, maybe we better give up."

Another volley of bullets sprayed the ceiling. Just then Gabriel heard the police siren, and they heard the door to the garbage room open.

BEN HEARD the sound of gunfire from 2 blocks away. Detective Harper drove right up to the apartment house. An NOPD squad car was already there. "Get down," yelled someone. Ben slid out of the cruiser and crawled to where a city cop was hiding behind his cruiser. One cop was lying on the pavement squirming. A bullet had shattered the windshield of the Slidell cruiser. Harper had followed Ben's lead and was hiding behind the car.

Ben looked at the cop who was down. He was holding his thigh and looked no older than a teenager. Ben pulled off his belt and cinched it around the leg. "What happened?" he asked the cop.

"We just drove up, and some guy started shooting from

the doorway. I ducked for cover, but Rollins here caught one in the thigh. Who the fuck is in there?"

"His name is Kane Nantois,"

"I've radioed for help. They should be here soon."

"There are civilians in there."

"Where?"

"There are 3 people in the top apartment, plus there might be more in the two apartments on the first floor." Ben pulled off his jacket and wrapped it around the man's leg, telling him he'd be fine as long as he kept pressure on the wound.

Detective Harper crawled over to them. "Looks like one shooter. I'm going to see if I can go around the back and come up from behind."

Ben nodded, "We'll cover." Harper nodded, and Ben started firing at the doorway where the cop had said the shots came from. Detective Harper was running all-out to the apartment house next door when more shots rang out, this time from the second-floor window. Harper didn't stand a chance and went down as he neared the sidewalk. He continued to crawl for a moment before he slumped to the ground.

The sound of sirens could be heard in the distance. The city cop looked at Ben with a frightened look on his face. "There's more than one bad guy in there."

CHAPTER SEVENTY

The sirens are getting closer, Gabriel thought. He went back to the vent that he'd kicked out and saw that there were two cruisers in front of the apartment. One was a black and white NOPD cruiser; the other was blue and white, likely from Slidell. He figured that Ben was down there, but he had no idea where the bad guys were.

Reloading his gun, Gabriel whispered, "Tray, I think they're on the first floor shooting at the cops. I'm going to see if I can come up behind them. Take Chevon and double back to the apartment."

Gabriel unhooked the stairs and pushed them down into the small room. With gun in hand, he climbed down into the empty room. He heard shooting again, coming from the first floor. Opening the garbage room door, he checked that the hall was empty. He slowly started down the stairs to the first floor. Halfway down he saw a man with his back to him. The guy was dressed in black leather and had greasy dark hair and ridiculous sideburns. The man started firing through the open door at something in the street.

Gabriel slowly inched closer until he was on the main floor. More shots, this time coming from the street.

"Okay, drop the gun, and I won't have to shoot you," yelled Gabriel, crouching down. The man stopped shooting and held up the gun in his right hand, his back to Gabriel. "Drop the gun," repeated Gabriel.

All of a sudden, the man turned and leveled the gun at where he'd thought Gabriel was standing. That split second before he realized that Gabriel was a foot lower, was all Gabriel needed. He put three bullets through the man's neck.

The man slumped to the floor in a pool of blood. There was more gunfire, this time coming from the upstairs apartment. *Oh, fuck!* Gabriel ran back up the stairs and could already see that the apartment door was open. *Were Tray and Chevon still in the attic or were they in the apartment?* He ran along the hallway to the apartment door; gun held pointed in front of him. He heard a couple of more shots coming from inside the apartment.

"Bingo fucktards, how'd you like them apples?" yelled a voice.

Gabriel silently pushed the door open and saw Tray lying in the hallway, blood pooling around his head. Gabriel bent and checked his pulse. Alive, but weak. The next sound he heard came from the bedroom facing the street.

"Your boyfriend is a real fucktard. I think he broke my nose and gave me a black eye. Maybe if I can get out of here, I'll take you with me. Show you my big black wiener."

Gabriel chanced a look in the bedroom where Chevon was sitting on the bed holding her arm. "I think you broke my arm, you idiot."

"Too bad I don't have time to teach you a few things."

The man was momentarily distracted by something down in the street.

Gabriel seized the opportunity to step into the room, gun pointing at the man. He recognized the man from his mugshot. Chevon's eyes went wide as saucers. "If you want to live, drop the gun on the floor."

Kane continued looking out the window but after a few seconds tossed the gun on the bed.

"Chevon, are you okay?"

"He hurt Tray."

"He's alive, but we need to call for an ambulance." Gabriel looked back at Kane who had turned to face him. He was a bloody mess, nose smashed and eyes almost shut with swelling. "Geez, what happened to you? Shit, that must have hurt."

"Can I put my hands down now?"

"You must be Kane. I just put three bullets into a guy with the same stupid sideburns. What was his name?"

A foul look washed across Kane's face. "Kerry, and who the fuck are you?"

"Just someone who wants justice for Glenn Wilson and Tommy Huffman's parents." Kane gave Gabriel a tough guy look. "Were you the one who killed Glenn Wilson?"

"Didn't have much choice, the punk would have talked."

"What about the Huffmans?" Gabriel circled closer to Kane.

"Now that was fun, I had me some fun with Mary, Mary the Milf. Then I gutted her like a fish."

Something was wrong. The guy put his hands down and was acting too cocky. "Did your brother help you?"

"Why don't you turn around and ask him?" Gabriel felt the barrel of a gun at the base of his neck. Gabriel turned his head to Chevon, "Is there a man behind me?" Chevon nodded. "Another brother? Which one is this?"

Kane reached down and picked up his Glock. "His name is Kiefer."

"Quite the family, I'm sure your Mama's proud. By the way, you use way too much *Hai Karate*, but the guy behind me," Gabriel pinched his nose. "He smells really bad."

"Real funny, aren't you little man? Too bad there won't be time for an encore. Throw the gun onto the bed."

Gabriel reluctantly dropped the gun on the bed, close to Chevon.

"Nice try, fuckwad." Kane picked up Gabriel's revolver and put it in the waistband of his jeans.

A noise from the hall, followed by a gun blast, and Gabriel saw Kiefer fall heavily to the floor, blood oozing from a wound in his chest. While Kane was distracted, Gabriel went for his gun hand. They wrestled for control of the Glock. The man was strong, too strong. Kane wrapped his arms around Gabriel, putting him in a bear hug. As he was literally having the life squeezed out of him, Gabriel head-butted Kane in the nose. Kane let out a yelp and threw Gabriel to the ground.

Gabriel looked up at Kane. His eyes were aflame with rage. He pointed his Glock at Gabriel.

Chevon grabbed the switchblade Ben had left by the bed. Letting out a hellish scream, she rammed it in Kane's thigh.

"AHHHHHHHH!" Kane looked at the knife sticking in his thigh, blood pouring down his leg. He looked incredulously at Chevon before he leveled his gun at her.

Ben came into the room, holding a revolver pointed at Kane, "Drop the gun."

CHAPTER SEVENTY-ONE

The following morning, Hollis Huntley was anxiously sitting in his office at Heritage Savings and Loan awaiting his special customers. Hollis reached into his desk drawer and palmed a couple of Excedrin, washing them down with a glass of water. He'd never liked Mayor Baxter. The guy was a bully. He expected perfection. Plus, Baxter had the emotional intelligence of a flea.

Yesterday Hollis had been surprised when Baxter, representing the Board of Directors, had asked him if he wanted Friesen's job. He'd said it was an offer Hollis couldn't refuse. "Believe me, Huntley, you'll make lots of money. It's going to be tremendous." Hollis had shown a proper amount of interest and then lied, saying he'd give the offer serious consideration.

A few minutes after the doors to the bank were opened to the public, Baxter once again waltzed into the office and sat down in the leather chair facing Hollis' desk. "Huntley, have you given thought to what we discussed yesterday?"

Hollis smiled. "It was a very fine proposition, Mr.

Mayor." Hollis' voice was shaking. He took another long gulp of water to calm his nerves.

"That's good, Huntley. Reznikov will be here shortly. I trust everything is set up?"

"The $500,000 line of credit?"

Mayor Baxter let out a sigh, "Yes Huntley, the line of credit. For your sake, there had better not be any mistakes."

Hollis patted a stack of papers on his desk. "All set. The Louisiana Trading Company."

A couple of minutes later, a short, well-tanned man with closely cropped hair walked into the office. He was wearing a gray linen suit with an open neck shirt showing off his gold chain and hairy chest. The smell of Aqua Velva wafted through the office.

"Well Baxter, is everything ready?"

Mayor Baxter stood up and extended his hand to the newcomer. The man allowed Baxter's hand to hang in the air and sat down. "Absolutely Mr. Reznikov, Hollis here was just telling me the papers are ready for your signature." Reznikov turned his attention to Hollis.

"How are you this morning, Sir?" Hollis asked, his voice quivering.

Reznikov had unwavering dark eyes. They were dark and as empty as an open grave. He looked down at the papers in front of him. "Very busy."

With a shaky hand, Hollis took another long sip from his water glass, then handed the man his Heritage Savings and Loan pen. "I put little yellow stickers where you're to sign. As you requested, a line of credit at a prime rate, backed by the property down at the docks."

Reznikov scribbled his illegible signature about a dozen

times before he put the pen down. Hollis noticed that he had a gold ring on each finger. "I want the money in cash."

"Huh...I'm sorry Mr. Reznikov, the mayor didn't say you wanted cash."

Reznikov looked at Baxter with a menacing sneer, then glared at Hollis.

Hollis recovered quickly. "It shouldn't be a problem. I'll just need some time to get that much cash together."

"Well then, make it fast."

After Hollis made a call to his head teller, he repeated the news that "It might take 30 minutes or so...maybe a bit more."

"Huntley here has agreed to accept the position as Branch Manager, and agreed to our terms," said Mayor Baxter, filling in the dead air. Reznikov continued to stare at Hollis and nodded.

"Er...," Hollis took another drink. "I did have a few questions."

"Hollis, this isn't the right time," Baxter reproached.

Reznikov waved off the mayor and gestured that Hollis should continue. He turned to Baxter, "Opey, close the door."

Once the door was closed, Baxter sat down again. "Alright Huntley, your questions?"

"You said, Mr. Mayor that I could make a 6-figure income in addition to my normal salary at the bank, is that correct?"

"Low six figures, yes."

"Would I be receiving an increase in salary as branch manager?"

"I didn't say that. I think your current salary is acceptable."

There was an uncomfortable moment before Frank

waived his hand. "For God's sake Opey, just make it happen."

"Could we go over the types of things you would want me to in return for the ...bonus?"

Frank decided to cut to the chase. "Just like this line of credit, I'm paying you to make things happen without a lot of questions. I value people who can keep their mouths shut. I have people who will be coming in regularly with large cash deposits; I don't want these people to be hassled. I don't expect unnecessary questions."

Continuing to stare at Hollis, Frank continued, "I plan to set up a brokerage account in the next couple of months and introduce an exciting investment opportunity. I'll be needing some letters and documents certifying to my credit-worthiness. The accounts for the new business will be held here. I may consider inviting you to get in on the ground floor. Now does that answer your questions, Mr. Huntley?"

Hollis looked out the window and saw some men get out of their cars in front of the bank. "I don't think I'll be able to accept it."

"What? I don't think I heard that correctly," said the mayor, annoyance written across his face.

Hollis slid an envelope across the desk. On the front of the envelope, he'd written "Resignation."

"What the fuck, Huntley? You're an ungrateful little wiesel." Mayor Baxter stood and pointed his finger at Hollis.

Frank continued to stare at Hollis like someone contemplating a Rubik's Cube.

A few moments later, the office door opened and Ben O'Shea entered, followed by an entourage of men in dark suits.

"O'Shea? This is a private meeting. What the hell is this?" Baxter said, eyes shifting from O'Shea to Huntley.

Ben finally spoke. "Mayor Baxter, you're under arrest for conspiracy to commit murder, defrauding the bank, accepting bribes, municipal corruption, and a bunch of other stuff. It's a long list."

Baxter's mouth was agape throughout. He mumbled something about speaking to his lawyer and that heads would roll. Throughout all of this Frank sat smugly in his chair. Finally, he turned to Baxter, and said, "Shut the fuck up, Opey."

Ben turned to Reznikov and said, "In addition to all the shit Baxter did, you actually get the bonus jackpot. Running a criminal enterprise, conspiracy to commit murder, witness tampering, stolen cars. Fuck, there's just so much, it's like a stew. Stand up and put your hands behind you." Ben signaled to one of the suits to cuff Reznikov and Baxter and read them their rights.

"You have nothing. My lawyer will have me out in minutes," boasted Frank.

"The Mississippi Bureau of Investigation tell me otherwise. Now to add a little spice to your stew, how is Kane Nantois? I guess, now that Kory isn't around to tell him what to do, he's talking up a hurricane." Frank looked like he'd eaten something bad.

After the cops escorted Mayor Baxter and Reznikov out of the Bank, Ben turned to Hollis and extended his hand. "Good work Mr. Huntley, Chief Willis told me that there was an insider in all this. The state cops told me it was you. Thank you."

"What's going to happen now?" asked Hollis.

"Raids are taking place here in Biloxi, right through to

New Orleans. As for the bank, the regulators will decide what to do. Prepare yourself; after all the dust settles, Heritage Savings and Loan might not survive."

DEPUTY CAGLE WALKED into the sheriff's station to find Chief McDiarmid there to greet him. "Good morning Cagle, we've been moving stuff around this morning, and I had to relocate your office temporarily."

"Oh, am I getting the corner office now?" joked the deputy.

"No, let me show you where you'll be hanging your hat for a spell." Cliff walked the unsuspecting deputy to the back of the building where the cells were kept.

Cagle stopped in front of the cells. "What's going on, Cliff?"

In response, Cliff took his key ring and unlocked the door, pushing Cagle in. "The whole list of charges has yet to be filed with the county prosecutor, but I know you were part of the Glenn Wilson cover up. A guy by the name of Kane Nantois specifically told us just how helpful you were."

"You're going to take the word of that hood over your own deputy?"

"Thought you said you never heard of him, Cagle?"

WILLIS WALKED into his old office carrying a plastic shopping bag. Murdock took his feet off the desk quickly and looked up at him. "Hey, Willis, how's retirement?"

"I'm not retired anymore. Maybe you haven't heard yet, but your friend Baxter has been arrested. The acting mayor asked me to lend a hand by taking my old job as chief of Biloxi PD back." Willis pulled the trophy out of the shopping bag and put it on his desk. "As it says, Murdock, I'm the fucking boss now, so get the hell out of my chair."

CHAPTER SEVENTY-TWO

"Your real name isn't Mangina is it?" Rachel asked. They were lying in bed after a spirited celebration over the closing of the case.

Don kissed her passionately and raised up on his elbow to look down at her. She was beautiful, even with the black eye which had turned a nice shade of purple. Speaking with an Italian accent, "What, you don't believe I'm Don Mangina from Locarno? I come from a long line of Italian lovers."

"You are such a bullshitter. Alright, you're a pretty good lover, but I want to know the name on your driver's license?"

"Alright, only if you promise that I can make love to you again."

"If you insist."

Looking at Rachel, "It's Don, ...Purplinsky."

CHAPTER SEVENTY-THREE

Two weeks later, Geoffrey Motten walked out of the detention center a free man. There to greet him was his lawyer Rodney Smith, and Arnie Sims.

"Took you long enough," Motten said, as he got into the back of Smith's Cadillac.

"Mr. Motten, you should say thank you to Arnie. It was because of his good work that the cops dropped the charges."

"Yeah, well thanks for nothing. Huedunit is closed, and I have no job, no money."

"I tried calling your wife to see if she wanted to join us for your release but I couldn't get ahold of her," said Arnie turning around to face him.

"I heard the bitch's traveling," Motten replied.

"That so? Where?" asked Rodney Smith.

"I hear she's somewhere hot."

"Like Mexico?" Arnie asked.

"Hotter. A lot fucking hotter. Which reminds me, which of you two can lend me a grand? I have a bill to pay."

CHAPTER SEVENTY-FOUR

Arnie, Rachel, Ben, and Gabriel sat in a booth at O'Shays having a drink. Arnie had just finished telling everyone about the night Bourbon met Bernice Cross. "So, I said to her, "I was getting a lot of pussy."

After the laughter died down, "Did Bernice start to throw things?" asked Gabriel.

"No, but thank goodness Grace was there, she didn't miss a beat, she told her that Bourbon was her cat and that she had named him after herself, because of his coloring."

"She sounds like a quick thinker, Arnie." Rachel said before taking a sip of her beer.

After a moment Arnie asked, "Ben, what's transpired with the mayor?"

"He tried to work something out with the DA. He fancies himself as some big deal maker. Because of all the evidence, the DA told him to take a hike."

"There's one thing I'm not sure of. Did Baxter blow the whistle on Friesen?" Rachel asked.

"Kane Nantois has admitted to killing Friesen. He said the order came from Reznikov. As for Baxter's involvement, we may never know."

EPILOGUE

Around the same time that Motten was getting out of jail, Ben O'Shea was sitting at a table by himself at *Les 3 Muses*. In front of him was half a glass of Canadian Club. Chevon and her quartet were on stage performing their rendition of *House of the Rising Sun*. Chevon had taken his advice and sang part of the vocals in between licks on the sax.

He let the rye and the music do their thing to chase the demons from his mind. *It's only been two weeks since I laid out my grand plan to Gabriel on how I was going to change my life. I haven't lost weight, my shoulder still hurts, and it almost cost us our lives. Picayune was a disaster. As for Chevon...well I just don't know.*

A memory flashed through his mind. *God, I promise if you help me get there in time, I will do anything you want. I'll become a nun. But how long would she be happy with a broken-down old cop twice her age? Would she even say yes?*

Ben had spent a couple of hours that day visiting the

Wilsons. They were very thankful for what had been done to find justice for their son. The *Herald* had done a feature on the story, giving Ben and the Agency even more publicity. In her heart, Mrs. Wilson had known all along that her son had been murdered, but she had known nothing of the Nantois brothers, Deputy Cagle, or Frank Reznikov.

From there, Ben had driven to Slidell and spent half and hour with a tearful Agnes Flowers. Fortunately, Astor and Basil were home for their father's funeral. That family had paid the ultimate price for what had happened that day in the woods.

Rachel was continuing to drive to Slidell most days to sit with Tommy, hoping for a breakthrough. She was positive that the young man was listening to her.

Willis was back in control as police chief and was on his fourth or fifth stapler. He'd begged Ben to come back, if only in a training or administrative role. Ben had put him off and said that consideration of the offer would get thrown on top of the pile, along with everything else he was dealing with.

Kane Nantois was at the detention center waiting for his permanent cell in Parchman to be ready. Although he'd told Ben that he had found Jesus K. Christ, Ben knew Kane would never again be allowed out.

The State Police were continuing to build their case against former Mayor Baxter and Frankie Reznikov. In a sobering moment, the DA warned Ben and Gabriel to be careful. They would be expected to testify if the case went to trial. Reznikov had a long history of making witnesses disappear.

Ben's thoughts were interrupted by Chevon coming to his table. He hadn't even realized that the quartet had stopped playing. Ordering her a glass of white wine, Ben congratulated her on the performance. "Your arm must be all better?"

"Still a little sore where he yanked it. Hurts like hell when I go to physio."

They sat in silence for a couple of minutes enjoying their drinks. Finally, Ben asked, "How's Tray?"

"He's fine. Daddy always said he was hardheaded." For a few minutes they were silent; it was like they had run out of things to say. Chevon finally leaned over and gave Ben a kiss. "So, Ben, have you made up your mind?"

"Yeah, I'm going to work at the agency with Gabriel, Arnie, and Rachel."

"That's good, but you know that wasn't what I meant."

"Picayune? I hope I never see that place again."

"No Ben, not about Picayune."

"Chevon, I promised God that if he helped me get to your apartment in time to help save you, I would do anything, even become a nun," he said looking into her eyes. "So, I am going to Sacred Heart Convent next week."

Chevon laughed but then gave him a look. "Ben, be serious."

"I sat down and did the pros and cons countless times. The con side of the page is long. The odds are stacked against us."

"And on the other side of the page?"

"Only one thing. I love you and want to spend the rest of my life with you." Ben pulled out the ring he had been carrying around with him for the past two weeks and then got down on one knee and said the words.

Chevon's face lit up with surprise. "Marry you?" She

started to laugh. "I was just asking if you had decided on supper!" A smile washed over her face when she saw the look on his face, "Seriously Ben, you deserved that. Of course, I'll marry you."

– THE END –

Dying to find out whether Ben marries Chevon? Will Dan Mangina ever tell Rachel his real name? Will former Mayor Baxter and Frankie Fingers get convicted and sent to the big house? Here is the Prologue of Book 6, *Eye on You - Right Place, Wrong Time* due to come out in 2019.

Monday, July 9th

WGNO TV Studio, New Orleans, Louisiana

The lights glared in Gabriel's eyes. He was conscious of sweating profusely, as he anxiously tried to prepare himself for what he knew was about to happen. He went over his planned responses and hoped that things didn't get too tough. *This should be Ben sitting here. Why did I let him talk me into doing this?*

The heavy-set make-up girl dabbed his face with powder and fussed with his dark hair. "If you don't stop sweating you're going to end up looking like a Picasso painting," she said, stepping back with a look of concern.

"I'm sorry, the lights are hot. Any chance we can turn them off?"

"They don't like filming in the dark," she replied, sarcasm dripping from her voice.

"I'll turn off my sweat glands then."

She started again with the powder, this time slapping his face a little too brusquely.

"Now I know how Tom Cruise feels. My wife tells me I look like him."

"Listen buster, the only way you'd look like Tom Cruise is if you taped his picture to your forehead."

When she was finished, Gabriel took a seat in the studio across from Susannah Collings, the reporter who had set up the interview. "It'll be great publicity for your business," she'd said. "My program is very popular with the white women over fifty segment. Just the kind of people who'd hire a private detective to check up on their cheating husband."

Susannah was a slim, attractive brunette with a perpetual sly grin on her face, like she knew your naughtiest secret. The news producer walked between them, holding out his hand and wishing Gabriel a good interview. Then he nodded at someone and counted down from five. As the channel five music started Susannah, likely picking up on Gabriel's terror, whispered, "You'll do great, easy, nothing but soft balls," she said making a cupping motion with her hand.

"Good morning New Orleans, and thank you for tuning into our program." Susannah stared into the camera. "Today we have a special guest with us. You may have read about his exploits in the press. I am pleased to have Mr. Gabriel Ross, owner and operator of the *Eye on You Detective Agency*.

Mr. Ross is here partly to promote his new location, opening up at 1300 Canal Street in our fair city. Welcome to the program, Mr. Ross."

"Uh, thanks and you can call me Gabriel," he replied, shifting in his seat.

"Is that chair okay for you? It's not too big is it?" she asked with a playful look.

"It's fine. I'm just a little nervous."

"Let's start with an easy one, then. Many of our viewers must be wondering, just how tall are you?"

"I'm over 5 feet," then because he couldn't think of anything else, "I'm not short, just concentrated."

Susannah laughed at the attempted joke. "Seriously Gabriel, how much of a handicap has being short been for you?" When she said short, she held her thumb and index finger about an inch apart.

Gabriel shrugged, "I haven't really thought of it as a handicap. Maybe some people underestimate me because of it. I just concentrate on rising to the occasion."

Susannah smiled again and crossed her legs seductively. "Did you always plan to be a private, 'dick?"

"Ah, no, I went to school to be an accountant." Gabriel turned away from Susannah to face the camera. "When that didn't work out, I came down to Biloxi and happened to meet Ben O'Shea. At the time he was working as a Biloxi Police Detective, and he must have seen something in me. He taught me the business."

"You recently concluded a case where the Mayor of Biloxi was arrested on a number of charges. The case also involved a well-known local businessman," Susannah said, her mouth seductively playing with the end of her pen.

"Yes, I can't talk about that very much as the matter is

still being adjudicated in the courts. But the case started off as a missing person's case and then developed into something else. Finding missing people is one of our main activities."

"Weren't you also part of an FBI task force, a couple of years back involving a man who became known as the Mardi Gras Killer?"

"Yes, Charles Bouvier, he grew up in New Orleans. He was working with an accomplice to abduct teenage girls. I was a consultant for the FBI at the time. Sadly, Bouvier never faced justice, or had to explain what happened to the girls, because he died falling overboard off his boat."

"When I was reading about your exploits, I came to the conclusion that your job sounded very dangerous," she stated showing concern.

"I suppose it can be, but most of the cases we handle involve doing reference checks, looking for missing teenagers, doing surveillance on a cheating spouse...Pretty tame stuff."

"I read that you investigated a local sheriff. You stopped him from burying his wife alive. Is that what you mean by tame?" Without waiting for a reply, she continued, turning to face the camera, "So you killed him and married his wife!"

So much for the softballs. "Hearing it that way, makes it sound like I made all that happen. No, I was hired by the sheriff's wife to watch the man. She suspected he was cheating on her. In the midst of the investigation, I learned that not only was he cheating on her, but he was also involved with a number of illegal activities with some bad people. I told his wife and she left him. He got upset and he kidnapped her. Ben O'Shea and I were able to save her in time."

"And you killed him."

"No, well yes. His wife, I mean ex-wife, and I developed a relationship after he was arrested. The FBI cut a deal with him in return for testifying against others and put him in the witness protection program. It was quite a bit later when he came back to Biloxi and tried to kill us. I had to, you know, put him down, kill him, you know with a gun."

"I sense some nerves over the whole killing thing Gabriel, which some of our viewers may find surprising. I have read in the papers that you've been compared to a short Charles Bronson, in *Death Wish*, or an itsy-bitsy Clint Eastwood in those *Dirty Harry* movies. Just how many people have you snuffed out?"

"I'm not keeping track, Susannah. I've never killed anyone who wasn't threatening to harm someone. Anyway, all of that is in the past. We've hired a retired New Orleans Police Detective to run the new office. Almost all of our cases are not dangerous."

Susannah gave him an incredulous look and smiled, turning to the camera, "There you have it, folks, coming to a location near you, our own, not dangerous, crime fighter/avenging angel. Thank you, Gabriel."